I0551818

HER WEREWOLF MATE

JODI VAUGHN

Copyright © 2017 by Jodi Vaughn under Fall of a Blood Moon

All rights reserved.

No part of this book may be reproduced in any form or by any electronic or mechanical means, including information storage and retrieval systems, without written permission from the author, except for the use of brief quotations in a book review.

❀ Created with Vellum

PROLOGUE

"*I* promise to love you until I take my last breath." Jaxon Taylor looked down into the soft blue eyes of the love of his life and soon to be mate, Ginny Wilson. His heart seemed to expand in his chest with the love he felt.

"You better, Jaxon Taylor." She smiled, her beautiful lips curving upward. The gentle spring breeze ruffled her brilliant blonde hair, sending an errant strand across her cheek. He reached down and tucked the silky tress behind her ear.

He gripped her slender hips, took a step forward and pressed her back against the trunk of the old oak tree in the middle of the pasture. The green grass and rolling hills were decorated with yellow wildflowers, making it one of their favorite places to be alone. Here, they could lock out the world. Here, only they existed.

He nuzzled her neck and inhaled her intoxicating scent. When he pulled back, she was looking at him with that smile that always made his heart trip.

God, she was beautiful. More beautiful than he deserved.

While other guys his age were enrolling in college or

1

planning a summer vacation to the beach, he was jumping to marry the only female he would ever love.

But then again, he wasn't just any male. He was a werewolf. And when a werewolf met his mate, nothing would tear them apart.

"What if I die before you?" She looked up at him and cocked her head. A slight smirk played on the corners of her full lips, lips that he was dying to have on his body. "Will you mate with someone else?"

"Not a chance. I will die when you die." He spoke with certainty and without flinching. His heart ached at the thought of being apart from her. He couldn't bring himself to imagine a life without Ginny.

"We're only eighteen. We've got years and years to think about that. First we have to make it down the aisle." Jaxon cradled her tight against his chest. He rested his chin on the top of her head.

She fit him.

She always had.

She always would.

In a few short hours, they would be married according to human law and mated in werewolf law.

"We could just leave now. Run away and mate and forget about the wedding," she suggested.

He wanted her like never before. He'd held off for months and had never pushed the issue of making love. As much as he wanted her, he wanted their first sexual encounter to be once they were mated and married, never to be torn apart.

"You've got too many human friends, and they'll think you're just shacking up with me." He smiled. As much as he wanted to mate with her right then, he wouldn't do it. He wanted their relationship to be different from any other. He wanted theirs to last through eternity.

"Getting tired of all those cold showers you've been

taking?" She trailed her finger down his chest and arched her perfect brow.

"You have no idea." His smirk slid off his face, and he narrowed his eyes a little. A flicker of worry gnawed at his gut. It was the same worry he'd felt when he'd woken up this morning. "You're not trying to weasel out of getting married, are you?"

Her smirk grew into a breathtaking grin. "Not at all. After this afternoon, Jaxon, you won't be able to get rid of me."

"That's exactly what I want to hear." He bent his head and covered her lips with his. He slid his hands around her waist and pulled her tight against his chest. He could feel the thrum of her heart beating against his chest in sync with the rhythm of his own.

She moaned and opened her mouth. He deepened the kiss. He touched his tongue to hers, tasting her sweetness.

His heart thudded in his chest, and his breathing changed to a pant. His body ached. He didn't know how he was going to keep from taking her right now up against the tree.

He pulled away, took a deep breath, and shook his head. "Woman, you're going to be the death of me."

"Don't say that, Jaxon." She covered his lips with the tips of her fingers. Fear flashed through her blue eyes.

"It's just a saying. I don't actually mean it." He snorted.

She shook her head. "You know how superstitious my grandmother is. If she'd heard you right now, she would have crossed herself and thrown salt over her shoulder."

"Come on, Ginny. You know I don't believe in that hocus-pocus bullshit." He tilted her chin with his fingertips. "I believe we make our own destiny and our own future. My future is with you."

Her expression relaxed, and she finally gave him a smile.

"You're right." She glanced down at the watch on her

3

wrist and sucked in a hiss. "I've got to go. I've still got to get my hair and makeup done before the wedding."

"You don't need to do any of that. You look beautiful right now."

She laughed and pressed her hand against his chest and stepped away. "Jaxon, I want to be perfect for you. I want the first day of the rest of our life to be perfect." She giggled as she ran toward her grandmother's car.

He grinned like an idiot as he watched her climb into her grandmother's old beat-up, gold Buick. She gave him one last wave before she pulled out onto the dirt road.

Today was the first day of the rest of their life together.

He liked the sound of that. He liked the sound of that a whole lot.

He didn't realize then that today would be filled with unimaginable pain and he would lose his heart forever.

CHAPTER 1

"**Y**ou sure she'll be here?" Jaxon narrowed his eyes at the large bartender standing behind the bar, who also happened to be a werewolf named Gary. Jaxon placed his hands on the sticky counter and leaned forward. The bartender's fear was overwhelming. "If I drove my ass all the way down here on a hunch, someone is going to get their ass handed to them. You feel me?"

"Easy, man. I told you she's been coming in all week. So far she hasn't missed a day." Gary frowned and wiped down the bar with a dark cloth. He put the bar towel aside and grabbed another longneck beer out of the cooler. He popped the top and shoved the beer at Jaxon. "I wouldn't give Barrett bad intel. That would be like signing my own death warrant."

"I'll give her a few more minutes, and then I'm leaving." Jaxon grabbed the beer off the counter and glared at the bartender. He pushed off the bar and headed to a small table near the rickety old jukebox. He flipped the wooden chair around, straddled it, and faced the door.

He studied the crowd, a mix of humans and werewolves in the Treetop Bar and Grill. The familiar scent of warm beer, stale cigarettes, and desperation filled the room. The jukebox wailed an eighties song while a few guys played pool in a dark corner. Older men sat huddled in the corner of the bar, talking about sports and women while nursing their beers before heading home for dinner.

There was a time he couldn't get enough of this place. He remembered hot summer nights playing pool and drinking beer and wishing the morning would never come. Back when he was younger and dumber and knew nothing about the true heart of a female.

He'd learned soon enough that a woman's heart was cruel and selfish, and that he'd been foolish enough to believe that love really existed.

It was a hard lesson to learn: the power a female could hold over a male when she had his heart in her hand.

He grabbed his beer and took a deep drink. His gaze landed on the familiar initials carved into the scarred table and froze.

Anger, hatred and bitterness swelled in his heart like ocean waves filling a hole at the beach.

J.T. loves G.W.

"Fuck." He stood so fast his chair fell over and smacked onto the wooden floor. The patrons barely gave him a glance before turning their attention back to their drinks.

"I heard that hot Pack Master is looking for me," the sultry, feminine voice whispered near his ear.

He slapped on a grin to hide the seriousness that was brewing in his head.

"Hello, Ella." Jaxon turned. "Or should I say, *Witch?*"

She narrowed her pretty green eyes at him for a fraction of a second and then glanced around the room. She was wearing a short black leather skirt, a skintight white shirt, and boots with come fuck-me heels. Her makeup was heavily applied, and her lipstick looked almost black.

"Keep your voice down," she scolded. "There are *some* humans in here, you know."

"I doubt anyone can hear us over all that noise." He cut his eyes at the jukebox, which was playing a song by Abba, and then looked back at her dark lipstick. He hadn't known the witch was into the Goth look.

"It's not noise. It's my favorite song." She narrowed her eyes and lifted her chin.

"You have no taste in music." He cringed. He knew all about the Witch of Yazoo City's preference in music from his fellow Guardian werewolf, Lucien.

"Really? I bet all you listen to is that metal stuff that makes your head hurt." She crossed her arms, forcing her breasts to strain over the top of her tight shirt.

"I'm not here to talk about music. I'm here to take you back to Mississippi." He took a drink of his beer without breaking his gaze from hers.

She shook her head and smirked. "I'm not going anywhere, Wolf."

"Now see, that's where we have a difference of opinion." Jaxon shoved one hand in his pocket and pointed his beer at her. "Tell me something. The curse should have brought you back to the cemetery, but it's been months now and you are still free. How'd that happen?"

Lucien had been sent to Ella to discover who was behind the torture of Arkansas Guardians, who were the protectors and defenders of the werewolf population. Ella had given them information but had escaped from her cursed prison in the cemetery when she stabbed Lucien's female, Catty. Only a blood exchange would allow Ella to break the curse, and it was only temporary.

"I need blood. I have to have someone's blood every week to keep the curse from pulling me back into that fucking graveyard." Her emerald-green eyes flashed in anger.

ly, and the hair on the back of his neck stood at attention.

"You may be hot, but you're one crazy bitch." His snarled, and the hair on the back of his neck stood at attention.

She leaned into his personal space and trailed a finger down his chest. "Aww, you think I'm hot." She arched her eyebrow. "I have the hots for your Pack Master, Barrett, but I don't think he'll mind me scratching my itch with you." She gave him a wink. "What do you say? Wanna give it a go?"

"I'm not here for a roll in the sack, Witch. I'm here to bring you back to Mississippi."

"So are the Arkansas Guardians bringing me in?" A look of surprise crossed her face. "Shouldn't it be the Mississippi Guardians?"

"Barrett wanted his men to bring you in since you escaped on our watch," Jaxon said. He knew Barrett wanted to handle this himself to keep the relationship between the state of Arkansas and the state of Mississippi on good terms. Things were volatile with the Louisiana Pack, and Barrett knew it was smart to stack up his allies in case shit went sideways.

"How noble." She studied her long pink nails and looked unimpressed. "I wonder if all that nobility falls to the side when Barrett's in bed. Bet he gets real nasty when he's horny." Her lips curled up into a wicked smile.

"Is sex all you think about?" She was beautiful. But she was also dangerous as fuck. A psychopath in heels.

"Don't try to talk to me about virtue, Jaxon Taylor. I've heard all about your reputation." She propped her hand on her hip and grinned. "Makes me wonder how hard you're gonna fall when you find the right female." She leaned in and placed her hand on his lower stomach.

He grabbed her hand. "Let me guess, you think you're the right girl."

"I'm the right-now girl. Not the right girl." She leaned in and smirked. "There's a difference."

8

The fact that he had a reputation wasn't news to him. The fact that even the Witch of Yazoo City knew about him made him uneasy. Still, it was better to be a man whore than to get his heart broken again.

He'd been down the road of heartache and heartbreak and had no fucking desire to make that trip again. He cut his eyes around the room.

This place brought back too many memories, too much pain to make him feel at ease. It was a place he'd sworn he'd never visit again. But when he'd gotten the intel that Ella was hanging at the dive, he'd had no choice but to go. He was here to get her and take her back to Mississippi before she could do any more harm.

* * *

GINNY MCGREGOR SAT in her Mercedes and tightened her grip on the wheel. Damn her husband, John, for making her come here to pass off some information about the Arkansas Guardians.

She knew he was testing her, testing her loyalty to him and the Louisiana Pack.

He had nothing to fear. Since her father had forced her to wed John seven years ago, she'd done nothing to give her husband a reason to doubt her. Her faithfulness to him wasn't born out of some undying love for him. No, she was faithful to him to make sure the one male she had loved would never be hurt.

Jaxon Taylor.

Once, she'd been full of hope and love and eternal optimism. That had all died the day her father killed her grandmother and forced her back to Louisiana.

The day of her wedding, her life had changed forever.

Now her life consisted of doing what was expected, not

getting angry, and sure as hell not having a voice. Those were the things that kept her alive.

"Get over it, Ginny. It's not like you're going to know anyone here." She grabbed the large envelope and her purse off the passenger seat and opened the car door. The Arkansas humidity slapped her in the face like a wet mop. If she weren't a Southern female, it would have been miserable. She'd long since acclimated to the weather and, in some respects, embraced it.

She headed toward the building, walking on her toes so her expensive heels wouldn't sink in the dirt. Despite her confident stride, her gaze was constantly searching the parking lot for anything out of the ordinary, anything suspicious.

It was still light, so only a few Harley Davidsons and a couple of pickup trucks sat in the grassy parking area out front. The bar was in the middle of nowhere. The nearest town was twenty miles away. The place used to be a hangout for underage teens, but it had lost its appeal when the law cracked down. Now it mainly catered to bitter old men and bikers looking to get drunk fast.

She quickened her footsteps and wished she could have worn something more casual, like jeans and a T-shirt, instead of the white pants and matching blouse she had on. Her feet ached from the high heels, and she couldn't wait to change into the ballerina-style flats she kept in her car. If it had been up to her, she would have worn something casual and comfortable.

But her life wasn't her own. It belonged to John, her husband, her mate... her owner.

John dictated everything about how she looked from her clothes and hairstyle—even the color she painted her nails. He insisted she look like the wife of the future Pack Master of Louisiana and not some common housewife.

She would give anything for a simple life, a life of her own where she could do what she wanted and live how she wanted. A life where she only had to worry about herself.

She took off her designer shades and patted the shimmer of sweat that had settled on her face. She took a steadying breath, opened the door, and stepped inside.

The wave of emotion washed over her so swiftly it almost knocked her back a step.

It was a place she used to meet him. The only male she'd ever loved. Anguish tugged at her heart, and she forced herself to swallow the knot in her throat.

She spotted the bar and made her way over. The sooner she delivered the parcel, the sooner she could get the hell out of the place.

If John asked her to come back here, she'd refuse.

Her stomach clenched. Who was she kidding? She wouldn't refuse John. She remembered what his punishments felt like in the form of bruises and broken bones.

Maybe one day he'd be so angry with her that he would end her life with a silver bullet to the skull. At least it would end her misery.

She stepped up the bar and placed the large envelope on the counter. She met the gaze of the bartender. His narrowed gaze tracked down her face, past her chest to her hand resting on top of the envelope. His eyes widened, just as she'd known they would. He'd seen the insignia ring letting every werewolf know she was the wife and mate of John McGregor, the son-in-law of Edward Boudier.

To the werewolf population, she was untouchable.

"Would you care for a beer, Mrs. McGregor?" The bartender blinked several times and took a step back from the counter, wringing the bar towel in his hands.

It was almost comical how frightened he was of her.

If only he knew the truth: that she herself didn't wield

any power. And if something happened to her, John probably wouldn't give two shits. He'd just move on to the next female he set his sights on.

She had once thought that protection was found in her last name.

Now she was beginning to doubt even that would be enough.

She should be heading back. But she wanted to enjoy a few minutes of freedom away from John. One drink wouldn't hurt.

"Do you have Chardonnay?" She glanced at the barstool, making sure it was clean before easing onto it.

He frowned and then caught himself. "Sorry, no. But I have some wine coolers."

"Beer is fine." She didn't normally drink beer. Maybe a glass of wine every few weeks, and only when she knew her husband would be out of town on business. Otherwise she didn't drink. She needed to be alert and on her guard around John.

"Thank you." She slid him a twenty.

"No, it's on the house." The bartender waved her away.

She nodded and stuck the bill back in her leather purse. She lifted the cold bottle and pressed it to the insides of her wrists before taking a drink.

The bitter brew on her tongue sent her back a million years ago. Back when she was young and without a care in the world. Back when nothing could ever go wrong.

Back to a time she was happy.

* * *

JAXON'S GAZE slid across the room to the woman who walked through the door. Her face was hidden from his view by the short silky blonde hair that curtained her face. He started to turn his attention back to Ella, but something about the stranger held his attention.

"She's way outta your league, wolf." Ella leaned in and sneered.

"What do you know about it?" He lifted his eyebrow, but didn't look away from the blonde at the bar. He usually stayed away from blondes. They were nothing but trouble. But he couldn't seem to tear his gaze away. "Do you know her?"

"Nope. I don't have many friends, and I sure as shit don't have women friends," Ella said defiantly.

"Maybe you should try to be nicer." He glanced at Ella and then back at the stranger, who was now sitting at the bar.

"I'm nice. I am. Who said I wasn't nice?" Ella crossed her arms. "It was Catty, wasn't it?" she huffed. "Jesus, it wasn't like I killed her."

"You stabbed her through the chest and left her pinned to a tree. Face it, you're not exactly a girls' girl." Jaxon glared.

Ella rolled her eyes. "Oh, please. It didn't kill her. She's a werewolf—I knew she wasn't going to die. Besides, I needed to get out of that hellhole."

"Which brings us back to why I'm here. I have to take you back." Jaxon reluctantly looked away from the stranger and back at Ella.

"You don't understand what it's like to be held prisoner in a place you hate. To lose everything you know and love and be expected to just accept that it's the way things are."

His chest tightened.

He knew that better than anyone.

"I'm here doing my job. Nothing personal." He held up his hands. He glanced over at the stranger at the bar, who was now picking up a beer.

There was something oddly familiar about her. Some-

13

thing so familiar it was wildly distracting. He shook his head and looked back at Ella.

"Not personal? Right. You Guardians don't know a thing about me. Yet you judge me. Believe me, it's personal." A hardness settled across her beautiful features. She truly looked like the evil witch he was here to capture.

Jaxon sighed. "I do know there have been fifteen deaths since your escape, and they all happen in places you've been spotted."

"I've not killed anyone. There's no proof." She narrowed her eyes and propped her hands on her hips. "You're not going to pin those deaths on me."

"Look…" he started to respond, but the woman at the bar made a familiar motion that caught his eye.

He held his breath. It couldn't be.

She tucked her hair behind her left ear, ran her hand behind her neck, and then rubbed her left shoulder like it ached.

It couldn't be.

Buzzing noise filled his ears. His gut clenched.

If he were standing behind her, he would see the spot on her shoulder that she rubbed, the scar she'd gotten when she'd gone to the beach and fallen on a seashell. A scar that had gotten immersed in salt water and hadn't vanished despite her werewolf blood.

It was her. It was Ginny.

The second her name popped in his head, she turned in his direction as if sensing him in the room.

Their gazes locked. Shock registered on her face. They both went perfectly still.

"Fuck." The curse slipped past his lips out into the dingy bar, where it was eaten up by the noise of the jukebox and the mumble of conversations.

He wanted to go to her, to pull her into his arms, to

scream and ask her why she did what she did. But in the end, he still had his pride. He did the only thing he could think of.

He wanted to hurt her back for all the pain she'd caused him.

He grabbed Ella around the waist and pulled her against his chest. She struggled for a second or two until she realized his intention.

"Well, it's about time, wolf." She purred as she ran her hands up his chest and locked her fingers around his neck.

He narrowed his gaze on Ginny, wanting her to feel a fraction of the pain that she had caused him every single day of his life since their wedding day. He wanted her to suffer as he had suffered. He wanted her to know how it felt.

He held Ginny's gaze and smirked.

CHAPTER 2

*J*axon bent his head and covered Ella's mouth with his. The witch eagerly rubbed herself against his body and kissed him back with an urgency he didn't feel.

Ginny's mouth dropped open and she covered her parted lips with her hand.

The unmistakable streak of shock and hurt flashed through her blue eyes.

His stomach bottomed. Revenge hadn't seemed so sweet after all. It only made him sick to his stomach.

Ginny fumbled on the bar for her purse before she snatched it up. She hurried to the door, her high heels clacking against the old wood floor.

She dabbed the corner of her eye discreetly before reaching for the door handle.

She jerked the door open and hurried out.

Shit. He'd made Ginny cry.

He tried to shove Ella away, but she opened her mouth and bit down hard on his lip. He held her at arm's length. He wiped his mouth and looked at the smear of blood on the back of his hand.

"You fucking bit me."

Ella smirked. "What's wrong, wolf? Your woman didn't like that act you put on for her?"

He jerked his head at her and narrowed his gaze.

"Did you really think I thought that kiss was for real?" She arched her brow. "I've kissed better wolves than you. I can tell when a guy is faking." She crossed her arms and let out a loud sigh. "So are you going to just stand there, or are you going to go after her?"

"You stay here." He pointed his finger at her and snarled.

"Where would I go?" She gave him an innocent look as she held her arms up. She shook her head and then turned her attention back to the jukebox.

There was nothing innocent about that witch. He stuck his hands in his jeans pockets. His fingers brushed against the metal keys.

He'd taken advantage of the kiss and pocketed her car keys from her jeans pocket when she'd kissed him. She wouldn't get far.

He jogged to the door and stepped outside into the heat. He scanned the parking lot for Ginny.

Judging by the expensive white pantsuit she was wearing, he bet she was driving a luxury car.

His gaze locked on a black Mercedes parked off to the side. It stood out, an expensive car among the handful of Harleys and trucks sitting in the parking lot.

The engine purred to life, and his heart jumped in his throat.

She was leaving.

He took off at a run, his hands clenched in a tight grip. Part of him knew he was opening a painful can of worms by even engaging with her. He knew he should just let her go. Hell, she'd let him go years ago.

But then there was another voice, a voice in his head. That voice needed answers. He needed closure.

She looked over the steering wheel, her familiar blue eyes wide with surprise and hurt and fear. Emotions he'd never seen her wear before.

He opened the door and peered down at her.

"What are you doing here?" Her voice quivered, and her fingertips shook slightly against the wheel.

"I could ask you the same thing, Ginny."

She looked away. Her perfectly manicured fingers white-knuckled the steering wheel.

When she looked back at him, she'd slid a mask of indifference over her expression.

"I'm here on business. For my husband."

A gunshot to the gut would have felt better than those last three words.

He let go of the door and stepped back a foot, trying to regain his breathing.

She'd literally knocked the breath out of his lungs without ever laying a hand on him.

"Husband. I didn't know you were married." He spat the words out. Bitterness lingered on his tongue.

"No one did." She gathered her hands in his lap and looked down. "Jaxon, why are you here?"

"I'm here on business as well." He wanted to tell her he was an Arkansas Guardian now, one of the elite werewolf solders who guarded civilian Weres of the state. He was a protector, a defender, a fighter.

"No, that's not what I meant." She licked her lips. "I mean, why did you follow me out here?"

"Answers." He kept his tone cool, neutral. He didn't want

her to see how badly she'd affected him. He still wanted to hurt her. He wanted to hurt her as much as she'd hurt him.

"I've got to go." She averted her gaze as she reached for the door. Her hand trembled as she grabbed the handle.

She was leaving.

He grabbed the door, preventing her from shutting it.

"Not yet," he said. "Our conversation is not finished."

"You don't understand." Her nervous gaze flitted around the parking lot. She turned and looked over her shoulder.

"No, *you* don't understand. You're not leaving until I have some answers. You owe me that much." He narrowed his eyes.

She jerked her head in his direction. "Owe you? Are you kidding me? What about that girl I just saw you kissing? You certainly got over me, so don't even act like you're still hurt. I know your type, Jaxon Taylor. You've had quite a lot of females in your bed since me."

His gut twisted. "How do you know? Have you been keeping tabs on me?"

"Not me. Someone else." She shook her head and waved him away. "Just go back inside to your redhead."

"She's not my..." He caught himself. He'd almost given himself away. Then he smiled. "No, you're not getting rid of me that fast. We have unfinished business, you and I. I have a lot of questions. Questions that only you can answer."

"Jaxon, I don't have time for this." She tried to tug the door toward her, but he held on tight.

"Seems like you don't have time for things that make you uncomfortable." His eyes roamed over the rich leather and the top-of-the-line navigation system in her car. "Not quite sure why you even bothered coming out here. This atmosphere doesn't seem like it fits you anymore." His gut tightened. "You don't live around here, do you?"

Had she been in Arkansas all this time and he'd never found her? Had fate been that big of a bitch to keep her under his nose while he nursed his heart and soul?

Her eyes widened and then narrowed. "I left Arkansas a long time ago."

Pain flashed behind her eyes.

"I've got to go." She pressed the engine button.

His eyes landed on the key fob sitting on the console. He reached in and grabbed it.

"What are you doing, Jaxon?" She jerked her head in his direction and glared at him.

His heart tugged at the sound of his name on her lips.

He shook his head. He wasn't going to do that. He wasn't going to let her get away without having that discussion with him. He needed to know.

"I'm taking away your leverage." He sneered and stuck the key fob in the front pocket of his jeans pocket. "I'm betting you won't get far." He scratched his cheek. "Actually, I've always wondered how far a car will go without the key fob. So why don't you try to drive away and see where you end up?"

"You're an asshole," she hissed and climbed out of the car. She fisted her hands at her sides while pressing her lips into an angry line. He bet his life her beautiful blue eyes were shooting daggers at him behind her expensive shades.

"And you, my dear, are... "

Yells erupted behind the closed door of the bar. Jaxon turned just as the door flew open and men came running out like ants.

"Shit." It had to be Ella.

Jaxon ran for the door. He stepped inside and looked around. The place was completely empty. He scanned the area and inhaled. Danger and the unmistakable scent of blood hung heavy in the smoky air.

His eyes landed on a pool of blood by the bar.

"What the hell happened?" Ginny stopped behind him.

"Go back outside." He scanned the room for any movement or any sign of Ella.

"Jaxon, why is there blood on the floor?" Ginny's voice cracked on the word blood.

"Ginny, please go back outside." He pulled her key fob out of his pocket and held it out to her.

She shoved her sunglasses on top of her head and shook her head. Something flickered through her eyes.

She was afraid. Something tugged at his heart.

"Fine. But stay close." He sighed, stuffed the key fob back into his pocket, and walked over to the pool of blood.

"What's this about?" she whispered from behind him.

"I'm going to guess that pretty little witch did this." He walked behind the bar and stopped.

"Your girlfriend is a witch?" Ginny jerked her head towards him.

"She's not my girlfriend." He glared and then looked back at the floor behind the bar.

Gary lay behind the counter, blood pouring out from a single gunshot wound to the head. Ella was nowhere in sight.

"Son of a bitch." He stood. He reached in the back of his jeans and pulled out his nine millimeter. He wasn't sure if a bullet would even hurt Ella since she was a witch with a curse. But a gun was better than nothing.

"Stay here." He shot Ginny a warning glare. He eased his way to the door leading to the back room of the bar. The door was cracked open.

Keeping his gun, he pushed the door open with his free hand.

"Jaxon," Ginny whispered.

"Shush." He kept his gaze trained on the dark room. Why the hell didn't Ginny listen when he told her to keep quiet? Jesus. It was enough to make him want to throttle her.

He strained to hear any noises coming out of that room. But it was silent.

His eyes dilated and adjusted to the dark. He scanned the room, searching for movement.

He eased into the room and flipped the wall switch. A beat-up couch and a desk sat off to the side. He saw a filing cabinet and a few boxes of beers, but other than that, the room was empty.

"How the hell did she get away? There's no back door," he muttered.

"I didn't think you would be so worried about your girl-friend getting away. Never seemed to bother you before," she muttered.

He turned, anger running through his veins. If she wanted to hurt him, she'd definitely found her mark.

"What do you know about it anyway? You didn't stick around to find out what kind of male I am," he snapped.

She flinched at his angry words. He felt the guilt for a second before reminding himself exactly who Ginny McGregor was.

To him, she was a total stranger.

To him, she was someone who had lied to him to get his guard down so she could steal his heart and then crush it under her heel.

To him, she was his worst enemy.

"I'm leaving. My key, please." She lifted her chin and held out her palm.

His eyes drifted down over her expensive clothes and manicured nails.

"Late for a massage? Or maybe it's your pedicure?" He dragged his eyes up to her face. "Looks like you don't like to get your hands dirty anymore. You're definitely not the Ginny I once knew."

* * *

"You have no idea," she muttered, curling her fingers into fists. Her nails dug into her palms, leaving marks, yet she barely registered the pain.

Dealing with physical pain was something she'd mastered over the last few years. She'd had to in order to survive.

"I think you know as well as I do there's nothing for us to talk about, Jaxon. We are two different people with two different lives. No need to catch up now." She tried to keep her voice calm, her expression indifferent. But she couldn't conceal the tremor in her voice.

His eyes narrowed, and the muscle in his cheek twitched. That familiar look of anger crossed his features. When they were younger, she had not seen that expression much, only on very rare occasions. Like that time when some biker had grabbed her ass in the bar.

Jaxon hadn't wasted words but had set his beer on the pool table and leveled the guy to the floor with one punch. For the rest of night the males, both human and Weres, made damn sure to keep their hands to themselves and their eyes off her ass.

"So what are you doing here, Ginny?" He crossed his muscled arms across his chest and glared.

"Just getting a drink." She shrugged.

"Dressed like that?" His gaze ran down the length of her body. She wanted to fidget under his stare, but forced herself to stay still. "No, you are here for some other reason. You might as well tell me before I extract the information from you."

Her eyes widened for a second before she composed herself.

"It's really none of your business."

"Well, sweetheart, as an Arkansas Guardian, I make it my business to sniff out trouble. And you smell like you are steeped in trouble."

Guardian? Holy shit, Jaxon was a Guardian.

She stepped back and tripped. He reached out and grabbed her before she could fall.

"What's gotten into you? You're as jumpy as a cat in a room full of rocking chairs." He narrowed his assessing gaze on her.

"Nothing." She cleared her throat and stepped back.

"Doesn't sound like nothing. Sounds a lot like you're in some kind of trouble."

"I have to go." When he didn't hand over her keys, she dug her hand in his jeans pocket.

She hadn't expected his alpha scent wash over her like it did. And she certainly hadn't expected to have the flood of bittersweet memories cover her like they did.

He grinned as he looked down into her eyes. "A little to the left. As I recall, you remember what to do next."

She jerked her hand out and shot him a glare so intense it should have scalded him.

"I don't remember you being quite so vulgar," she spat.

"I don't remember you being so cold." He shrugged. "People change, I suppose."

"Yes, they do."

"I'll give you your keys back on one condition," he said.

"What's that?"

"You are going to tell me why you left me on our wedding day without saying goodbye."

The hurt streaked behind his eyes. Harshness etched into the lines around his eyes, and bitterness clung to his cruel mouth. She wanted more than anything to reach out and touch his lips, soothe away the hurt, and make him hers again.

Like they used to be.

But they'd existed an eternity ago where reality didn't intrude and where pain did not exist.

No, she and Jaxon were nothing more than a memory now.

"I wasn't ready to settle down. I wasn't ready to get mated, let alone get married." She lifted her chin to deliver the final blow. "You were never going to make me happy, Jaxon, and I knew I was the last female in the world to make you happy."

His gaze darkened. He leaned into her.

She flinched. It was a conditioned response after the last few years of her life. She knew what was coming next. She braced herself for the pain.

"Ginny, you are so full of shit." A hard smirk played on his lips. "You forget, female. I always know when you are lying."

She curled her hands into fists and turned. He grabbed her elbow just as her phone chirped in her purse.

She felt the blood drain to her toes and she quickly grabbed it and checked the time. "Oh, god. I'm late."

She hit the answer button. "Hello?"

But the call had already gone to voice mail.

Her stomach dropped.

"Late for what?" Jaxon frowned.

"I should have left thirty minutes ago." She hurried out the back room and raced for the front door. Her heart leapt into her throat.

"Ginny, what's got you so scared?" He grabbed her arm, preventing her escape.

"Nothing. I'm just late for a meeting." She tried to snatch her arm away, but he only tightened his hold.

She flinched and sucked in a hiss.

He reached down with his free hand and tugged the sleeve of her shirt up.

"What are you doing?" She tried to wiggle free.

"What the fuck?" He darkened gaze landed on the dark blue bruises dotting her arm.

"It's nothing. I fell," she lied and snatched her arm away. She rolled her sleeve down and studied the floor. She could feel his gaze burning her with his disgust. At what she was. At the life she now lived.

"Who did this to you?" His gaze darkened, furious rage lying behind his blue eyes.

She tried to swallow, but her throat was tight and achy. She wanted to look away from his eyes, to hide from his condemnation, but she couldn't. If she looked away, he'd see the lie.

She had made a vow to herself all those years ago never to let him know.

She'd walked through hell, sacrificed her soul, and bled tears.

She didn't do all that for nothing.

"I said I fell." She lifted her chin, narrowed her eyes, and muttered the words through her clenched teeth.

"Don't fucking lie to me. You know I hate a liar."

"If you hate me so much, it shouldn't matter to you how I got these." She turned for the door, needing to get away.

She grabbed the doorknob and opened the door. His hand slammed down on the door and slammed it shut before she could get out. "We're not done, Ginny."

Anger rose up in her chest like a thousand fires. She was sick and tired of being told what to do.

She was supposed to be broken, to come to heel like an obedient pup. But she was all out of submission.

She rounded on him and shoved him back as hard as she

could. She could feel her wolf rising inside her body, wanting to be taken off the leash and wanting to lash out.

Her head fell back, and she dug her fingers into her palms. "Jaxon, leave it alone."

"I can't…" His phone rang, diverting his attention.

She squeezed her eyes shut and focused on sucking in deep breaths to calm her rampant heartbeat. She would not shift. She would not shift.

"Hello?" Jaxon kept his gaze on her as he spoke. His eyes narrowed, warning her she'd catch hell if she tried to leave now.

She never remembered him being quite so unforgiving. The Jaxon she knew was generous, kind, and endearing.

The years had left their mark on him. No doubt all of it had been her doing.

"Fine." He ended the call and stuffed the cell phone back in his jeans pocket.

"Jaxon, I really need my keys back. I need to get home."

"And where is that, I wonder? Home? Is that where you got those bruises?" His gaze darkened. "Did your husband do that to you, Ginny?"

"Leave it alone, Jaxon." She held out her hand. "You don't know what you are talking about. We are not in each other's lives anymore. Just leave it."

"Well, if pain is what you're into, you should have just said so. I guess I was too gentle for you back when we were together. Maybe that's why you left."

She flinched, his words slamming across her in outrageous indignation and pain.

So that's what he really thought about her.

"Good thing we didn't last then," she countered and forced herself to shove away her emotions.

She couldn't do this right now. Not with him.

She needed to get away from him and get back to her home. Otherwise the punishment would be severe.

"Is that what you want? To be away from me? You got it." Jaxon shoved his hand in his pocket to retrieve the key fob. "I don't force my presence on any woman. Human or Were."

He frowned and pulled his empty hand out of his pocket. "I could have sworn I stuck it in that pocket." He checked both pockets of his jeans.

"Jaxon, that's not funny." Anxiety rose in her chest.

"They must have fallen behind the bar." He walked back over to the counter as she followed on his heels.

Panic rose inside her like a typhoon. Her heartbeat amped up and fear settled in the pit of her stomach.

He searched the floor behind the bar and the room behind the bar. She grabbed her phone and turned on the flashlight app to illuminate every nook and cranny where they might have fallen out.

His hand landed on something hard. He grabbed it and stood.

"Here." He dangled the plastic fob between his fingers. She snatched them out of his hands.

A car engine started outside. He frowned. "I thought everyone left."

"They did. I saw them all pull out when we were running inside." An uneasy feeling settled in her stomach.

Jaxon hurried to the entrance.

"What? What's wrong?" She ran up behind him just as he flung open the door. They both watched as her taillights disappeared down the driveway and onto the main road.

"That fucking witch took your car. How the hell did she take the car when we have the fob?" He ran his hand down his face and growled.

"Oh, god." She stepped back. Nausea rose in her stomach, and she raced for the bathroom.

"Ginny? Are you okay?" Jaxon called after her.

She heard him trying to get into the bathroom, but she had locked the door behind her. She didn't want him seeing her like this.

A few minutes later, she walked out of the bathroom.

"Are you okay? Are you ill?" He placed his hand on her forehead. He frowned, concerned etched into the set of his mouth and corners of his eyes.

"No. I'm pregnant."

CHAPTER 3

"*F*uck." Betrayal struck through him like a hot blade of a silver knife.

Pregnant.

Of course she'd probably be pregnant. She was mated, wasn't she?

"Jaxon, I need to get home." Her gaze darted to his, and he saw something flicker through her eyes.

"I'm sure your mate... husband... whatever will understand that you'll be late."

"No, he won't." Her hand went to the arm where he'd seen the bruises.

"Ginny, those bruises aren't from some sex game, are they? Does he... abuse you?" What the fuck kind of monster was she with? How'd she pick that over him? How could a male abuse his mate? It didn't make sense.

"It's none of your business, Jaxon. It really isn't."

"Protecting civilian Weres is my business. You are a civilian Were, so this is my business."

"I'm not in the state of Arkansas. So this technically falls outside your jurisdiction. Which makes me not your business." She lifted her chin and wrapped her arms around herself like armor.

"What state do you live in?"

"Louisiana."

He felt his blood boil. Knowing how big a dick the Pack Master of Louisiana was, Jaxon figured he wouldn't force any of the Weres to stop abusing their mates.

"Have you ever thought about leaving?"

"No. I can't do that." She shook her head and glanced down the empty driveway. "Right now I've got to figure out how to get home."

"I can..." His cell phone screeched to life, interrupting their conversation.

He pulled his phone out of his pocket and tapped the screen.

"Hello?"

"Jaxon. I need an update." Barrett Middleton's deep voice came over the line. His Pack Master was known for getting things done and tying up loose ends.

"Tell me you have that witch," Barrett said.

"I wish I could say that. But unfortunately I can't." His clenched his teeth. He hated letting his Pack Master down. He hated not coming through for Barrett.

"Did she not show?" His voice changed, became harder. "Because if that bartender gave us some bad intel, I want him handled. If you get my meaning."

"That's not it." He took a deep breath. How could he explain that a ghost from the past showed up and distracted him?

"Then what's the story?"

"The witch showed. She did admit to taking blood from her victims. But she said she's not responsible for the killings." He ran his hand through his hair, imagining

Barrett's face turning red with anger. "There was an incident at the bar tonight. Bartender got killed."

"Did she do it?"

"I didn't see her actually do it. But my guess is yes." He shook his head. "She stole a car and got away."

"Let me get this straight. We have a psychotic witch on the loose who not only is wanted for murder, but now she's wanted for grand theft auto?" Barrett's tone was even, but Jaxon could only imagine the look his Pack Master was giving him through the phone.

"In a nutshell, yes." He grimaced.

"That's not good enough!" Barrett growled. "I want that witch found by my Arkansas Guardians by the end of the week. I'm tired of that bitch getting away!"

"You got it, boss. I won't let you down again."

"See to it, Jaxon. Make it happen," Barrett growled.

The phone went dead.

"I take it by the look on your face, that call didn't go well." Ginny looked at him under her lashes.

"You'd be correct. I need to get that witch back now." Jaxon glanced up at the sky. The sun was dipping low, and soon it would be dark.

"I need to get my car back."

"Seems we are in the same boat. It looks like we are stuck together."

* * *

"Fuck." Barrett ended the call with Jaxon and slammed the cell phone on his desk.

"We don't have her, do we?" Ryker looked up at him from his seated position and steepled his fingers together.

"No. Jaxon saw her, but she got away."

Ryker tensed and sat up in the chair. "How the fuck did that happen?"

"He didn't elaborate." He rubbed his temple and tried to rein in his temper. Jaxon had been eager to go on this mission, to bring back the Witch of Yazoo and get her back to Mississippi. Barrett didn't want the relationship with Jack Welbourn, Pack Master of Mississippi, in peril. Alliances were broken for lesser offenses.

Barrett had made a promise to Jack, and he intended to fulfill it. He needed to capture that witch.

"Shit. Bet he got distracted by a piece of ass." Ryker hissed.

"With Jaxon, it's always a woman." He wasn't sure why that was. He knew about Jaxon's past and how he'd been heartbroken over some female. This was long before Jaxon had joined the Guardians. Before he'd made his commitment to the state of Arkansas.

If some woman had broken Barrett's heart, Barrett sure as fuck would steer clear of females. Not Jaxon. Whenever the Were had time off from a mission, he had the females lined up. A new female every time Barrett turned around.

Yet another reason why Barrett intended on never mating. He wasn't getting sucked into the female mind fuck.

"Want me to go down and handle it? He's in the southern part of the state, right?" Ryker looked at him.

Barrett nodded. "Yeah, head on down there, but keep it on the down low. I want to see if Jaxon makes up for this and gets her on his own. But keep me updated on what's going on."

"You got it." Ryker eased out the chair and grabbed his sunglasses off the desk before heading out the door.

Barrett eased back into his leather chair and reached for a file on the corner of his desk: Jaxon's file.

Maybe if he researched Jaxon's past a little bit, he could get a better read on how to help his Guardian.

He flipped through the pages until he came to the very last page. His finger stopped on a name that had a familiar ring. Ginny Wilson.

He turned his computer on and typed her name into his database of werewolves. A few short seconds later, her picture popped up on his screen.

Ginny Wilson, AKA Ginny Boudier

"Fuck." It was like a punch in the gut.

Ginny Wilson wasn't just the girl who had broken Jaxon's heart.

Ginny was the daughter of the most dangerous Pack Master in the States. She was the daughter of Edward Boudier, the Louisiana Pack Master who'd managed to capture, torture, and kill two of his Guardians.

He'd never actually seen Boudier's daughter, and people rarely mentioned her. In fact, it had been years since someone had brought up Ginny's name. As the years had gone by, Barrett had just assumed the daughter had died.

He took a deep breath and shook his head. Jaxon had been lucky to dodge that bullet. If he had ended up with Ginny, then who knew how his life would have turned out.

At least he wasn't with her now and hadn't been for years.

Jaxon's ex was their enemy.

CHAPTER 4

Ginny watched Jaxon walk over to his Harley. The muscles across his broad shoulders flexed with each step he took, reminding her how powerful he really was underneath that cotton T-shirt. She remembered how it felt to be wrapped up in his arms, held against his chest. It was the safest place in the world. She'd not felt like that in a thousand years.

She studied his motorcycle. It was shiny chrome with hints of red painted on the gas tank and the fenders. It was a far cry from the '69 Mustang he'd driven her around in when they were younger.

He'd gone from a motorhead to a badass biker.

As if feeling her eyes on him, he turned and looked over his shoulder. When he realized she wasn't following him, he shot her a glare.

"Come on." His tone was hard, and even from this distance she could see the muscle twitching in his cheek.

"I'm not going with you." She clasped her shaking hands together and glanced around. They might look like they were out here alone, but it didn't feel like they were alone. John always had eyes everywhere.

Jaxon rubbed the back of his neck and studied the ground. "I don't have time to argue with you, Ginny. We've got to leave now." His voice was even and calm, but she could still hear the anger concealed just under the surface, waiting for its chance to burst through.

She shook her head and swallowed. "I can't go with you." If she did, it would be a death sentence.

He let out a string of colorful curses, words she'd never heard him say in front of her, and headed in her direction.

His face was a storm of dark emotions. She'd seen that look before. She'd seen it on John's face right before his hand would strike her.

She took a step back and cringed.

"Do you think I would hit you?" Hurt flashed through his eyes, and he propped his hands on his hips and stared.

She swallowed back her fear. She hated herself in that moment. She'd hated what she'd become. Scared and unsure. She never used to be either of those things.

"Tell me, Ginny. When did I ever hit you?" His stare hardened.

"Never." She lifted her chin.

"You don't get the right to be mad at me. I'm the one who gets to be mad. I'm the one you destroyed," he said.

And I'm paying for it every day of my life.

"I'm not mad at you, Jaxon." She forced her arms to relax at her side and held his gaze.

"Well, you don't look exactly happy." He folded his arms over his chest.

"My car is stolen. I have no way to get home." She narrowed her gaze. "You'd be a little put out if that happened to you."

"I wouldn't be put out. I'd be fucking pissed." He arched his brow.

She snorted and then bit her lip to keep from laughing.

"Ah, see. There's a glimmer of the girl I once knew." A slight smile played at the corners of his beautiful lips.

She shook her head and let the smile go. "No, that girl is gone." She'd been gone a long time.

He opened his mouth and looked like he wanted to say something. But then he shrugged and looked over his shoulder at his bike.

"Well, we both need to find that witch. She has your car, and I need to take her in." He looked back at her. "Go inside the bar and call someone to pick you up."

The flesh on the back of her neck crawled. She couldn't go inside and call John. She was looking at a punishment as it was for being late getting home. But if she told him her car had been stolen, that punishment would be a thousand times worse.

"Do you really think you can catch her?" she asked.

"Absolutely."

"Well, what are we waiting for?" She walked past him toward the Harley. "Let's go."

* * *

JAXON SHOOK his head and followed Ginny over to his bike. He didn't get women. Honest to God, he didn't know what made a woman tick.

First she was mad as hell to see him. Then she acted like she expected him to beat her. Now she was standing by his bike, wanting to go with him.

Something was up. Once they got the witch secured and on her way back to Mississippi, he was going to have a one-on-one talk with Ginny and get to the bottom of things.

He strode over to the bike. He wished he had a helmet for her, but he didn't wear one.

"Your hair's going to get all messed up." He smirked. In her white pants and pink shirt, she looked like a Harley was the last place she belonged. "Need a bandana?"

"Yes." She sighed and fashioned the material around her head.

"I'm ready now." She held his gaze.

He fought a smile. She didn't look like she belonged on a Harley, but he wasn't going to tell her that.

He straddled his bike and waited for her get on.

Her hands rested on his shoulders as she climbed on behind him. His heart sped up, and his muscles tensed at her warm touch.

Despite all she'd done to him, he still wanted her in the most carnal of ways.

Sometimes being a werewolf was a bitch.

He started the engine and the bike roared to life. He never got tired of hearing that sound.

He pulled out of the dusty parking lot, turned onto the road, and increased his speed.

Her hands slid from his shoulders to his waist. She wrapped her arms around him and held on tight as they raced down the back roads of Arkansas.

The sun was fading fast. Soon they would lose daylight. He had no idea where the witch could be headed or how far she'd gone. The only thing he could go by was his heightened sense of smell and his gut instinct.

He approached a four-way intersection and stopped. The land was flat and each direction was surrounded by rice fields.

Ginny leaned closer to her ear. "She went to the right."

"How do you know?" He frowned and shot her a look over his shoulder.

"I have a tracker on my phone." She held up her cell phone.

"Why the hell didn't you say that before we pulled out of the parking lot?"

"You seemed to know where you were going. Besides, you didn't ask." She smirked.

He faced the road.

She thought she wasn't the same girl. But her last comment had proven something.

Ginny was there. She was just hidden under a whole lot of makeup and bruises.

* * *

"WHAT'S BEEN GOING ON, GRANNY?" Ava tried to keep her tone casual as she looked at the older woman over the magazine she'd picked up and pretended to read. Ever since the Valentine Day disaster where Granny had gone on a blind date with a fugitive, everyone near the old woman had been keeping a close eye on her to make sure she didn't get into any more trouble.

Granny put down her knitting and gave Ava a hard stare.

"Ava, I know what you're doing, and it's not working."

"What do you mean?" Her eyes widened and she blinked.

"You want to know if I've had another date since Valentine's Day." She narrowed her wise old eyes and pursed her lips. "You've been staring at me over that magazine you're holding upside down for the past fifteen minutes."

She frowned and glanced down at the magazine. Granny was right. She'd been holding the magazine upside down.

She threw the magazine on the coffee table and sank back on the couch.

"Fine. You're going to make me beg. I'm not above

begging, you know." She gave Granny her best puppy dog eyes.

"No kidding." Granny studied the ceiling before looking back at her.

"Well? Have you had any more dates?" Ava sat up.

"You're too nosy for your own good, Ava," Granny scolded.

"Says the pot to the kettle." Ava smirked.

"Fine, sassy pants." Granny sighed and relaxed back in her favorite green-and-white upholstered chair.

"After Valentine's Day"– she narrowed her eyes– "I didn't get back on that dating site. Sounded like a whole lotta fruit-cakes on there." She shook her head in disapproval. "My curiosity finally got the better of me the other day so I went and checked on my profile, you know, just for kicks and giggles."

"And?" Ava leaned forward.

"I had four hundred hits." She frowned. "Is that what you call it? Hits?" She cringed. "Sounds like doing drugs."

"Holy crap, Granny! Four hundred? That's a hella lot."

"Language, Ava." Granny pursed her lips together.

"Sorry. But seriously, that's lot of responses." Ava said. "Are you going to go out with any of them?"

"I don't know. I read most of them and they all seem so… needy. Like they are looking for a wife. I'm not looking for a husband. Just some companionship from time to time."

"Like a booty call?" Ava giggled.

"Really, Ava? I don't need a man for that with all the merchandise I can get my hands on," Granny deadpanned.

Ava barked out a laugh.

Granny sold adult toys and made damn good money too. She wouldn't tell anyone exactly what she made, but Ava knew it was in the six figures.

"So are you going to answer any of them?"

"Probably not. I still can't shake the one who lent me his RV." Granny frowned. "I returned that thing in one piece, and he still had the nerve to call me a tease. He had no idea I was in deep cover."

Ava bit back a grin. Granny had showed up in New Orleans and saved Barrett and his Guardians after Lucien had been captured and tortured. Granny had managed to commandeer an RV from an older gentleman who'd offered it in exchange for a little romantic time with Granny. Needless to say, Granny did not hold up her end of the bargain. She'd taken the RV, rescued the Arkansas Guardians, and driven them to safety. Barrett had returned the RV to the man so she didn't have to see him again. But he was a persistent gentleman and had found her home phone number and left message after message.

"Seriously, if he's bothering you, let Jayden or Damon take care of it." Ava sat back in the couch and studied the old woman.

"I don't need anyone to take care of it. I've got a concealed carry. I'll shoot him right in the pecker if he dares to show up here." She crossed her skinny arms across her chest. "I told him that too. I think he liked it. Seems like he's into that BDSM stuff."

Ava frowned. She wouldn't classify shooting a man in the dick as the same as BDSM, but she wasn't about to argue with Granny. She knew she'd never win.

"You and the boys should come over for dinner Friday night." Granny relaxed. "I can make a pot roast. I know that Lucien is fully recovered from his injuries. We've haven't had a proper dinner since all that happened in Louisiana."

"I don't know who all is in town. I know that Damon and Jayden have been working surveillance for Barrett. He won't tell me where he is or what's he's doing." Ava frowned. "It's very irritating."

"Hmm. It probably has something to do with Louisiana." Granny raised her eyebrows.

"That's what I thought." After finding out that Louisiana had been behind the attacks on Arkansas Guardians, Barrett had been very close-lipped about what action he was going to take next.

"I'm not so sure I want to know this time." Granny's voice was but a whisper. Her eyes crinkled on the sides as she frowned.

"What do you mean? If Barrett gathers enough intel on Louisiana, won't he just bring it before the other Southern Pack Masters?"

"It's not that simple, Ava," Granny said. "I've seen a lot of Pack Masters come and go. The bad ones always outlast the good ones. I'm concerned what kind of retribution Barrett will face if he pursues this."

"But that's not right. Louisiana can't just commit a crime like that and get away with it." The heat rose in Ava's face.

"Life isn't always fair, honey."

"Well, I trust Barrett and I know that he always gets what he wants. He's been the best Pack Master I've ever met. He won't let us down, Granny. That I can promise you."

CHAPTER 5

*J*axon tried to ignore Ginny's soft hands clinging to his waist. He tried to ignore the sweet scent that drifted over his nose every time he turned his head to the right just a tiny bit. Most of all, he tried to ignore the way his heart sped up in his chest, not because they were chasing the witch, but because she'd always made his heart speed up whenever she was near.

The first time he'd laid eyes on her, he'd known she was the only female for him. Now she had become his Achilles' heel.

"Take a left," she said near his ear and held out her phone to show him the direction the arrow was facing on her tracker system.

He slowed his Harley so he could take the curve. She tightened her arms around his waist and leaned into him. Her pert breasts pressed into his back and he groaned, hating how much he was still attracted to the woman who had not hesitated to rip out his heart.

He increased his speed down the desolate country road.

The quicker he found the witch, the quicker Ginny would get her car back and drive out of his life forever.

His gut twisted.

The bruises. How had Ginny gotten involved with someone who hurt her? How had the girl he'd once known, or thought he'd known, end up with a male like that?

Fuck. He needed to stop overthinking shit. Ginny had made her choice. And she didn't chose him.

Still, he knew that he couldn't just let her ride out of Arkansas and back into Louisiana until he had the whole story about what was going on, even though he knew he couldn't make her leave a dangerous domestic situation. Hell, he'd hung around Braxton enough to hear how that shit turned out.

Braxton, a fellow Arkansas Guardian, had tried to get his mother to leave his abusive father for years. When the old man had been found dead, Braxton had been blamed. After the real killer was found and taken back to stand trial, his mother still hadn't left Louisiana. She still mourned the male who'd beaten the hell out of her every day of her life.

He'd seen the hurt in Braxton's eyes when talked of how his mother had cut herself off from him. Braxton had offered to move her to Arkansas to live with him and his mate, Kate. His mom refused. So he quit trying to be part of her life. He still sent her money every month, but she never responded.

Was that how Ginny was going to end up?

Nausea rolled around in his gut. He knew he couldn't just let her leave until he gave her a way out. A female shouldn't have to live her life in fear.

"Fuck me." He scrubbed his hand down his face. If he didn't watch it, he was going to get sucked back into being vulnerable with her. That was something he couldn't afford to do.

* * *

Ginny didn't suppress her grin. She'd never been on a Harley in her life. But something about the speed and the wind rushing across her skin made her feel alive, something she'd not experienced in a very long time.

The heat from the exhaust scorched her ankle, and she tried to hold it away. Jaxon turned and threw a scowl over his shoulder. He must have felt the shift in the balance of the bike, but she wasn't worried. He was clearly an expert rider. He knew how to handle a bike. He knew how to handle her.

He slowed down as they approached a gas station. He turned in and pulled up beside a pump.

Planting her hands on his shoulders, she got off the bike. Her heel caught on a pebble and she stumbled. Jaxon dismounted and caught her before she fell.

"I'm fine." She stepped out of his embrace and stared up at him.

He said nothing.

"We need to hurry if we're going to catch the car." She glanced around the gas station. It was a habit of hers, looking around and surveying her surroundings. These last few years, her life had consisted of surviving, and she made a point to not let her guard down. Letting her guard down could cost her.

"We're not going anywhere until we get you some different clothes to wear." His gaze drifted down her body to rest at her feet. "Last time I checked, heels were not exactly considered riding gear."

"If you have a bandana or rag, I can tie it around my ankle. No need to get new clothes." She might look like she had a million dollars, but she didn't have a cent to her name. The times she did spend money on something, it was

45

through a credit card. She wasn't allowed to carry cash. She knew why. It was just one more way John could control her.

"Well, you're ruining my image, sweetheart. I can't have a female on the back of my bike looking like some fancy lawyer."

"So you'd rather have a biker chick." She crossed her arms over her chest.

"There was a time you might have liked being a biker chick." He leaned in and smiled.

Her stomach warmed and turned to Jell-O. It had been years since they'd seen each other. He shouldn't still have this effect on her.

"I don't have any money. I can't buy any clothes." She couldn't use the credit card. He could track her down within an hour, and there'd be hell to pay. She was in enough trouble as it was. She didn't need to make it worse.

"Are you kidding, sweetheart? No money? That ring alone looks like it could be worth at least twenty thousand." His gaze narrowed on her wedding ring.

"Thirty," she corrected him and twisted the ring on her finger. Remembering her insignia ring, she shoved her right hand into her pocket before he could get a good look. Jaxon would hate her if he found out who she really was.

If she could be a big enough bitch, then he would be more than willing to let her go after they found her car. He'd probably count himself lucky that he hadn't ended up mating with her.

Her throat tightened. She felt her heart break a little more.

She lifted her chin and reminded herself that she was doing this for Jaxon. That she had to keep this up. If she wanted Jaxon to live she could sacrifice herself.

Something flashed behind Jaxon's eyes, yet he said nothing. She knew that hurting him now would save her trouble down the road.

"Go inside and see what kind of clothes they have." His voice was low and void of emotion. He pulled out his wallet, tugged out a couple of hundred-dollar bills, and shoved them at her. He didn't wait for her to argue or watch to see if she complied. Instead he turned his back and reached for the gas pump to fuel up his Harley.

She turned on her heel and sauntered inside the gas station. The cashier glanced up from reading his paper. He gave her a nod of acknowledgement before his gaze drifted back down to his newspaper. To the left was an area that served freshly made sub sandwiches. To the left were the snacks and coolers for drinks. She glanced toward the back of the gas station and noticed a door going into a different area of the store.

She passed the snacks and stepped into the next room. There were a few racks of secondhand clothes and some shoes, along with some secondhand furniture. An older lady looked up from the counter and smiled.

"Can I help you, dear?"

"I... ah... I was looking for some clothes." She nodded toward the racks.

"Oh." The smile on the older woman faded as her gaze drifted down Ginny's blouse and dress pants. "I don't think we have anything that you would like, honey. They're mainly jeans, T-shirts and boots."

"Actually, that's perfect." She nodded and walked over to the rack of jeans.

After poking around and checking the tags, she found jeans in her size and pulled them off the rack. They had sequined pockets and were a popular brand found in malls. She slung the jeans over her arm and turned toward the T-shirt rack. She settled on a sleeveless racerback T-shirt in black.

She needed boots that would at least protect her ankles from the heat of the bike. She spotted a pair of Harley Davidson boots that came up a few inches over her ankles. They had a lot of wear on them, but she wasn't concerned about the looks. She picked them up and took her findings to the counter.

After changing clothes in the bathroom, she studied her reflection in the mirror. Her gaze drifted down to her insignia ring. She tugged off the jewelry and stuffed it in her pocket.

A few minutes later, she was walking out of the gas station in her new biker clothes with her old clothes folded in her arms.

Jaxon lifted his gaze from his phone and did a double take.

Longing filled his eyes, and she knew that he was remembering how they used to be, the times they'd had together. Back then, they were invincible. That was before she'd learned about life and death and reality.

"All of it was under a hundred dollars." She held out his money. "Here's the rest of your money."

He took it and stuffed it back in his jeans pocket, his gaze never once leaving her.

"Are we ready?" Anxiety pounded in her chest, and she glanced around the gas station. She didn't like staying in one place too long. She knew they needed to get back on the road.

"You certainly look different," he finally said. His gaze landed on her boots. "Nice boots." A slight smile played on his lips.

"I didn't have much choice. I needed something to protect

my ankles." She handed him her clothes, and he stowed them in his saddlebags.

He secured the bags and stood. "It doesn't look like you are trying to protect everything." He reached out and turned her arm over, making the bruises visible. His thumb traced the slight purple marks across her forearm.

She jerked her arm away.

"Ginny, have you ever thought of leaving him?" He cocked his head.

"And finding you?" She smirked. "Don't give yourself so much credit." She had to hurt him, to make him stay away. It was the only way she could keep him safe.

"No. Not to find me." He let out a sigh. "Have you ever thought of leaving so you could feel safe?"

She said nothing. She couldn't. If she did, she would give herself away.

"You must love him very much to tolerate what he does." He glanced at the ground and then back at her.

"You know nothing of love, Jaxon." She swallowed and narrowed her gaze. "Don't try to pretend like you do."

He fisted his hands at his sides, and for a fleeting second she was afraid. No so much afraid that he was going to hit her. She didn't think Jaxon would ever lay a hand on her. But she was afraid of herself. Of what she might say if she caved in. She was afraid of revealing the truth.

Once Jaxon saw the truth, there would be no way to stop him.

And it would end with his death.

CHAPTER 6

"I'm going to meet with the Pack Masters of the Southern States." Barrett studied Damon across his desk. "I'm going to need you to fill in for me while I'm gone."

Damon frowned. "Me? What about Zane or Ryker?"

Barrett narrowed his eyes at the werewolf. "I'd rather have you. Don't get me wrong, they are both capable, but not for this assignment."

Something had shifted since Damon had come into the Pack. He was no longer the loner that Barrett had once seen. He was becoming more entrenched in the Pack, and Barrett wanted to see how much responsibility he could handle.

He held up his hand before Damon could open his mouth. "And don't start telling everyone that I don't think Zane is reliable."

"Wasn't going to."

"Zane wouldn't do it, even if I asked him too. He's still making sure he doesn't go rogue again and start shifting in front of humans." Barrett sighed. "I had the best doctors run test after test on him. They're all saying the drug that was in his system that made him shift out of control is gone. But he still doesn't trust himself. And now is not the time to stress him out over it."

"It'll just take time. He'll get his confidence back." Damon shrugged. "Besides, I'm sure he doesn't mind all that attention that Skylar is giving him."

"No doubt." Barrett grinned. "Not to mention he's been helping finish up SKYLAR'S HOME. It should be open within a month."

"Pretty impressive. So she wants to make it open for both human and werewolf girls who are runaways?" Damon scratched his chin. "It's going to be difficult to keep the humans from finding out about our species. I'm not sure this is a good thing."

"Skylar insists on being inclusive. She wants to protect endangered girls regardless of species. She said that she'll be able to keep the girls' identities secret." Barrett leaned back in his chair. "I told her to handle it and let me know if there's anything I should worry about." Barrett reached under his desk and opened a drawer. He pulled out a thick file and shoved it across the desk to Damon.

"What's this?" Damon frowned.

"A little information on what's going on politically in the great state of Arkansas." Barrett smirked.

"Shit, man. I thought you just sat here in your office all day drinking cappuccinos and scowling. Didn't realize you had all this shit to deal with." Damon sighed.

"You have no idea." He tapped the folder. "Open that up."

Damon turned to the first page.

"That's the drug that Zane was infected with. It's the same drug that those red rogue wolves gave Ava when they kidnapped her."

Damon growled.

"We know it's being made and sold in Louisiana." Barrett narrowed his eyes.

"So the Pack Master Boudier…"

"That fucker is probably in on it. They are probably paying him enough to keep his head turned the other way. I wouldn't put it past him to do something like that."

"Why the hell is he even in power?" Damon shook his head.

"Because once a Pack Master is in power, it's hard as hell to get him unseated." Barrett leaned back in his seat. "Virtually impossible, actually."

"But what about the Council?"

Barrett snorted and shook his head. "The Council may act as the government, but they don't hold much power. Back in the early days, hundreds of years ago, they played a bigger part in ruling. But as stronger Pack Masters arrived, the Council started handing over more and more power to them. They don't mind doing that, as long as the state is running smoothly. But once the population starts bitching or crime goes up, civilian Weres start bitching about how the Council needs more power to protect them."

"So what exactly does the Council do?" Damon shook his head. "I know they take part when we hold Tribunals for crimes committed against our kind. But as far as sending out Guardians and patrolling the state, do they do any of that? Do they offer suggestions?"

"Nope. They are happy to get paid to sit in their mansions and get drunk every night. They get paid as much as the Pack Master, with none of the responsibility."

"Sounds like things need to change," Damon groused.

"Yeah." Barrett looked at him. He couldn't agree more. "Right now I have another fire I have to put out, and it involves that fucking witch from Yazoo City."

"Lucien feels real bad about that happening, Barrett." Damon shook his head.

"He shouldn't. It wasn't his fault. That witch stabbed Catty in order to escape. I had heard stories of the Witch of Yazoo but didn't know she was that vicious." She better hope he didn't cross paths with him, or she'd wished she'd never escaped Mississippi.

"She's psycho," Damon said.

"For sure. I have no doubts that we'll get her." He always got his target. This situation was no different.

Barrett took a deep breath. "Something has to be done about Boudier. Louisiana is in the shitter. There's more violent crime involving werewolves and humans, and in the last three months I've had an influx of civilian Weres flooding into Arkansas. The state is going to explode if we don't do something about the Pack Master."

"Which is why you have constant surveillance on Boudier. Me and Jayden didn't get any new intel on him, but we'll keep trying."

"Do that. I'm hoping to gather enough physical evidence before calling a Tribunal of the Southern states." Barrett stated.

"Shit. That sounds serious." A shadow crossed Damon's face.

"It is serious. There's only been one Tribunal that I even know about involving a Pack Master," Barrett said.

"Oh, yeah? How'd it turn out?"

Barrett held Damon's gaze. "They ended up sentencing him to death."

* * *

"Fuck, fuck, fuck," Ella gripped the steering wheel and pressed her foot against the gas.

"You need to slow down." Nyx said and dug her cat claws into the leather of the passenger's seat.

"Where the hell were you when the shit hit the fan inside the bar?" Ella took her eyes off the road long enough to glare at her familiar.

"I don't visit establishments like that. It's dirty and stinky and full of stupid humans." Nyx glared back. "Why are you on this road anyway? I told you to take a left ten miles back."

"I know where I'm going." No way in hell would she tell Nyx she was lost as a goose. The cat would never let her live it down.

"Where's that envelope at?" Ella looked at the seat and then glanced at the floorboard.

"Keep your eyes on the road." Nyx hissed. "You're gonna kill us both."

"Well that's kind of hard to do since I'm immortal and you have nine lives." Ella shot back. She took one hand off the steering wheel and felt around under Nyx.

"What are you doing?" Nyx swatted with her paw.

"Where's that envelope? Your smelly ass better not be sitting on it." Ella glared.

"My ass is not smelly. It's quite fresh. Besides, what's so important about some stupid paperwork?" Nyx lifted her chin in the air.

"That paperwork is my ticket to freedom." Ella's heart pounded in her chest. This day was going to shit, fast. She hadn't expected she was going to have to kill a werewolf. She may spill blood to keep out of her paranormal prison, but she never killed any of her victims.

"Slow your ass down. You're going way too fast." Nyx dug her claws deeper into the rich leather seats and hissed.

"Have I ever told you how big a pain in my ass you are?" Ella took her eyes off the road for a second to scowl at Nyx.

She glanced back at the road. The car was on the wrong

side of the road and the bright lights from an oncoming vehicle blinded her. She screamed and turned the wheel hard. The car overcorrected and left the road and landed with a sickening thud in a deep ditch.

* * *

"I DON'T UNDERSTAND why we haven't found the car yet," Ginny yelled in Jaxon's ear. According to her phone, they should be pulling up behind it any second. She looked over Jaxon's shoulder at the road ahead.

There were no taillights in front of them. The road was completely dark.

"I'm stopping," he answered.

"No, you can't..." She tugged on his shirt, but he was already slowing down.

He pulled off the isolated road and onto a gravel driveway before he killed the engine. She reluctantly climbed off, and he followed.

"Why did you stop?" She glanced around in the dark and then let her gaze rest on him.

"Let me see your phone." He held out his hand.

"Fine." She shoved it into his palm and crossed her arms. The cool night air brushed across her skin like a caress, and the only sound in the darkness was the hoot of a far-off owl.

He narrowed his eyes on the phone and then looked back at her. "Hmph. Just what I thought."

"What?" She took her phone and looked at it again.

"According to the tracer, the car should be about twenty feet from here."

"But I don't see any taillights. Maybe it's not working." She gnawed on her lips. If John couldn't track her, then he'd send out his men to find her. Finding her with Jaxon would mean an automatic death sentence for him. She couldn't let that happen.

"Not necessarily." He went to the saddlebag and pulled out a flashlight. He walked down the road shining the light off to either side.

She followed.

"There," Jaxon said after walking less than twenty feet down the road. He aimed his flashlight along the steep drop off the right shoulder. Something metallic reflected the light.

It was the trunk of her car. She recognized the license plate.

"Oh, God." She ran past him to the vehicle.

"Wait, where are you going?" He reached out and grabbed her waist, preventing her from going any farther.

"My car." The words rushed past her lips as she continued to stare at the car.

"You can't get in it. It needs to be pulled out by a wrecker." His voice, low and deep, was way too close to her ear.

"Stay here and let me see if that witch is in there." He released his hold and stepped around her. She watched as he made his way down the embankment toward her wrecked Mercedes.

She glanced back at the road. Still no headlights or taillights. They were in the middle of nowhere. Why had the witch stayed on the smaller roads? It would have been quicker if she'd gotten onto the highway versus taking back roads where there was nothing.

It didn't make sense.

"She's not there." Jaxon's voice drifted to her through the darkness. He walked back toward her, stopping a few feet away.

"Is the car damaged? Did she hit something? Is that why she ran off the road?" Despite the heat of the night, goosebumps popped up along her arms, and she rubbed her hands up and down her arms to soothe herself.

"Doesn't look like she hit anything. I'm guessing she figured out you had a tracking device on the car and ran it off the road to throw us off her trail." He glanced back at the car. "And the way the car is sitting, you need a tow truck to pull it out."

"So call a tow truck." She glared.

"Why don't you call a tow truck?" he shot back.

"Because I don't know where the hell I am," she screamed. "And I don't have roadside assistance."

Surprise touched his handsome features, and his glare intensified. "You don't know where you are?" He pointed to a mailbox by a gravel road. The box was partially hidden by overgrown grass and weeds. "You don't recognize the mailbox? Or maybe you know exactly where you are and just don't give a shit." He turned and headed back to the Harley.

"What are you talking about?" she murmured as her gaze landed on the mailbox. Something familiar tugged her gut. Compelled by some unknown force, she walked over to the rusted box.

She held up her phone and shone the light on the metal. With careful fingers, she brushed back the weeds.

Cold dread settled in the pit of her stomach, and her heart thumped hard.

How had she not known? How could she have forgotten?

Madeline Wilson.

She dropped her hand, and the weeds once again hid the mailbox from sight. She looked up the gravel driveway. She couldn't see anything—it was too dark. But she didn't need to see. She already knew where she was.

Fresh chills broke out across her arms as she walked up the gravel driveway. The gravel crunched under her boots as she carefully made her way up the hill. She could remember a time when she'd loved running down this driveway to get the mail. She remembered laughing and racing to see what had been delivered by the mailman. Not tonight. Tonight her path was unfamiliar and unsure. She didn't really want to see what awaited her at the end of the drive.

But the ghosts of her past called to her, demanded that she keep going.

"Ginny. What are you doing?" Jaxon called after her.

She barely heard Jaxon's voice over the buzzing noise between her ears. She swallowed, but her mouth had turned to ash.

She turned on the flashlight app on her cell phone and held it out in front of her. The light illuminated the desolate white house.

The small white house with the front porch stood against the overgrown yard and vines trying to creep through the windows.

She didn't want to go any farther, but her body didn't know that. She took a step as chills marched up and down her spine and nausea curdled in her stomach.

Her foot touched the first creaky step and then the next step until she was standing on the front porch.

"Ginny." Jaxon's voice was low and determined.

Ignoring him and feeling the pull of her past, she touched the knob of the front door. A mass of stringy cobwebs brushed her palm as she twisted the doorknob.

The door creaked as it swung open, revealing the pitch-black hallway. She held up her phone, letting the light shine into the interior of the house. Unable to stop herself, she stepped inside.

The house had long been abandoned. Dirt and dust clung to the old wallpapered walls, and trash littered the floor. Old pictures, their glass cracked, hung at an odd angle.

"What are you doing?" Jaxon called out.

She walked farther toward the kitchen. She stepped into the room and her foot hit an old mason jar, sending it rolling across the heart-of-pine floors. She slid her light over the old, yellowed countertops. Sadness engulfed her, and a hundred memories of her standing on a chair and rolling out cookie dough with her grandmother washed over her in an instant. Laughter had been an ingredient in this kitchen. She couldn't remember a time when she hadn't been happy here.

She turned toward the back door and pushed open the screen door.

Terror and horror filled her chest as she stepped outside.

She remembered one time when this house was devoid of happiness. The one time when she hadn't felt safe.

Grief, hard and sharp, cut into her chest as that one memory crashed into her as she stepped back inside the house.

That was the day her father showed up and killed her grandmother.

CHAPTER 7

*J*axon followed Ginny into the house. His stomach twisting.

He'd once loved this house. Once upon a time, this was a second home to him. But that was many years ago, and like all things tarnished with the passage of time and betrayal, it was nothing but a shell of painful reminders.

"We need to go," he said. He was no longer in a gentle or a forgiving mood. He didn't know what kind of female Ginny had turned into for showing him this, reminding him of how his life hadn't turned out. But he knew now that he no longer knew her. Hell, maybe he never had.

"I said, we need to leave," he said, this time more forcefully.

She turned, and he expected her to retort with some smart-ass reply. But when he saw her pale face illuminated by her phone, he knew something wasn't right.

"Ginny, what's…"

Her eyes rolled back in her head. She slumped forward.

He lunged for her and scooped her up in his arms before she hit the floor.

Her phone slid out of her hand and hit the hardwood floor with a thud. Surrounded by darkness, he blinked, adjusting his keen eyesight in the darkness.

He walked over to the broken window toward the back of the house. The musty lace curtain fluttered in the breeze and stirred a strand of hair against her cheek.

She was even more beautiful than he'd remembered. She'd obviously lost weight and she looked pale, but in her relaxed state with her eyes closed, she looked peaceful, all the stress he'd seen in her face now gone.

The urge to lean down and press his lips to hers was overwhelming. He'd been doing his best to control his body ever since he'd laid eyes on her. Now it was all he could do to stay sane.

Her eyelashes fluttered open and she moaned. She met Jaxon's gaze and frowned.

"What happened?" She turned her head toward the window.

"You fainted. That's what happened." He cocked his head. "Think you can stand if I put you down?"

"Yes, of course." The scowl was back on her forehead, and she pushed at his chest to get him to release her.

He eased her to the floor but held his hands on her arms.

"I'm fine, Jaxon. You can let go." She shoved at his chest, but he didn't move.

"Just making sure you don't hit the floor." He studied her eyes. "What's going on?"

"Nothing's going on."

"Right. Like nothing's going on with those bruises on your arms." His narrowed gaze drifted down.

She flinched out of his grip and shook her head. "You

need to focus, Jaxon. I need to know how to get my car out of that ditch, and fast." She blinked rapidly.

He rubbed his chin with his fingers. "Well, I can call for a wrecker. But that's going to take hours. Or I could just take you home myself."

"How am I going to explain my car?" Her eyes widened and her breathing increased as she stared off.

"Just tell him the truth. That it was stolen." He studied her expression. It was a look he'd never seen on his Ginny before. She wasn't his. She hadn't been for quite a while. Maybe she never had been.

She swallowed. "I can't."

"You can't what?" he cocked his head.

She met his gaze and pressed her lips into a thin line. She took a deep breath and slid her mask of confidence right back over her pretty little face. "I need to get home." She picked up her phone off the dirty floor and cringed at the time. "I'm already pushing it as it is."

"So where is home?"

She bit her lip as if debating whether or not to tell him.

"Ginny, I can't leave you here by yourself."

"I can't ask you to take me when you are obviously on a mission to find that witch." She shook her head. "What did she do that was so bad anyway?"

"She hurt a lot of people. And I'm trying to capture her and take her back where she belongs before she can hurt anyone else."

"Maybe she had a reason for what she did." Ginny's voice was soft.

He knew she must have been feeling some guilt. He felt vindicated in a way. He'd been hurt over her for a very long time.

"There's never a good reason to hurt anyone. Ever," he spat out.

She flinched like he'd slapped her across the face.

He took a deep breath and blew it out. "She escaped from where she was being... contained. Since her escape, she's left a trail of bodies, not to mention she managed to stab a female Were. I need to capture her and bring her back to Mississippi..."

"Mississippi?" Her head snapped up. "Are you saying she's the Witch of Yazoo City?"

"Yeah. You know her?"

She shook her head. "Personally, no, but I've heard the stories. I just always thought she was a legend."

"Nope. She's very much real. And she needs to go back to the cemetery."

"She's imprisoned there, right?" Ginny cocked her head. "How did she leave anyway? I always heard she was under a curse."

"She is. She managed to stab Catty, who happens to be the mate of one of the Arkansas Guardians, when they went to inquire about some shady shit going on in Louisiana. Apparently when the witch spills blood from a paranormal, she can escape the cemetery. She has to keep spilling it to keep from being sucked back into the graveyard."

"She's under a blood curse then." Ginny's eyes grew wide. "I always heard a blood curse was for the most dangerous criminals."

"Or the craziest." Jaxon snorted.

"So what did she do to get cursed in the cemetery?" She folded her arms over her chest.

"How the hell should I know?" he fired back. "Whatever it was must have been pretty serious though."

"You're so damn judgy."

"Judgy? Me? Are you kidding? What about you in your expensive clothes and Mercedes? You're the one looking down your nose at me." His anger boiled, and he curled his fingers into fists at his side.

"I've never looked down on you." Her eyes widened and her arms dropped to her side. "Why would you even say that?"

"I wasn't exactly rolling in money when we met."

"You were just a kid. We both were. I didn't expect you to be rolling in money." She turned and glanced around the darkened room. "I didn't grow up with a silver spoon in my mouth either."

"Well, you are certainly living a life of luxury right now." He glanced down at the large rock on the ring finger of her left hand. "I guess the ring I bought for you was too small."

She placed her right hand over her left, concealing her ring. She met his gaze with renewed focus.

"I need to get home. I don't have time to dredge up the past. I have to get home." Her gaze darted around the room. "If you can't help me, then at least give me your phone and I'll call a cab."

"A cab?" He rubbed his eyebrow and considered his words. "There is no way a cab is going to come all the way out in the middle of nowhere." He shrugged. "Even if you did manage to get one out here, it would take half the night. You wouldn't make it back before dawn."

"But I have to make it back before dawn. I have to..." Her voice quivered and trailed off.

She was scared. And after seeing the bruises on her arms, there was no way in hell he was going to let her go home without seeing what the hell kind of mess she was in.

He couldn't make her leave her husband. Being pregnant complicated things even more. He'd heard enough stories from Braxton to know that abused females rarely left their males. He also knew she would hate him forever if he forced her to do something she didn't want to do.

Her life was her life. If that was what she'd chosen over him, that's what she wanted.

He hated himself for even thinking about going down this path with her. He'd never forgotten her, but he had managed to put together a life for himself. He found that being single suited him. He could date or fuck whoever with no strings attached. He made damn good money working for Barrett as a Guardian in Arkansas, and he actually enjoyed his job. Protecting the civilian werewolves of the state gave him purpose, and at night he could put his head on the pillow and know he'd done a good job at making someone else's life safer, better.

The only time he thought of Ginny was when Granny gathered all the Guardians together for dinner or the holidays. He would glance around the table and notice how the other males were slowly being mated with females. First there was Damon and Ava, then Braxton met Kate and they mated. Jayden was next and he not only mated Haley, he wanted to marry her as well. That had brought up old memories, as that's what the plan had been with Ginny. Zane mated Skylar and now Lucien and Catty had mated around Valentine's Day. The only ones in their little group of friends that were still single besides himself were Ryker and Barrett.

At least he knew Barrett would never mate. The Pack Master had stated that on several occasions.

"What are you thinking?" Ginny asked.

"I'm thinking I'm going to live to regret this." He shoved his hands through his hair and studied the ceiling. "I'll take you back to Louisiana. If we leave now, I can get you there before sunrise."

CHAPTER 8

"It's from Jaxon." Barrett frowned at the cell phone in his hand. He read, then reread the message he'd sent. A female Were was in trouble and he had to help her out. He said he had to take her to Louisiana and would be back late the next day.

Unease settled over him like thick fog.

He punched in a text and sent it. *Who is the female?*

"That asshole better not be getting any pussy," Damon snarled and then crossed his arms over his chest. He'd been in the office with Barrett going over what he needed to do while Barrett went to the meeting with the other Pack Masters.

"He knows better. Jaxon might be a skirt chaser, but when it comes to his job, he's focused." Foreboding snaked around Barrett's gut. It had nothing to do with Jaxon. He trusted the Were. What he was feeling was something else coming down the road that he couldn't see. Too bad he didn't have that fucking witch in custody. He could get her to do some kind of magic and tell him what future event had him on edge.

His phone buzzed, and he glanced back down at Jaxon's reply.

Her name is Ginny.

"Motherfucker." He'd bet his soul it was Ginny Boudier McGregor.

"What is it?" Damon looked up from the paperwork and frowned.

Barrett looked at Damon and held his stare. "Apparently Jaxon is helping a female werewolf."

"Yeah, you said that already." Damon shrugged.

"And her name is Ginny."

"Who the fuck is that?"

"Edward Boudier's only daughter." He squeezed the phone in his hand and struggled to make sense of what Jaxon had just done.

"Fuck."

"We're the ones who are going to be fucked if Boudier finds out." Barrett sent a quick text back to Jaxon. A message in red popped up saying it wasn't delivered.

"Shit."

"Now what is it?" Damon stood. "Does Jaxon know who he's dealing with?"

"I don't know. I sent him a text to let him know, but it's not going through." He forked his hand through his hair.

"Do we send someone down there?" Damon frowned.

"I've already sent Ryker. He's trying to find that witch." He sat down in his chair and leaned back, steepling his fingers together.

"We can pull another Guardian," Damon said.

"No." He shook his head. "Ryker is on the border of Arkansas and Louisiana. He knows not to cross the state line. I have a bad feeling that Jaxon is already in Louisiana. If we send another Guardian, it's going to add fuel to the fire with

Boudier. If Jaxon can get out of Louisiana before Boudier realizes one of my men is there, we still might have a chance."

"A chance of what?" Damon asked.

"A chance of avoiding all-out war with Louisiana."

"War? The Packs haven't been at war since, hell, I can't remember when."

"Boudier would start a war if his steak wasn't prepared the way he wants it. Boudier thinks of nothing but himself. His Guardians are just hired soldiers, there at his beck and call."

"Sounds like a bigger fucker than I remembered him to be," Damon said.

"That's right." Barrett cocked his head. "You used to be a Louisiana Guardian."

Damon snorted. "Before I got kicked out. Best thing that ever happened to me."

Barrett leaned forward and studied the Were. "When you worked for Boudier, did you see what it was about him that made his Guardians so loyal to him?"

"Well, first of all, I was only a Guardian in that state for less than a year before getting kicked out. And I never met the Pack Master. I was offered the Guardian position through one of his Assassins. Boudier never had Guardians in his presence, only his Assassins. The Guardians were never allowed to discuss Boudier or talk smack about him." Damon shook his head. "I don't think it's loyalty they feel toward him. They're afraid of him."

"That's what I figured. If Boudier catches a whiff that I have a Guardian in his state, he won't hesitate to retaliate. It's what he wants." Barrett walked over to the map and studied the boundary line between the two states.

He wanted his revenge against Boudier, but he sure as shit wasn't about to sacrifice his own Guardian.

He needed Jaxon back in Arkansas without Ginny.

It was the only way to save the future of their Pack.

* * *

GINNY TIGHTENED her arms around Jaxon as he tore down the highway toward Lafayette. It had taken her four hours to drive to El Dorado in her car. But judging by how fast Jaxon was pushing his Harley, she figured he was going to shave that time down by at least forty minutes.

She welcomed the night air that blasted her face. Her hair had long since come undone and was swiping around her face and impeding her vision. She didn't mind. She didn't need to see the road. Jaxon was in charge, and she felt safe in knowing he'd do what he promised and get her home.

Home. The overgrown house she'd stepped into tonight was the only home she'd ever known. Where she was heading now wasn't home. It was a prison.

Her mind flew back to the day her life forever changed. What was supposed to be her wedding day had turned into a funeral.

Not only had her grandmother died trying to protect her from a father she didn't know, but her future had died as well.

She didn't have a life. She existed. She existed so others could live.

It was a life she wouldn't wish upon her worst enemy.

Her stomach pitched as they passed a highway sign for Lafayette. The skin on her arms pebbled with terror. She was almost home.

City lights came into view, and Jaxon slowed his speed. Instead of staying on the road, he turned into a gas station.

Her heart lurched into her throat.

"What are you doing? We can't stop. Not now." Her heart beat against her chest.

"I need gas," he said over his shoulder and pulled up beside a gas pump.

Her gaze darted around at the few people milling around their cars. She inhaled deeply. According to their scents, none of them were werewolves.

It didn't matter. John employed humans as well as werewolves. He had eyes all over the state of Louisiana. The fact that she'd just pulled into a gas station on the back of a bike with a man who wasn't her mate would get back to John. This was not going to end well for her.

She needed to get out of sight. She hoped off the bike and fumbled with the saddlebags. Finally she opened one and gathered her clothes into her arms. She dug in her pocket for the insignia ring and slipped it on her the index finger of her right hand.

"What are you doing?" Jaxon grabbed her arm and narrowed his eyes.

"I can get home by myself now. Thank you for taking me this far." She glanced around, looking for any familiar faces.

"But it's still a few more miles."

"It's fine. I have to go." She jerked out of his grasp and hurried down the side of the road. It was late and there was hardly any traffic, so she should be okay. The streetlights illuminated her path, and she knew if she stuck to the light she'd be safe enough from any harm.

The funny thing was, she was safer out here on the streets than she was at home.

Because once she got home, there'd be hell to pay.

* * *

"THAT IS the most hardheaded female I've ever come across," Jaxon muttered under his breath as he gassed up his Harley. He was running on fumes and knew he had to get gas before going after her. He kept glancing up to keep an eye on her as she walked away. The few people who were out didn't bother her. One sketchy-looking human eyed her and then started to walk close to her but then changed his mind and ran in the other direction.

It was like they were afraid of her. Or afraid of what would happen if they got too close to her.

When he'd pulled into the gas station, he'd had a gut instinct that she was going to try to run away from him before they reached her house, and he'd already made up his mind to follow her until she got home. Maybe she was too embarrassed about the abusive situation she was living in. Maybe she really loved her mate and didn't want to leave.

Who the fuck knew. He'd thought he knew women. But Ginny was proving him wrong.

He hung up the pump and trashed his receipt. He knelt and secured the saddlebags Ginny had left open.

"Nice bike, man." A big, burly human with muscles and a bald head sauntered up to him. "I'm in the market for a bike like that."

"Not for sale." He straddled the bike.

The man stepped in front of the Harley and grabbed the handlebars. "Well then, why don't you give it to me?"

"I'm not giving you shit. But I will crack your head in for you," Jaxon snarled.

The guy let out a laugh. "Look, you little piece of…"

"I don't have time for this shit." Jaxon placed his feet on the ground and stood. He hit the guy between the eyes.

The man blinked and then fell back like a tree, his head smacking against the pavement with a sickening sound.

Jaxon started the engine and the bike roared to life. He sped out of the gas station, running over the guy's fingers.

He drove as far as he remembered seeing Ginny walking

and then inhaled, using his sense of smell to follow her deeper into town.

He rumbled past rows and rows of mansions, looking and smelling for Ginny's scent. He noticed the houses all had state-of-the-art cameras aimed at the driveway, and some even had gated entrances.

The large houses were quite different from what Ginny had grown up in. She'd been a country girl through and through and preferred going fishing and having picnics to shopping or going out for a fancy dinner.

She was a shell of who she used to be.

He slowed his bike in front of large mansion. The gate had been activated, and the gates were swinging closed. He saw her small figure walking up the driveway. Without thinking, he drove through the gate, barely making it inside before they closed.

There were no lights on inside the house. Unusual for someone expecting their wife to come home after being gone all day.

The gate slammed shut behind him.

"What the fuck am I doing?" he muttered to himself. Now he was trapped on the wrong side of the gate with no way to open it without waking the house.

But he'd started this journey, and now he needed to see it through to the finish.

CHAPTER 9

*G*inny held her breath as she opened the back door to her house. The lights were off and it was eerily silent.

That was odd.

Though she'd never been late getting home, she'd fully expected John to be waiting for her at the door, eager to dole out his punishment.

She hated John with a vengeance. The only thing that kept her tied to this place was that promise she'd made so long ago.

She glanced down at her clothes and cringed. Appearing in front of John dressed in jeans and biker boots would flame the fire of his rage.

She headed into the half bath off the kitchen and quietly shut the door. She cringed when the hinge creaked.

When she didn't hear any footsteps on the hardwood floor, she turned on the light and hurried to change her clothes.

She glanced at her reflection in the mirror and froze. Her eyes sparkled instead of looking dead. Her normally pale face was flushed from the exhilarating ride on the back of the Harley, and her lips were pink from thinking about Jaxon.

She'd never thought in a million years she'd ever see Jaxon again.

She'd never planned what to say to him if she ever did.

Today had been a big shock to her system. Like her grandmother's home in Arkansas, her relationship with Jaxon had died long ago.

She'd seen to that.

"Ginny!" John yelled.

Her heart jumped in her throat at the sound of his voice.

She stuffed the clothes in the cabinet underneath the sink behind a stack of toilet paper and monogramed hand towels. She finger-brushed her hair and looked at her reflection. There was no time to even think about a lie John would believe.

The door swung open. John stood there, his large frame filling in the doorway and sucking the oxygen out of the room.

Her heart pounded in her chest and her eyes widened.

"Where the fuck have you been?" He narrowed his blue eyes and curled his perfectly manicured fingers into fists. He was still wearing a button-up shirt and tan slacks, both devoid of wrinkles. John always demanded perfection, from how he looked right down to his wife. Appearances were important to him.

His angry gaze raked over her disheveled appearance.

"My car was stolen." She lifted her chin. At least that part wasn't a lie.

"I had to find a way home. I tried to get here as fast as I could." She swallowed. "I knew you would be worried."

"Why didn't you call me?"

"Because my phone died. My charger was in the car and I had no way to charge it." The lie rolled out easy enough.

He cocked his head and studied her. Testing to see whether she was lying or not. She'd learned that she could tell a lot about how hard he was going to hit her by looking in his eyes.

She braced for his next question.

"So how did you get home?" He crossed his arms over his chest and waited.

To the casual observer, John was handsome— more than handsome. With his dark hair, blue eyes, and body made of muscle, he looked like the perfect male specimen. He could have gone into modeling and done quite well. But if they could see inside John's body and stare into his mind muddled with evil and a heart coated in sin, they would see something else.

He was not just a werewolf. John was a monster, a blood-thirsty monster with no conscience.

"I caught a ride with a biker." She took a deep breath. "It was the only option I had. There was no one else on the country road."

She swallowed. "I had no choice."

"Who was this biker?"

Ginny shrugged. He didn't act like he knew Jaxon had brought her into Louisiana. But he was also one to guard his expressions like a snake. He would strike when she least expected it.

"Just some stranger."

"Did he touch you? In any way?" He narrowed his gaze.

"No. He was very polite. He didn't make a move to do anything."

"What about the envelope?" His eyes widened slightly. "Did you deliver it to the bartender?"

"Yes, I gave it to the bartender as you instructed. It was at the bar that my car was stolen." She looked away. Fuck. She'd totally forgotten about the envelope after the bartender had been killed.

"Stolen by who?" He stepped out of the way so she could walk out of the bathroom.

She released the tension in her shoulders. If he was focused on the envelope, then maybe he really didn't know about Jaxon.

She walked into the kitchen and grabbed a glass out of the cabinet. She held it in the door of the refrigerator and filled it with ice-cold water and then took a drink before turning back to him.

"I don't know. Someone said it was some witch."

His hand slammed down across her face. She dropped the glass and it shattered on the floor. Pain exploded behind her eyes and she literally saw stars. She cradled her face in her hands and dropped to her knees, cradling her stomach to protect the baby.

He loved hitting her in the stomach. The bruises there weren't visible to the public.

He rarely hit her in the face. He didn't want to leave bruises on her face.

If he found out she was pregnant, he'd kill the baby. He'd make sure he didn't have an heir that might take away his future as Pack Master.

"You lying bitch." He grabbed her by the hair and lifted her head. He slammed his fist into her stomach. The breath whooshed out of her lungs and she crumbled to the floor. Her arms went around her stomach as she struggled to breathe.

"John, please." She wheezed out. What had she said? What had she done wrong?

"That's not some witch. It's the Witch of Yazoo City. That same bitch that Barrett Middleton has been trying to capture since his Guardian let her get loose out of that cemetery."

"I didn't know that." She cried out. The pain in her stomach spread like white-hot fire.

"And according to my sources, not only did she steal your car. She killed the bartender. And took my envelope." He gritted his teeth and curled his fingers to fists.

She curled herself into a fetal position and braced for the next blow. With him, she never could tell how hard it would be.

"I'm sorry. I'm sorry," she whispered, unsure if he even heard her. Images of Jaxon flashed through her head. "I did everything like you asked me to. It's not my fault she stole it."

"It is your fault, Ginny. You should have called me after you knew the car was gone." He kicked her again in the stomach. She screamed.

"You should have told me it was the witch that had stolen it." He walked around her body and kicked her in the lower back near her kidney. She cried out again in pain.

"Most important of all, you stupid cunt, you should have told me it was Jaxon Taylor who gave you a ride home."

She almost forgot the tremendous amount of pain racking her body.

He knows. He knows. He knows.

Those words danced around in her head like flames of a fire, unable to be contained, unable to be controlled.

She slammed her eyes shut.

She'd known fear since becoming John's wife. She'd known terror since living in his home. But now, right now in this moment, all she could see was death.

Hers and Jaxon's.

CHAPTER 10

*J*axon eased closer to the mansion, careful to keep hidden in the shadows. His keen vision had alerted him to every single camera around the house, and he knew how to avoid getting caught on video.

Whoever this fucker was had money up the ass.

Despite all the cameras and the gate in front of the house, he didn't see any guards. That felt off to him.

Glass shattered inside the darkened house, and he quickened his steps to get closer.

Maybe Ginny had knocked something over while stumbling around in the dark. He'd waited about ten minutes after she entered to see if she turned on a light. She didn't. While he waited, he made sure no one was watching him.

A scream tore through the house. Every muscle in his body tensed. His heart rate amped up and his breathing increased. He hurried toward the back of the house where he'd seen her enter. He heard something rustling in the trees behind him. He stopped and turned.

Something black jumped on his face and dug its claws in.

"What the fuck." He grabbed the black fur ball and pulled it off. He slung it to the ground and glared. "A fucking cat."

"I'm not just a cat, you asshole." The black cat hissed and then pawed at him.

"A talking cat, perfect," he said.

"That's rich coming from a talking wolf." The black cat turned and padded off into the trees.

He started to go after it to find out if the cat was a spy, but just then he heard another scream.

Ginny.

He ran toward the back and stopped just as the door opened. He slid behind a large tree in the back yard and waited.

A large man hurried down the steps toward the car parked around back. He looked back over his shoulder. "If you fucking leave this house before I get back, I'm going to make you wish you were dead, Ginny."

Anger rose up in Jaxon's chest like kerosene and splashed into his heart.

He was going to kill that fucker.

The male jumped in the car and sped out of the driveway.

Jaxon ran inside the house and froze. A small form was huddled on the floor.

"Ginny?" His voice quivered.

"Oh, god, Jaxon, you have to leave." She tried to push herself up on her elbows, but she slipped.

He reached for the light switch.

"No. Don't turn on the light."

He knelt by her side. Gently, he helped her up into a sitting position. She wheezed and cradled her stomach.

"I'm picking you up."

"No, wait. Just give me a minute." She shook her head and then drew in a pained breath.

"Jesus, Ginny. I guess I don't have to ask if that was your

husband who did this to you. You're not fucking staying here." His voice cracked. His stomach literally churned at seeing her beaten and bruised.

"You don't understand, Jaxon."

"That you stay with a man that hits you? No, I don't fucking understand. Look, I don't care if you never want to see me again. I'm not asking you to come live with me. What I am asking you to do is leave this place. Ginny, I can take you away and you won't ever have to see this guy again." Jaxon swiped at the tears running down her cheeks.

"You don't understand, Jaxon." She sniffed.

"Then tell me, Ginny. Tell me something to help me understand. Make me understand. Do you love him that much? That you would allow him to beat the shit out of you? You know that's not love, right?"

"I don't love him, Jaxon. I hate him with a passion." She looked up at him. "Help me stand."

He helped her to her feet but kept his hand around her waist to steady her. She felt frail and thin, much too thin. This wasn't his Ginny.

But he wanted to help her find her way back.

"So you hate him," he said.

"Like you wouldn't believe."

"Yet you stay with him." He shook his head. "This doesn't make sense, Ginny. You're not making any sense." He narrowed his eyes. "Are you on drugs? Has he drugged you?"

"I'm not on drugs, Jaxon. I rarely ever drink." She smiled a little. He swiped a cut on her lip with his thumb.

"So tell me then. Make me understand."

"I don't have a choice. If I leave him, he will kill my mother." She looked into his eyes.

He shook his head. "But your mother died when you were a baby. So did your father. That's why you were living with your grandmother."

"That's what I thought. I thought I had no parents." She turned her head from him.

"Are you saying they are both alive?" Her words didn't make any sense at all.

"Yes," she said softly.

"So why was your grandmother raising you?" He shook his head.

"My mother ran away from my father when she was close to giving birth. Once she got to my grandmother's house, she went into labor." She shook her head. "There wasn't time for a doctor, so my grandmother delivered me. My mother planned on leaving the next day, running as far as possible. She wanted to go to Alaska and raise me without fear of my father ever finding us."

"What happened?"

"The next day, my mother saw my father driving up the driveway. She gave me to my grandmother and made her promise, made her swear to run into the woods and hide. She made my grandmother promise to protect me with her life." She looked into his eyes. "So that's what she did."

"My father came into the house, outraged that my mother had fled, had left him. When she'd found out she was pregnant with me, she was scared of bringing me up in a house with him as a father. So that's why she left." She winced as she touched her bruised face.

"He found your mom." He shook his head. "But why didn't he try to find you?"

She smiled a little. "My grandmother is a very smart woman. When my mom showed up and gave birth to me, she knew my father would be coming for me. She knew he would catch up to my mom. After I was born, she went out in the backyard and she started digging a hole. She dug all night until the hole was deep enough for a grave." She looked at him. "She had a wooden crate in the barn. She had a calf

81

that had died the day before my mom arrived, so she wrapped the body in sheets and put it in the crate. She buried it six feet down and then marked the 'grave' with a wooden cross."

"So your grandmother was going to tell your father that your mother had died in childbirth and you hadn't survived." He'd always liked her grandmother. The woman was wise and kind.

"Yes. So when my father arrived, my mother lied and said that I had died, that I was stillborn." She shook her head. "He didn't believe her until she showed her the grave. If it hadn't been for my grandmother's quick thinking and planning, he would have hunted her down until he found me."

"So your father took your mother away with him, and for eighteen years you were hidden from him." He took a step back, shocked at the story she'd just told him.

"Yes."

"So when your father found you and brought you back, why didn't your mother take you and leave? You both could have left together."

"My mother was too conditioned by then. Living with him for eighteen years had changed her, made her almost mad. Made her loyal to him. When he found me and brought me back here, she begged me to promise never to try to leave."

"I don't understand that." He shoved his fingers through his hair.

"It's not meant for you to understand, Jaxon." Her voice was quiet and sad. "It's just how life is sometimes."

"So you just plan on staying here, living here with your abusive mate?" Anger curled in his gut and flowed to every muscle in his body. Ginny was supposed to be his. He was supposed to be Ginny's mate.

"He's not my mate. Not in ways that count," she said.

He didn't say anything. He just nodded.

"So how did your father find out that you were alive?" He needed to know the rest of the story. He needed to hear.

"When I was planning our wedding, I got really emotional one night with my grandmother. I told her that the only thing that would make my wedding day perfect was if I could have my mother there. I was just a girl wanting my dead mother to share my special day. I had no idea I would regret saying that out loud." She looked away and shook her head. "My grandmother thought she could get a letter to my mother without my father finding out. She still had some people in Louisiana she trusted. She wanted to tell her about the wedding. It was going to be a surprise for me. I was at home, upstairs in my room. I heard a car coming up the driveway. I didn't really pay any mind to it. I was too busy trying on my…" Her words tapered off.

He knew what she was going to say before she uttered the words.

"Your wedding dress," he said. A heaviness settled in his chest, something that felt a whole hell of a lot like grief.

She nodded and studied the floor. She wrapped her arms around her waist.

"I heard my grandmother talking to someone downstairs, and when the yelling started, I ran down to see what was going on."

"The second he saw me, he grabbed my grandmother and wrapped his arms around her head and snapped her neck." A sob bubbled out of her, but she regained her composure and waved him away when he moved toward her. "As my grandmother slid to the ground, he told me he'd always hated the bitch. He then put a silver bullet in her head."

A desire for revenge poured through him until all he could see was red. To kill a female was unheard of. To kill an elderly female was worse.

"Where does your father live, Ginny? I want his name," he demanded.

She shook her head. "No, Jaxon. He will kill you."

"He can try. And he might succeed. But that fucker's going in the ground with me." He didn't care if he died. All he wanted was the chance to rip that fucker's throat out and decapitate him.

But first he was going to kill her husband in the most painful of ways.

"Jaxon." She placed her hands on his chest. The sky outside was starting to turn a gray-purple color that heralded the impending dawn. She turned to look out the kitchen window, and he could see the swelling of her cheek.

It fueled his rage and determination.

"I will kill your father, Ginny."

"You can't. He's very powerful. Everyone is afraid to turn on him. It's how he's kept his power all these years."

"He doesn't care that your husband beats you?" The thought made him sick.

Her wide eyes met his. "They are cut from the same cloth. My father knew John was a violent man, but he didn't care. John is wealthy, as you can see. John inherited all his money. He didn't earn anything. All my father cares about is how much more power he can grab. He knew that by marrying me to John, he could have an unlimited supply of wealth."

"First your husband goes, and then I kill your father."

"This is not some small-time criminal. He's very powerful." She shook her head and then froze. "How did you get in here, anyway?"

"I drove in before the gate closed. I saw you go into the house and wanted to make sure you were okay." His gaze dropped to her cheek. "And judging by the looks of things, I was right. Things aren't okay."

"God, Jaxon." She paled. "If you had come in while he was here, he would have killed you."

"I was on my way when I heard you scream. But a cat jumped out at me in from the tree line." His stomach dropped. "I should have been here for you, Ginny."

"I'm glad you weren't." She squeezed her eyes shut. "John could have killed you and made me watch."

"You don't have a whole lot of faith in me, do you?" Her lack of it was starting to irritate him.

She shoved away from him and cringed. She cradled her stomach and took a few steps back. "Why do you think he has gates outside?"

"To keep people from getting in here to kill his ass."

"You've got it wrong." She shook her head as tears ran down her face. "He has those gates outside to keep anyone from getting out." She looked up. "I don't know how you are going to get out of here. Jaxon, you're trapped."

CHAPTER 11

*B*arrett dug his ringing cell phone out of his brown leather jacket and answered it before sliding into his red Mustang.

He usually preferred riding his Harley, but he chose to take the car tonight instead. Tonight he needed music and a fast car.

"Hello?" He turned the key and the engine roared to life. The sound seemed to soothe his soul.

"Barrett…"

He froze when he heard the feminine voice on the other end of the line. It was a voice he'd only heard a few times in his life.

"Barrett, we need a little help in Vermont," she said softly.

He frowned. "Vermont or any New England state is not my territory. Never has been, never will be." He had enough trouble on his plate without adding to it. He needed a vacation. A long vacation on a beach with a couple of naked females to fuck his brains out.

That's what he needed.

"I understand. And you're right," she said softly.

He growled. "You know I'm not allowed to interfere in the dealings of other species. I am Pack Master of Arkansas. Werewolves are who I command in my state. Not..."

"Not fairies?" She laughed. "We don't want you to rule the Fae in New England. That's not why I'm calling."

"Then what is it? I'm trying to keep the peace and prevent a civil war from breaking out down here. I'm stretched pretty thin as it is." He felt like every day more bad shit was happening to draw Louisiana and Arkansas into a war of the Packs. Arkansas might have the fortitude and determination, but Louisiana had the firepower.

"Well, I know you can't give us an army. But I was wondering if you could spare any of your Guardians," she said.

He racked his brain, trying to come up with an excuse. Werewolves and Fae did not get along. They had nothing in common except an aversion to metal. Where iron was toxic to fairies, silver was deadly to werewolves.

"Ryker. I'll send Ryker." He accelerated and shifted gears as he increased his speed. He needed to get Ryker out of the southern part of the state anyway. Ryker always did have a hard time with instructions, and if he knew how close Jaxon was to danger and who he was with, Ryker wouldn't hesitate to cross the state line into Louisiana to save his fellow Guardian.

Barrett couldn't take that chance.

"I appreciate this, Barrett. I really do."

"Sarah, you owe me. Big time." He ended the call and threw the cell phone on the passenger seat.

* * *

"So you're going to be in charge? Stepping in as Pack

Master?" Ava ran her hand down Damon's chest, feeling each toned muscle under her fingertips.

"Just while Barrett's gone." He wrapped his arms around her waist and pulled her into his chest.

"I've never slept with the boss before." She unbuckled his belt and slid her hand down the front of his pants. Even without an erection, Damon was big.

"Ava," he warned in that tone he used with her when he was trying to maintain control. But she knew him better. She would just squeeze him a little harder and he would lose all restraint. She'd get him wild and out of control. Just how she liked him.

"Clothes off now," he growled.

"Huh?" She gave him an innocent smile while her body tingled under his command.

"Take your fucking clothes off now before I rip them off." His gaze raked over her body. "I know how much you love that top. But don't think I won't rip it off and buy you another one."

She stepped back and gave a squeak. "Wait! I just got this shirt." She glared but quickly rid herself of the top.

She stuck her hands in her jeans pockets and thrust out her breasts.

"And the jeans. Take the jeans off too." His lust-filled eyes narrowed.

"Whatever you say, boss." She smirked and took her time sliding her jeans down her hips. She didn't need to look to know he was watching her. She could feel those hot eyes on her body like fire.

The second she kicked her jeans off, Damon grabbed her hauled her across his shoulder.

"I'm done waiting." He smacked his hand across her ass.

"Damon." She sucked in a hiss at the sharp bite of pain.

"No talking." He walked over to their bed and laid her in

the middle. "The only sounds I want to hear coming out of your mouth are moans."

She met his gaze and felt herself go wet.

He crawled onto the bed and hooked his thumbs in her panties. He dragged them down her hips and tossed them across his shoulder.

He buried his face between her legs feasted on her sensitive flesh.

She bucked her hips and moaned as his tongue flicked across her clit. She threaded her fingers through his dark hair and held his face against her. He looked up and held her gaze as his mouth teased her.

"That feels so good." She moaned as her heart rate went through the roof.

He growled between her legs and then sucked her clit into his mouth.

Pleasure streaked through her body, and she let out a scream as she rode out her orgasm. He looked up from between her legs, his mouth shiny with her sweetness, and grinned.

He crawled up her body, trapping her underneath. He plunged inside her with one quick motion.

He stretched her, filling her with his largeness. She dug her fingernails into his back, needing him closer, needing him near.

He looked at her, his eyes filled with love so intense it made her want to weep. She was beyond lucky that she had Damon. She was blessed.

He threaded his fingers through hers and raised her hands above her head, moving against her body with rhythmic seduction.

His body moved, and she felt every tightening of his muscles against her stomach. She wanted to touch him, run her hand down his back and grab his butt, but he held her captive.

"Damon," she whimpered and wrapped her legs around his waist. She gasped as she felt her second orgasm rising to the surface.

"Come for me," he demanded, his voice hoarse and rough.

That was all it took.

She fell into a blinding orgasm so intense that it streaked across her body like a white light shooting across the sky. She trembled against his body as her orgasm flew through her. He quickened his thrusts and buried his face in the crook of her neck. He bit her as he spilled his hot seed inside her body.

Hot and sweaty, he pulled back to study her face.

"It never gets old," he whispered and placed his lips across hers.

"It never will." She smiled and slid her hands down and squeezed his ass.

* * *

"WHAT DO YOU MEAN, we're trapped?" Jaxon jerked his gaze around the room but didn't see anything.

"I mean, didn't you find it strange that no one stopped you from entering?" Her eyes were filled sadness.

"I found it strange that you came home willingly. Ginny, you had freedom outside these gates and walls. You could have kept going. Instead, you came back here."

"You don't understand. It's not that simple." She looked away.

"Then make me understand." He placed he tip of his finger gently under her chin. "If I got you out tonight, would you come with me?"

"He would only come after me if I left. Besides, there are other people in danger if I leave."

He cocked his head. "Like your mother."

"She's one of them." She shook her head.

"Then make your mother come with us. She doesn't have to live like this. You both can be safe."

"I've tried to tell her that. But she is brainwashed and so scared of him."

That was fucked up beyond anything he'd ever heard. A mother should always protect her child, even with her own life. Ginny's mother had failed her in a major way.

"Then it's her choice to stay. She can't guilt you into staying for her. It's selfish as hell," he ground out. He didn't care if it pissed her off or not. "Who else did he say he would hurt if you left?"

She looked at him, her eyes heavy with unshed tears. She'd probably learned a long time ago how to take the pain, how to take a beating and not let her husband see her cry. She knew it would show weakness.

Men like John would feed off weakness.

"Tell me, Ginny." He leaned in. "Tell me who he is using to keep you so in line."

"You, Jaxon. He'd told me he'd kill you if I ever left."

Coldness hit his core, spreading upward into his chest until he was panting. He dropped his hands and curled his fingers into fists as he looked at her.

"Me?" He shook his head. "But I thought…"

"You thought I had second thoughts about our wedding, about our mating." She shook her head. "No, when my father showed up and killed my grandmother, he told me if I didn't come with him, he would kill you. He said he was powerful enough to find you anywhere."

She swallowed and wrapped her arms around her tender stomach. "I was young and I believed him. So I left. And once I got to his house, he forced me to marry John. He said he needed the alliance because John had wealth. I didn't know it at the time, but John hoped to be next in line for Pack Master."

The hair stood up on the back of his neck. "Ginny, who is your father?"

She held out her right hand and looked into his eyes. His chest tightened when he saw the insignia ring for the state of Louisiana. Only Pack Masters were given insignia rings. He'd seen Barrett's sitting in a bowl on his desk. He never wore his.

"My father is Edward Boudier." She swallowed and looked away.

"Fuck." He stared at her for a long time. "Edward Boudier is your father." This was more serious than he'd thought. Barrett was going to flip the fuck out.

"I am your worst enemy, Jaxon. I'm sure you will want to retract your offer of help. I don't blame you. I'm ashamed that I have his blood running through my veins." Silent tears slid down her cheeks.

"Jaxon, please leave before John gets back. If he finds you here he will kill you."

He shook his head. "I can't leave you. You know that." He forked his fingers through his hair. "So your husband thinks he's next in line for Pack Master?"

"Yes. My father promised him the position if he would marry me."

"I can't imagine Edward Boudier giving that up any time soon." Jaxon snorted. He knew Boudier. He knew the depths the fucker would go to keep anyone from taking what he considered as his rightful place.

"My father won't. Right now, John has the honor of being the son-in-law, the presumed next in line for Pack Master. It gives him power that his wealth didn't. And my father has the wealth he's always needed to keep paying people off to keep him in his position." She swiped at her lip and looked at the smear of blood.

"I don't have a choice." She looked at him. A tear slid down her face and fell to the floor.

"You always have a choice." He pulled her into his arms. She went willingly, without a fight.

"John knows you brought me home, Jaxon. He knows everything." Her hands went around his waist, and she sobbed silently. "We can't escape now. He's going to kill you and make me watch."

"Someone's going die, but it sure as hell won't be me, baby."

She stiffed in his arms, and he immediately caught the scent of her fear in the air.

"He'll be coming back soon. You have to leave." She shoved out of his arms and stepped back, her wild-eyed gaze darting around the room.

"Then I'll handle him."

"No!" She shoved at his chest, catching him off guard with her strong reaction.

She grabbed his hand and pleaded. "Listen, if he catches you here in his home, he will kill you. Please don't make me watch him do it."

"I can't leave you with him."

"He won't hurt me, not again today. Once he comes back and sees the condition of my face, he will not hit me again. He knows he can't take me out in public looking like this." She spread out her arms.

"But..."

"At least leave the house. Go hide outside somewhere, or if you can, get out over the walls," she said. "If you are serious about getting me out of here, then I need to get my stuff in order. I need to tell my mom. Surely you have to let me talk to my mom first."

"We don't have time." They needed to leave now.

"Jaxon, do you trust me?" She grabbed his hand and put it to her chest.

"Ginny." His heart tumbled, and he knew he hadn't stopped loving the woman standing in front of him. Time had passed, but it had not weakened his love for her. He realized he loved her more now than he had all those years ago.

"Jaxon, please. I can't lose you a second time." Tears streamed down her face. He couldn't take it another second. He gathered her in his arms and pulled her close, pressing his lips against her.

She kissed him back, gently and cautiously. She opened her mouth under his lips, letting him taste the sweet recesses of what he'd missed all these years.

He groaned and felt his body go hard with lust.

She wound her arms around his waist, holding onto him like he was her lifeline.

He held her, careful not to press too hard against her injures. God, he'd waited so long to get some satisfaction as to why she'd left him.

Now with her in his arms, he realized she hadn't left him. She had tried to protect him by taking the abuse on her own body. He'd never let her get away again. He swore in his heart he'd always protect her, protect her with his heart and his body and his life.

Hope rose in his chest and crested over his heart, washing him in sheer determination to make things right with her.

He kissed a trail from her mouth to the corner of her cheek. He closed his eyes and whispered near her ear. "I love you."

"I love you too, Jaxon. I never stopped loving you." Sobs

racked her chest as she buried into him. "I'm so sorry you thought I left you. I never meant for you..."

"Shush. Shush. There's no need for words. Not now." He pressed his lips to hers, silencing any more words.

He moved back, taking his lips from hers, and gazed into her eyes. "Is there anyone else in the house with you?" With a house this big, there had to be staff.

"No, but my mom comes over every morning." She glanced over at the clock on the microwave. "She should be here any minute."

He nodded.

"Jaxon, I told you no one ever leaves."

"Well, I'm not exactly no one. And we're getting the hell out of here. I'll go outside and check the perimeter. While I'm outside, you need to talk to your mom, convince her to leave with us. Tell her I can provide you both with protection from the Arkansas Pack Master." He was making promises on Barrett's behalf. He was going to catch hell from his Pack Master, but there was no way around it. He'd take the consequences.

"Jaxon..."

He pressed his fingers to her lips to silence her. He saw the uncertainty in her eyes and heard the tremor in her voice. He also knew underneath that fragile shell lay the girl he had fallen in love with as a teenager. She was only other person on this earth that would complete his life.

He wasn't about to let her go.

"Trust me," he whispered.

She blinked, and a tear slid down her silky cheek. He swept his fingers across her cheek and wiped away the wetness.

"I trust you, Jaxon. I always have," she whispered.

A lightness, a feeling he'd never felt before, filled his

chest. This was going to work out. They were going to work out. Everything was going to be okay.

The sound of a car pulling into the driveway caught his attention, and he jerked his head toward the kitchen window.

"It's okay. It's just my mom." She looked at him. "I need to talk to her alone."

He nodded. "I'll be back after I survey the fence."

He gave her a quick kiss and bounded out the back door before her mom pulled around back.

He ran toward the fence, using the thick cover of trees to conceal himself. He ducked behind an oak tree just as the car stopped near the back door. He watched briefly as a small woman carefully got out of the Mercedes and looped her purse over her arm.

From this distance, he could tell that Ginny resembled her mother. She was blonde and beautiful just like Ginny. But there was something missing from her face—it was devoid of any smile lines. Even her eyes were dull, as if her soul had been eaten away many years ago.

He had to get them out and fast. He wasn't going to let Ginny end up dead—or worse, end up like her mother.

CHAPTER 12

*G*inny held her breath, bracing for her mother's reaction when she walked in the door.

Caroline Boudier opened the door and stepped inside.

Ginny's gaze swept over her mother, and she was reminded just how much her mother looked like her, except Caroline Boudier was nothing like her. Not where it counted.

"Hello, Ginn..." Her mother's words trailed off. She closed the door behind her. She squinted in the dim room and then flipped on the light switch.

Her gaze landed on Ginny's face. Concern flashed through her eyes, and then her mother shook her head and sighed. "I see your face is bruised. What did you do this time, Ginny?"

Ginny bristled at her mother's question. Usually she didn't feel any emotion when her mother chided her for getting beaten. But now, after being around Jaxon for a few short hours, her emotions were rising from that deep place where she'd buried them long ago. Jaxon had apparently awoken the beast within.

"What if I told you I didn't do anything?" she countered.

"He doesn't hit you for no reason." Her mother placed her expensive bag on the quartz counter and looked up at her.

"What if I told you I lied to him?"

"Then I suppose you know better than to lie to him. Lying has its consequences. You know that, dear." Caroline sighed heavily, walked over to the cabinet, and pulled down a coffee mug. She popped the coffee pod into the coffee maker, placed a mug underneath, and pressed the button.

"When did it happen to you?" Ginny swiped her lip and glanced at her fingertips. No blood. Which meant her body was healing quickly from the beating.

"When did what happen?" Her mother drew her tired gaze up to her.

"When did you decide it was okay for a man to hit a woman? What the hell happened in your head to make that okay?" Barely concealed anger pulsed just beneath the surface of her veins. She curled her fingers into fists and met her mother's surprised gaze.

"You don't understand. It's survival." Her mother narrowed her eyes and reached for her coffee cup.

"It would have been better if you had killed me when I was born." Ginny spat the words out, unable to conceal her anger or her hurt.

"That's probably true." Her mother took a sip and then sighed. "Should've, could've, would've."

Stunned at her mother's words, Ginny took a step back. "You're more fucked up than my father or my husband."

"We are all dealt certain circumstances in this life. We must bear them as best as we can." Her mother set her coffee cup down and waved her hands around the room. "Besides, you don't have it bad here, Ginny. You live in a mansion, drive a Mercedes, go shopping every day. You don't have to work, you don't want for anything. All you have to do is run an errand for your father or John every now and then." She shrugged her slender shoulders. "Sometimes I think you are just ungrateful."

"Sometimes I think you turned into a monster. My father, your husband, killed your own mother. He broke her neck in front of me, and you don't even care." She stepped toward her mother. She clenched her trembling hands into fists.

"My mother shouldn't have stayed in that house." Caroline shook her head. "I don't know what possessed that woman to not take you and leave when she had the chance. But no. She stayed there, knowing full well that he knew where she lived."

"She wasn't some woman. She was my grandmother. She thought she could keep me safe." Ginny's heart clenched as she thought about her grandmother.

"I'll admit, she kept you safe for a brief while." She shook her head. "She never should have sent me that letter informing me of your wedding and mating to that werewolf, what's his name? Started with a J. Jack or something."

"Jaxon. His name is Jaxon."

"Your grandmother should have known that Edward would intercept that letter. That he would come looking for you. You are his only child, his only heir in this world." Her mother lifted her chin.

"He's a monster," Ginny hissed.

"He's still your father." Her mother looked away.

"Mother, if you could leave, and be promised safety in another state, would you go?"

"There is no such thing as safety. Edward Boudier owns me, and he owns you. He even owns your husband. Don't ever forget that." Her mother glared and wagged her finger in her face.

"You're a coward."

"I'm a survivor. And I know when to count my blessings and to be grateful for what I have." She lifted her chin and glowered.

Ginny barely recognized the woman standing in front of her. "For years, growing up, I would always ask my grandmother about my mother. I longed to have a mother." She shook her head. "All she told me growing up was that my mother and father were killed by intruders with silver knives. It never made sense to me why someone would do such a horrible thing to good people like my parents."

Ginny walked around the kitchen counter. She needed distance from her mother.

"Finally, one day my grandmother told me the truth. It was a week before my wedding to Jaxon. She told me that my parents were both alive but my mother had hidden me with her to protect me from my father. She said that my mother gave up her freedom for me."

"Ginny…"

Ginny held up her hand to silence her mother. She had a lot to say, and she was going to damn well say it.

"Do you know what my father did as soon as he saw me?" She cocked her head. "Do you?"

Caroline sighed. "You've already told me this story before, Ginny. Why must you drag up the past now?"

"We're going to talk about it because you never wanted to hear the story. Now you will hear the story." She curled her fingers into fists. "Your husband, my father, grabbed my grandmother, your mother, and broke her neck. Right in front of me. Then he put two silver bullets in her head to make sure she was dead. Do you know what your husband said to me after that?"

She wasn't going to give her mother a chance to answer. "He stepped over my grandmother's body and grabbed me.

He said that I could come with him and he would leave Jaxon alive, or if I refused, he would have him killed within a day. Our wedding day."

"The past is the past. We must focus on the present," Caroline said firmly.

"I came to know what a monster my father really is. I have a husband who is as cruel as my father is in every single way. Now I'm beginning to think they're not the only monsters in my family." She glared. It was all she could do not to slap her mother's stoic face.

"Are you done being dramatic? If so, can we please have some coffee in the dining room so we can go over your schedule? There are a lot of upcoming social events that require your presence in New Orleans."

"I'm not going." Just saying those words had a lightness dancing around in her chest.

"You don't have a choice." Her mother picked up her coffee mug and walked in the direction of the dining room.

"You mistake me, mother. I'm not going to be here to be able to attend those functions." Her heart hammered in her chest.

"Do you have a trip planned that I'm not aware of? Milan? Paris, perhaps?" Her mother kept walking.

"I'm leaving. I'm leaving today, and I'm leaving with Jaxon." The words themselves empowered her, and she could feel her body trembling with excitement, motivation, and sheer determination.

Her mother made it to the dining room and stopped. She slowly turned and fixed her wide-eyed stare on her. "What did you say?"

Ginny licked her lips and lifted her chin. "I said I'm leaving and I'm leaving with Jaxon. I know you've lived like this for so long that you don't know how else to manage. But there is another life out there. A life without fear, a life without terror, and a life without pain. He has told me that he can get us out, take us to Arkansas, and we will be under the protection of their Pack Master, Barrett."

"Barrett Middleton?" Her mother sucked in a breath and glanced around the room.

"Is Jaxon here? Tell me he's not in this house." Her mother's face went pale, and her gaze flitted around the room.

"Not in the house. But he is outside."

"You selfish bitch." Caroline slapped Ginny across the face.

Ginny sucked in a gasp and palmed her face. Her mother had never raised a hand to her, ever. It had always been the men in her life.

"Make him leave now. There's still time to fix this before John finds out." Her mother grabbed her by the arms and shook her like a rag doll.

"Get your hands off me." Ginny shook off her mother's hard grip. "I'm leaving and I'm leaving today. If you want to stay here in this hellhole, then stay. But I refuse."

"You don't know what you are saying." Caroline shook her head violently. "John will track you down and find you. When he finds you, he will kill you. You have to know that."

She did. She knew that all too well.

Her chest ached and her skin crawled as a thin sheen of sweat cropped up over her flesh. She couldn't stay here another second even if she wanted to. She couldn't. She'd go insane.

Jaxon had given her hope, and it was that thin thread that she was clinging to.

"You can't go." Her mother's eyes went wide and she ran in front of her, trapping her in front of the dining room. She put her hands on her hips, preventing her from going any farther.

"You can't stop me." Ginny tried to walk around her mother.

Caroline grabbed her arm, digging her long nails into Ginny's flesh.

Ginny snatched her arm out of her grip, shocked and angered at her mother's display of aggression. She'd never seen her act like this before.

"What the hell has gotten into you?" Ginny cocked her head at her mother. The hair on the back of her neck stood on end. She had a very bad feeling.

"You are no daughter of mine. My daughter would do anything to protect her mother. She would sacrifice herself for the good of the family. I can't let you walk out that door." Caroline narrowed her eyes.

"A real mother would protect her daughter. You might have been that kind of mother a long time ago, but not now. Now you think of only yourself. You're no mother. You're sure as hell not my mother. My grandmother was more of a mother than you," Ginny said.

Caroline's hand came down across her cheek. The echo of the slap against her skin echoed in the empty room in the dark morning.

Ginny gritted her teeth at the hard sting of pain that set the nerve endings on her face on fire. She cradled her cheek in her hand and narrowed her hard gaze on the woman.

"You can't leave. I won't let you." Caroline's eyes grew wide and frantic, like a caged animal ready to attack. Her chest heaved rapidly as her breathing turned to a pant and her nostrils flared.

"You can't stop me. I'm leaving today or I'm going to die trying." Ginny lifted her chin and turned to head to the bedroom to pack a few things. If she was leaving Louisiana for Arkansas, she needed to make sure that her father would be stopped.

"You selfish bitch!" Caroline screeched.

Glass shattered.

Ginny spun around at the crash. Her china setting lay on the floor in a thousand shards. Her mother picked up another china plate off the dining room table and threw it on the floor next to Ginny's foot.

She met her mother's hate-filled eyes and shrugged. "I always hated that pattern anyway."

She turned to walk away. She'd always stayed and taken the abuse, believing she was protecting her mother. She'd always thought she was doing the right thing, being a good daughter. She'd listened to her mother's advice about how to act, what to do to avoid getting beaten by her husband.

Now she realized she'd been lied to. Now she realized that she'd died the day she'd left Jaxon. But today she was going to get her soul back. Today she was going to choose life.

She felt the blinding sting of something sharp between her shoulder blades. Then the pain.

She coughed and struggled to catch her breath. Panicked, she turned around. She caught her reflection in the mirror above the buffet table. Her mother had stabbed her with a silver fork.

Her mother stared at her with wide eyes. She held up her hands and shook her head. "I can't let you go. You know that."

"So you try to kill me?" Pain gathered in her back and spread through her chest.

"The silver fork won't kill you if I pull it out."

Ginny tried to reach around and grab hold of the fork. But the angle was wrong. She couldn't grab it. Pain and fear and panic raced through her body. Her breath came in short pants and she could feel her heart beating fast, so fast she thought it would burst.

"I can't breathe," she struggled to say. Her legs tingled, and she knew in a few more seconds she'd be on the ground and incapacitated. She was trapped.

"Don't fight it, Ginny. Once you pass out, I'll take the fork out. You can heal your body from the silver." Her mother's voice was eerily calm and not like anything she'd ever heard.

She grabbed her mother by the collar of her perfect unwrinkled white button-up shirt. Her mother's eyes were unfeeling and dead. She had the feeling she was looking at something from a horror movie.

She stumbled and fell against her mother, shoving them both against the wall. Unable to stand, Ginny crumpled to the floor. She expected to hear her mother's voice, full of condemnation for messing up her shirt and shoving her. Her mother was always concerned with appearances. She was much like John in that respect. She'd often wondered if her mother should have married John instead of her.

Unable to sit up, Ginny rolled to her side and braced herself for her mother's wrath.

She looked over at her mother. Her stomach knotted. She screamed.

Her mother's body was pinned to the wall by the silver antlers flanking either side of the buffet table. The antlers had gone through the back of her head and come out between her eyes.

Ginny had always hated those antlers. She hated having anything silver in the house. It was bad enough having sterling silver flatware. John knew the antlers intimidated her, scared her and their guests. So he kept them hanging on the wall. He would often shove her face close to the cold silver horns when he got angry to show her what it would be like it she displeased hm. He'd threated to hang her on the antlers like a side of beef until she died slowly from silver poisoning.

Her mother had been more fortunate than to suffer a

slow and agonizing death. The silver had penetrated her brain and killed her instantly.

Blood dripped down her face in thick red trail. Her eyes were still open, her mouth slightly ajar as if she couldn't believe her fate.

Her mother was dead.

There was no coming back from this.

Ginny crumpled to her side on the floor and screamed.

CHAPTER 13

A chilling scream erupted from the house.
Ginny.

Jaxon raced for the house, sprinting across the driveway. He bounded into the kitchen, but the room was empty. He hurried farther into the house, his booted heels echoing loudly against the hardwood floor.

"Ginny!"

"Jaxon." Her voice cracked as she spoke.

He entered the dining room and his stomach turned. His gaze landed on her small form lying on the floor. She was lying on her side, facing away from him. Blood dripped down her shirt and onto the floor. Something silver was sticking out of her back

Nausea and fear curled in his gut.

A silver fork.

He couldn't find her just to lose her all over again. It would destroy him. He wouldn't let this happen. He couldn't.

He knelt by her side and brushed the hair out of her face. "What the hell happened? Did John come back? Did he do this to you?" How had he missed John coming into the house? He'd been watching the gate so carefully. Maybe there was a second entrance that he didn't know about.

"No. My. Mother…" she struggled to say. She pointed. He turned and followed her gaze to the dining room wall, where her mother was pinned to the wall. Dead.

Fuck. He sucked in a breath but didn't say a word. He didn't give a shit that the mother was now dead. The bitch had tried to kill Ginny. He was glad she was dead.

He turned back to her. "I need to get this out of you."

"Wait." She gripped his hand preventing him from pulling out the utensil.

"It was an accident, Jaxon. I didn't mean for her to die." Tears swam in her eyes and rolled across her cheek onto the floor, mingling with the blood.

"I know, sweetheart," he said softly.

"I stumbled into her and she fell against the antlers." She struggled to speak and breathe.

"Shush. Stop talking and let me get this out."

"I'm going to die for this. Jaxon. It's the law." Her fearful eyes met his.

"No, you're not. You only face the death penalty for purposely killing your parent. This was an accident."

"No one will believe me." She closed her eyes.

"I believe you. And trust me when I say you're not going to be killed for this." He knew the werewolf law dictated that the punishment for killing one's own parents was death. He'd never seen a Tribunal where a Were was found innocent. They had all been found guilty of murder and sentenced to death.

Not Ginny. He had to find a way to get the Tribunal to see she was innocent. He had to.

"This is going to hurt." He tightened his grip on the fork and pulled it out in one swift motion.

Ginny screamed and slumped to the floor. She'd passed out from the pain.

He took a deep breath. He was racing against time. He had to get them out of there before her husband showed up.

"Well, well, well," a male voice called out from behind Jaxon.

Jaxon stood and spun around, ready to face John.

A slow smirk crossed John's evil lips as he met Jaxon's glare. "Ginny's right, you know. She's going to die for killing her mother. I'll make damn sure she does."

"It was an accident." Jaxon stood and curled his hands into fists.

"Not if I say it wasn't." His smirk slipped. "I'll have that bitch skinned alive before I put a bullet in her head."

"Not if I kill you first, fucker." Jaxon rushed John. His instinct to shift to wolf and kill was so powerful it made his body hum.

Jaxon lunged in midair, shifting into wolf form as John braced himself for the impact. They collided with such force it rattled Jaxon's teeth.

Jaxon sunk his teeth into John's shoulder. John screamed in pain and hit Jaxon in the head. Jaxon released his hold. He wanted to sink his teeth into the fucker's throat so he could rip it out.

John threw his head back and shifted into wolf. He was larger than Jaxon, but size didn't matter to Jaxon. He was going to kill John for laying his hands on Ginny. He was going to make him suffer like never before.

Jaxon lunged, aiming for John's throat. John leapt through the air and twisted his body, catching Jaxon on his shoulder with his teeth.

Pain blazed through Jaxon's body as muscle tore and bone broke. He'd been in fights before, been bitten by other wolves before, but this pain felt different. It was like it was draining him, weakening him.

"His teeth, Jaxon," Ginny screamed.

He cut his eyes in her direction. She had managed to sit up and was struggling to get to her feet.

"His teeth are silver." She met his gaze. Fear scraped across her beautiful features. Her eyes widened, and he could see the loss of hope in her blue eyes.

The fucker had silver teeth. No wonder the pain was so intense.

He wasn't going down like this. No way. No how.

He threw his weight back against the Were. John loosened his hold on Jaxon's shoulder and fell to the floor.

Jaxon blinked and shoved back the burning pain in his shoulder and the weakness filling his veins. The silver wasn't in his body, but he'd still feel the effects of it until after his body had a chance to heal.

Jaxon glanced around, looking for a weapon just as effective as John's teeth. His gaze landed on the table. He rammed into it. The plates and silverware crashed to the floor. He bent his head and grabbed a knife between his jaws and spun around to face his attacker.

John threw his head back and growled, revealing two large silver canines. He was a lethal weapon to any werewolf walking.

He ran toward Jaxon, baring his silver teeth.

Jaxon bent his head, feigning submission. His muscles tensed and his heart pounded as he waited for the perfect moment.

John leapt in the air. He landed on Jaxon.

Jaxon tightened his hold on the knife and rammed the blade into John's heart.

John stumbled back and looked down at his chest. Jaxon knew what the werewolf was thinking. He was going to shift back into human and pull out the knife. In wolf form he couldn't pull out the blade with his paws.

Jaxon still couldn't shift back, not yet. The silver from the bite had taken its toll on his body. He'd have to heal from the bite before he could shift.

John growled and forced his body to shift back into human form.

Jaxon jumped and landed on John, shoving the knife farther into his enemy's chest. John, now fully human, screamed and wrapped his hands around the handle of the blade, but Jaxon was faster. He bit down on his throat, ripping the tissue and cartilage.

Blood spurted and pulsed, dripping onto the expensive hardwood floor. Jaxon jerked his head back, ripping out John's throat and tossing it on the floor.

John blinked, shocked at Jaxon's move, and tried to pull the knife out. The properties of the silver were keeping John from healing and were slowly poisoning him to death. With his throat gone, death was only seconds away.

John's wide-eyed gaze frantically searched the room. When they landed on Ginny, he narrowed his eyes.

Jaxon felt his body weakening. It had taken all his strength to stay on top of the knife. He slipped in the blood. If John got that knife out, both he and Ginny were done for.

John bucked Jaxon off his body and grabbed the knife with both hands.

Jaxon roared and forced himself on his feet but slipped on the blood.

John looked at him and grinned. He slowly pulled the knife out of his chest. He scrambled to his feet and held the knife above his head, ready to strike Jaxon.

What a fucking way to die, Jaxon thought to himself.

"I won't let you hurt him, John," Ginny said.

"Shut up, bitch, and watch while I kill your wolf." He snarled, not even bothering to turn around to face her.

"Not today." She brought a flash of silver down across John's head. He blinked and then crumpled to the floor as the silver antler sconce implanted in his skull.

John lay motionless as the blood dripped from his head, forming a red puddle on the floor. Ginny ran to Jaxon's side.

She nuzzled his furry neck and clung to him as tears fell from her face onto him.

Jaxon closed his eyes, feeling his strength return to his body. When he finally had enough energy, he shifted back into human form.

He opened his eyes. He found Ginny staring back at him.

"I thought he was going to kill you, Jaxon." She sobbed.

He pulled her into his embrace. "It's okay, sweetheart. I'm all right."

The pain in his body was intense, but holding Ginny in his arms made the pain bearable.

"Everything is okay now. You're safe," he whispered against her ear. "What about the baby? Is the baby okay?" He pressed his hand to her stomach.

"Yes." She pulled back and stared at him, horror etched into her features. "But you're wrong. I'm not safe. Not now." Her tearstained gaze swept the room, first locking on the impaled figure of her mother against the wall and then her dead husband sprawled on the floor with the second antler sconce sticking through his skull.

"Ginny..."

"Jaxon." She pulled out of his embrace and stood on shaky feet. "There's no turning back from this. There's no reprieve for me." She shook her head. "No one kills their mother and their husband and lives."

He gritted his teeth, forced his legs under him, and stood. Pain shot through every cell, setting his body on fire. "I need you to trust me on this, okay? I need you to do what I say and everything will be okay."

Since their failed wedding day, he had gone through life existing, not really living. They had only a few more hours, days at best, before the evil that had pulled them apart was going to hunt them down and force them to pay up.

He knew what he must do. This time he was going to make sure Ginny was safe. Even at the cost of his life.

"You don't…"

"I don't what? Understand?" He cocked his head. "I know that you were married to a ruthless man and that your father is the most depraved Were there is. But the Pack Master in Arkansas is good. He has done miracles, stood in the gap for his Guardians. When we go there, I will explain what happened. That this was all self-defense. That you were abused."

She dropped her gaze to the ground.

"And when Barrett knows the whole story, he will do everything possible to make sure you are found innocent. That you won't be harmed. I promise you this, Ginny. I promise you this on my life."

Her gaze met his. A flicker of hope flashed through her eyes like a candle flame.

He knew Barrett would do whatever he could to help them. He also knew that he was willing to pay the price for Ginny. The rules of the werewolf law were very strict. Almost unbreakable. He knew that blood had to be spilt to satisfy the code.

He wouldn't let Ginny get hurt. Not again.

He was willing to sacrifice his life, using his blood to pay her debt.

CHAPTER 14

"Fuck," Barrett groused as he turned into the driveway of Jack Welbourn's house. Jack was the Pack Master of Mississippi, and Barrett considered him a friend.

What he wasn't looking forward to was seeing the rest of the Weres who were supposed to attend tonight. He knew the meeting of the Southern Pack Masters had to include everyone. Including Edward Boudier from Louisiana.

That fucker had managed to capture some of Barrett's Guardians out of Arkansas. He'd even had the gall to skin and kill one before feeding his body to the gators.

There wasn't any substantial evidence linking Boudier to the actual act. Just a whole lot of testimony from Lucien and his brother Lorcan, one of Boudier's lethal Assassins who had helped Barrett escape out of New Orleans.

He hadn't heard from Lorcan since the Assassin had ratted out his boss about all the dirty dealings the Louisiana Pack Master was into. After he'd helped get Lucien and the rest of the Arkansas werewolves out of New Orleans, he'd split.

Barrett had been grateful for the help, but he sure as shit didn't trust Lorcan. As far as he was concerned, he was still connected to the Louisiana pack, and he couldn't be trusted.

"Barrett." Jack greeted him at the door. "Come in, come in."

"Jack. Thank you for hosting this meeting." Barrett walked into the foyer of the Mississippi plantation. There was something different about Jack. Although they had never been the best of friends, Barrett had always felt he could count on the Were if he needed him. Tonight, something seemed off.

"Found my witch yet, Barrett?" Jack cocked his head and narrowed his eyes.With the Witch of Yazoo City still on the loose, Jack was going to hold Barrett's feet to the fire until she was found.

"We had her in the southern part of Arkansas. My Guardian is trailing her now." Or so he hoped. If Jaxon didn't get that witch bitch soon, Barrett was going to look like an incompetent leader.

That was something he could not afford.

"So you let her go?" Jack's furrowed brow grew deeper.

"No. She got away." Barrett turned and faced the Pack Master head on. No way was he going to let Jack intimidate him, despite how much he respected the Were.

"I don't need to stress to you the amount of trouble she can cause if she's not caught and returned to the cemetery."

"No, you don't." Barrett glared. "Like I said, my Guardians are on the case. She'll be found and returned to Mississippi."

Jack blinked and then gave a final nod. "It's not like I don't trust you. But that witch has left more bloodshed in her wake than you can imagine. She's a blemish on Mississippi and reflects poorly on me."

"What did she do to be cursed to that cemetery, anyway?" He'd always wondered, and Jack had always avoided the specifics on that topic. Barrett had heard different tales over the years. He'd never put much stock into what others said. He always trusted the truth. The truth was a rare commodity these days.

"Would you believe it has to do with a man?" A slow smirk played at the corners of Jack's lips.

"Isn't it always?" All he knew was Ella was dangerous and he needed to bring her in. "Don't worry about her. I've got my best Guardian on her. He'll get her. I promise you that."

Jack let out a breath, and Barrett could see the tension slip off the Pack Master's shoulders.

"I know, Barrett. You've never let me down before. You won't let me down now."

"Damn right," he said and then looked around the massive living room. Jack's home seemed like a house out of *Gone with the Wind*. The Pack Master had kept his Mississippi plantation home in the same style for as long as Barrett had known him, never updating his home to the latest style.

"Everyone is already here. They're out back." Jack put his arm on Barrett's shoulder and smiled. "I had the outside area redone. New fire pit and living area put in."

"So you did update something in this old place." Barrett smirked.

"Damn right I did." Jack laughed good naturedly. "Come see. Plus, we have drinks."

"Better not be a cash bar."

"I resent that statement. You know it's not hospitable in the South to have a cash bar. Why, any self-respecting Southerner would be shocked and outraged at your statement."

"Yeah, yeah," Barrett groused.

Jack opened the back door and waved Barrett out.

Barrett took a breath and stepped outside. The humid Mississippi air stung his lungs and had him immediately on edge.

A small group of gentlemen stood around the fire pit. A lone man stood near the bar where a bartender was busy mixing a drink. Though Barrett couldn't see his face, he knew who the Were was. Edward Boudier.

He tensed his muscles and had to restrain the wolf inside.

He turned his attention back to the men at the fire and made his way over.

"Barrett. Good to see you could join us." Charles Price, the Pack Master of Tennessee, smiled and held out his hand. Barrett accepted it in greeting.

"Charles, good to see you, man," Barrett said. Charles had been amiable, but he was soft on certain topics. He didn't like to stir the pot, and he sure as shit didn't like to get involved. He was Switzerland when it came to hard topics like Louisiana.

"Hey, Gerald, how you doing?" Barrett turned to the Pack Master of Alabama and shook his outstretched hand. "Heard Alabama is doing well."

"It is. Crime is down, and that's always a good thing." Gerald Davidson smiled and took a sip of his whiskey. "Heard you got Arkansas in good shape."

"It's a constant job, I assure you," Barrett murmured and glanced over at the bar. "Talked to Boudier?"

"Nah. He's been hugging the bar since he walked in. He knows better than to come over here and start his shit." Gerald took another sip. "I don't want no trouble. But if that fucker tries to start something with me tonight, then I will sure as shit finish it." He narrowed his eyes.

Barrett grinned. He knew he'd always liked the Alabama Pack Master. He wasn't much on social graces, but he drew a line in the sand when it came to his priorities.

"I don't think he's going after you. I think he has a different Pack Master in his sights." Barrett knew without a doubt that Boudier was gunning for him. Barrett was getting his game plan ready for when that happened.

"Guess I should go over and say hi," Barrett growled.

"You do that. And give him a swift kick in the balls for me while you're at it," Gerald said.

Barrett walked over to the bar, his gaze trained on Boudier. His gut tightened as he got closer to his enemy. He'd never hated anyone as much as he hated Edward Boudier, and that was before the Were had tried to kill Lucien. When he'd killed Heimy, Barrett's hatred for the Pack Master of Louisiana had been cemented. It was then he'd spent every waking minute planning his revenge. On how he would take him out. Make him pay for what he'd done. Boudier needed killing. Barrett would be making the entire world safer by taking Boudier out.

No one cared if Boudier lived or died. He was just a waste of space.

"Barrett." Edward Boudier slowly turned from the bartender and looked at Barrett. "I was wondering when you were going to come over and extend your welcome to me."

"Fuck off," Barrett spat out and then glared at the bartender. "Give me a bourbon."

"Yes, sir." The bartender nodded and quickly poured the dark liquid into a glass and placed it in front of Barrett.

Barrett placed a ten-dollar bill into the tip jar. The bartender nodded his thanks. He then shot a glare in Boudier's direction. Barrett knew the Louisiana Pack Master didn't tip. Boudier had once said that servers didn't deserve extra money for doing their jobs.

"Ah, your genteel Southern manners always make me feel warm and fuzzy inside, Barrett."

"How about I rip out your fucking liver. Bet that would get you a raging hard-on."

Boudier burst out laughing. "Come now, Barrett. We are not at war. We are neighbors, after all."

Barrett slammed his glass down on the bar. The glass shattered, silencing all the voices around the fire. "We are at war, Boudier. We went to war when you skinned and killed my Guardian."

"That's only hearsay. There's not a shred of evidence to prove that was me or that I ordered that." He lifted his chin. "Besides, sounds like a disgruntled employee who wanted to paint me in a bad light." He narrowed his eyes, all his false humor gone.

Now Barrett was seeing the monster behind the mask. Now he was seeing the true Edward Boudier.

"What's this?" Jack walked over, his expression pinched and pained. "We are here to discuss the future. The future of our Packs. Not to bring up old grievances."

"Seems Barrett doesn't know how to have an adult conversation. He's pouting over some Guardian he lost."

Barrett's anger boiled over into every muscle in his body. He plowed his fist right into Boudier's face, knocking the Were back onto the ground. His head made a sickening crack as it met the concrete.

Gerald Davidson laughed and tossed back his drink.

Charles Price stood up from his seat and glanced around, his face worried. He looked like he was going to be asked to take sides and everyone knew Charles Price didn't take sides.

"We're not here to start taking swings at each other," Jack bellowed. He cut his glare from Boudier back to Barrett.

Barrett wanted to do more than take swings at Boudier. He wanted to gut him.

"He started it," Boudier whined and then cut his eyes over at Jack. "I gave him no reason to hit me."

"Skinning and killing one of Barrett's Guardians is more

than a reason to hit you, Boudier." Gerald wasn't afraid to stand up to Boudier.

Barrett's blood boiled.

"There's no evidence of that claim. And if you keep saying shit like that, I'm going to bring you before a tribunal for slander and libel," Boudier growled.

"Are you that much of a psychopath that you can kill without feeling?" Barrett snarled. He fisted his hands at his sides. He knew Boudier liked to fight dirty, and he was waiting on the Pack Master to shift into wolf and lunge at him.

Barrett was ready.

"Enough!" Jack slammed his fist down across the counter of the bar. "This is not why I called you here tonight."

"But shouldn't it be the real reason we are here? I mean, come on. We can keep dancing around the issues of what Louisiana has done, or we can straight-up address them." Gerald stood and threw back the rest of his drink. He set the glass down on the edge of the fire pit.

"There are differences and grievances between the states. If we don't start working together to work them out, then we will end up destroying each other. I, for one, don't want to see that happen." Jack gave everyone a hard stare before finally resting his gaze on Barrett.

There would be no working with Louisiana. Not with Boudier in charge. Barrett would never forget what had been done to his Guardians.

"We as Pack Masters of our states need to start working together. We have to, or we will all fail," Jack pleaded.

"What about justice? What about honor?" Barrett addressed Jack but kept his eyes on Boudier.

"What about having factual evidence?" Boudier glared. "Bringing accusations against another Pack Master without substantial evidence is suicidal." A ghost of smirk played on his lips.

"I like suicidal." Barrett leaned in and growled.

"I'd like to take some odds on that one." Alabama smirked. "I bet ten thousand dollars that Barrett will rip your throat out without even shifting." He glanced around to Charles and smiled. "Any takers?"

"You're not helping, Gerald." Jack snarled. He stood between them and placed a hand on each of their chests. "If you can't get along with each other, then I'm going to ask you both to leave."

"Don't bother." Barrett shoved Jack's hand away. "I'll leave." He shot Boudier a glare and headed for the house. Quick footsteps followed behind him.

He didn't need to turn to know that it was Jack.

"The only thing I will apologize is for trying to fight him on your property. I should have waited until it was just the two of us before taking his ass out." Barrett stormed through the house and headed straight for the front door.

"Barrett."

He tensed at the sound of his name. He took a deep breath before turning around to his old friend's face.

"This situation is way out of hand." Jack leaned in and lowered his voice. "I know you're upset about Heimy, but think of the best for the majority."

He curled his fingers into fists. "Fuck yeah, I'm upset about Heimy. I'm upset about Mitchell and Lucien too." He cocked his head. "Do you know how long it took Lucien to heal from his scars? And for his mate Catty to see him like that? To see his flesh flayed from his body? What about their justice?"

Jack swallowed and licked his lips.

For the first time, Barrett got an uneasy feeling about the Mississippi Pack Master.

"What happened is very… unfortunate. For all involved." Jack admitted.

His unease grew tenfold.

Barrett took a step back. "Unfortunate?" He turned to leave, but Jack grabbed his arm.

He rounded on the older male.

"What's wrong with you, Jack? This isn't like you. You used to be a male of great respect, of great integrity. The Pack Master I knew would demand immediate justice."

Jack shook his head. "We took a vote, and the Pack Masters didn't have enough votes for an investigation into the alleged incident."

"What vote? I didn't hear about a vote. Why wasn't I told?" Barrett asked.

"Because since you filed the complaint, you can't vote. Boudier was disqualified as well. It came down between Alabama, Tennessee, Kentucky, and Mississippi. You only had one vote in your favor." Jack shook his head.

"Let me guess who sided with me. Alabama." Barrett swallowed back the knot that had developed in the back of his throat.

"Listen, just let me talk to the other Pack Masters without Boudier around. I know Kentucky would like to see Boudier gone, but he feels like he doesn't want to start trouble since Boudier has left his state alone. Tennessee isn't going to go up against Edward Boudier for anything."

"What about you, Jack?" Barrett cocked his head. "Where do you stand in all this?"

Jack's eyes bulged. "You know where I stand. How can you ask me that?"

"Before I walked in here tonight, I would have sworn that you were on the right side of all this. That you were on my side. But now, I'm not so sure."

Jack took a step back and pursed his lips. "I take great

offense at your statement, Barrett. I've always been a good friend and a supporter of the state of Arkansas. I refrained from voting because I figured it would be a conflict of interest since everyone knows I'm your friend." He lifted his chin.

"Yeah. Well, things change. People grow weary of doing the right thing. They want to do the easy thing." Barrett walked through the front door and slammed it behind him.

CHAPTER 15

"*D*o you have enough strength to ride? Are you sure the baby is okay?" Jaxon stepped away from the window and turned back to Ginny. Her bruises from where John had hit her were now healed, and only the dried blood on her shirt showed evidence that she'd been stabbed by her psychotic mother. He stepped closer and rested his hand on her stomach.

"I can ride. The baby is werewolf. He'll heal." She narrowed her eyes at him. "What about you? You're the one bitten with silver."

He rolled his shoulders where John's teeth had sunk into his flesh. He was still sore, but the wound was closing up fast.

"I'm good." He narrowed his eyes on the corpse of her husband. "I can't believe that fucker had his teeth coated in silver." It was a sadistic move. "If he had bitten his own cheek, he could have poisoned himself."

"He had it done right after we were wed. He said he wanted every part of his body to be a weapon so any werewolf who went against him would feel the bite of death." She swallowed and looked away.

"Ginny?" His gut clenched.

"Yes."

"Did he ever use those teeth on you?" He forced the words out, needing to know the truth. "Did he ever bite you?"

"Every time he forced me to have sex." Her voice was distant but soft.

He took a step toward her, but she held up her hand to stop him.

"I need you to know that I never mated with him. Never. I was forced to wed him and act the wife to him." She shook her head. "But I was never his. Not in ways that it mattered." She looked up at him and lifted her chin.

"I don't expect you to want me after this, after he's had me. I know I'm ruined. I'm not that perfect girl you once knew." She shook her head. "But if we get out of here, then I can have some kind of peace, away from this life, away from this violence. Then that will be enough for me." She licked her lips.

"Ginny"— he took a step—"we're getting out of here. And then we're going to talk. If you think you can get rid of me this fast, you don't know me very well." He glanced at the floor. "Besides, it's not like I've been lily-white. I've had other women. You need to know that." He looked at her. "I never felt the same way about any of them that I do you. They were just there to try to fill a void. But they never could. You need to resign yourself to the fact that you're not getting rid of me. Not now, not ever. As far as I'm concerned, you are the only mate for me."

Her blue eyes swam with unshed tears and her lip trembled. It was all he needed.

He closed the distance between them and covered her lips with his in a promise-filled kiss for the future. When he pulled back, he looked down into her face.

"I promise you that we are getting out of here and back to Arkansas. It's safe there. Barrett will see to that. I promise my life on it."

* * *

"THANK you for inviting us over for dinner. Sorry Damon couldn't make it." Ava wrapped Granny in a big hug. The scent of old-lady perfume and dessert had Ava smiling.

"Come on in. Lucien and Catty are here. So are Jayden and Haley." Granny waved her in toward the dining room.

The aroma of home-cooked food made Ava's stomach rumble. She smiled when she saw her friends already seated around the table.

"You're here," Jayden groused. "We can finally eat."

Haley giggled and stood up and gave Ava a kiss on the cheek. Ava liked Haley. She thought of her like a sister and knew that she was a good match for Jayden.

"Hey girl." Ava hugged Catty and then turned her attention back to Lucien. She patted him on the chest. "Looks like you are as good as new."

"I am." He grinned and pulled Catty into his embrace. "It helps that Catty knows how to make a werewolf get better quick."

"Maybe I should go into medicine instead of law," Catty quipped.

"When do you start college?" Ava sat down in the dining room chair and looked around for Granny. The older woman had disappeared back into the kitchen.

"In the fall. But I'm already reading up on everything. And talking to my dad." She grinned. "He's glad at least one of his children decided to follow in his footsteps and go to law school. He thought it would be Zane, but it turns out, to everyone's surprise, it will be me."

"I'm not surprised." Ava placed her napkin on her lap and suddenly wished Damon were with her. Now that he was filling in for Barrett, she was getting lonely. Looking around the table at the couples made her a little sad that her mate wasn't with her.

"I do miss my partner in crime, though. I mean, who's going to go on chocolate runs at ten o'clock when I need something sweet?" Ava crossed her arms and feigned a pout.

"I thought that's what Damon was for." Jayden snorted. He sighed with relief when Granny walked out of the kitchen carrying a large plate of roast beef.

"Not anymore. Not since he's filling in for Barrett while he's gone doing whatever it is that he does." Ava sighed and held her empty wine glass up. Catty smiled and poured a liberal amount of red wine into her glass. Thank God Granny always had an abundance of wine with dinner.

"So where did Barrett go?" Granny asked and sat down at the head of the table. She passed the beef to Jayden, whose eyes grew wide, and Ava was pretty certain she saw a bit of drool on the corner of his mouth.

"Some Pack Master's meeting. I think they were having it at Jack Welbourn's house in Mississippi," Ava said and then took a sip of wine and cringed at the sour taste. She grabbed her water instead.

"Jack Welbourn. That's a nice-looking gentleman if I ever saw one." Granny grinned a little. "And if I were a few years younger, I just might take a crack at him."

Jayden's fork clattered to his plate and he gave his grandmother a look of horror. "Absolutely not! You got yourself in enough trouble with that little Valentine's date from hell."

"How was I supposed to know he was a criminal?" Granny shrugged.

"Maybe by the look in his eyes." Jayden frowned.

"To be honest, I thought he looked constipated. I figured

once we had dessert and coffee that would loosen his bowels up a bit. Figured after a trip to the bathroom, he'd come out a different man."

"Jesus, Granny." Jayden flinched. "I'm trying to eat here."

"Watch your language at my table, Jayden." Granny narrowed her eyes on him. "You're not too old for me to take you across my knee."

"Actually, I am." He pointed his fork at her. "Plus I'm faster. I can get away from you."

Ava burst out laughing. Whenever she felt a little down, she knew a visit to Granny would perk her up.

"So how long is Damon filling in for Barrett?" Lucien cut his eyes at her. The large Were might look big and intimidating, but he'd always been kind to her. He'd been through a lot in the last few months after being captured and tortured. But his mate Catty was bringing him back to life again. They both seemed to help heal each other from their painful pasts.

"Not long. Just until he gets back from this meeting with the Pack Masters." She shrugged. She didn't care for this side of Pack business. She preferred Damon doing his missions and coming home to her. It was a simpler life than the political bullshit that Barrett had to muck through.

"I'm kind of surprised that he didn't ask Zane to fill in." Catty frowned and then spooned some potatoes onto her plate. "I thought he was Barrett's right-hand guy."

That thought had crossed her mind. She looked up at her friend and shrugged. "I don't know. I think he felt like Zane had enough on his plate with getting SYKLAR'S HOME ready to open."

Catty averted her eyes from Ava.

Unease settled in Ava's gut. She looked at her friend. "Catty, are you upset that Damon is doing this rather than your brother?"

"It's not that, Ava." Catty set her fork down and sat back in her chair.

"What is it?" She looked at everyone around the table to see if they knew where this conversation was headed.

"Is the reason Barrett didn't offer the job to Zane because of me?" Catty met her gaze.

"What are you talking about? Why would that have anything to do with you?" Ava asked.

Catty lowered her gaze to her lap. "Look I know that people put a lot of stock into what you do with your life. And the fact that I used to be a stripper…"

"Wait." Ava held her hand up to stop her friend from going any further. "Stop right there. I can honestly tell you from the bottom of my heart that your past had no bearing on why Damon was put in charge."

"Catty." Lucien turned and wrapped his arm around Catty. He pulled her into his protective embrace. "Why would you even say that?"

"Because I know what mistakes I've made in my past. I own them. They are what made me the person I am today. I just don't want my family to pay for my choices or my mistakes." She lifted her chin and looked round the table.

"And you know our Pack Master." Jayden nodded and stopped eating. "He would never judge someone by their past. He's not like that." He cut his eyes at Ava. "I agree with Ava. Ever since Zane and Skylar hooked up, I see a change in Zane."

"A change?" Catty frowned.

"I mean, he's still a hard-ass," Jayden admitted.

"Jayden, language." Granny scowled.

"Sorry, Granny." Jayden looked back at Catty. "But I see something else in him. He seems calmer now. I mean, he's over at SKYLAR'S HOME for children every chance he gets. He loves his job as Guardian, but being over there with

Skylar, I think he's a different Were. I don't think he wants to be next in line for Pack Master."

"Whoa. Hold on. Wait a second." Ava set her water down. "What Damon is doing is just filling in. Not prepping to take over for Barrett on a permanent basis." She grabbed her fork and pointed it to everyone around the table. "Let's get that straight."

"Wouldn't you like to be the wife of the Pack Master, Ava?" Haley grinned and took a sip of her wine.

"Ah, no." She shook her head and concentrated on cutting her roast. She didn't like the direction this conversation was headed in.

"Why not? I bet you'd get invited to a whole lot of parties and balls and..." Granny had a dreamy look in her eyes as she spoke.

"Balls? Parties?" Jayden's eyes grew wide. "This ain't no President of the United States. This is Pack Master. Why Barrett's lucky if he gets an invite to a barbeque." He snorted. "And have you seen his home?"

"Barrett has a home?" Catty sat up and paid attention.

"Well, he has one in Fayetteville when he wants to go see a football game. It's an older home but it has been updated." Jayden had stayed in that house when he'd been protecting Haley from a stalker.

"What about here? I never see him leave that office of his. Does he have a place to sleep in there?" Granny frowned.

"I bet he does. I bet it's behind one of the walls. Like that secret gun room." Lucien nodded.

"He's got a secret gun room?" Granny sat up in her chair.

"Yeah. And you're never going to see it, so get that out of your head right now." Jayden scowled.

"I personally don't think he sleeps." Lucien shrugged, forked some roast beef into his mouth, and chewed thoughtfully. "I mean, I've never actually seen him leave the

Compound unless it's on business or for some meeting. He's there when everyone arrives and there when everyone leaves."

Ava frowned. She crossed her legs and took a sip. "I don't think being Pack Master would suit Damon."

"You mean it wouldn't suit you." Granny gave her a knowing look. "I can't imagine you two parted for any length of time."

"Yeah, me either." She crossed her arms and fidgeted. She hoped Barrett would hurry his ass on back to Arkansas so Damon would come home to her. She was proud of her man, she really was. She just didn't want to be put on the back burner for a job.

"Granny, mind if I take a plate to Damon?" Ava asked.

"Sure, honey. After we eat I'll fix a big plate. And don't let me forget to get you a big piece of hummingbird cake to go along with it. That will put a big smile on your mate's face."

"I don't need any cake to do that, Granny. I can manage that on my own." Ava smirked.

CHAPTER 16

*J*axon knew they were racing against time. They were literally behind enemy lines and needed to get out now.

"I want you to open the gate." Jaxon looked at Ginny standing in front of her dead mother.

"John had the code. He changes it every day, first thing in the morning, in case I ever tried to leave." She looked at him.

Jesus. What kind of hell had she endured these last years?

"We are limited on our options. Well, we can climb over the fence and stay on foot until we get a ride."

She shook her head vehemently. "That won't work. My father has eyes in this town. Cameras on every street corner, people working for him who would turn a bit of information over to him for money. The only person I ever trusted in this town was my mother." She looked back at Caroline. "And apparently I was wrong about her too. I thought she cared. Thought she loved me."

"Sweetheart, your mother's mind was poisoned a long time ago by your father. He brainwashed her." He took a deep breath. "Right now, we need to think about getting out of here. Since you don't have the code, I can try to disable the gate long enough to drive my Harley through."

"It will set off an alarm. It goes straight to my father." She shrugged and studied the ground. "I heard my father tell John about it. And how he could control every move I made."

Jaxon nodded. "I figured there would be an alarm, but there's also got to be a delay. Probably only a minute or two. But it would give us enough time to get the gate open and drive though and get across town if I haul ass." He cocked his head. "Are you strong enough to hold on?"

"Yes." She nodded.

"Hurry and change back into the clothes you were riding in. I'll get the Harley close to the gate. Once I open the gate, we need to go." He stepped closer and touched his fingertip to the bottom of her chin. "No turning back."

"No turning back." She smiled.

He gave her a quick kiss and then headed out the back door. He scanned the area, making sure he didn't see anyone, and then headed back to the tree line to get his Harley.

The dawn was breaking, casting its soft gray light across the dark ground. Soon the sleepy town would be wide awake and on alert.

He walked his Harley down the driveway. When he got close enough to the gate, he dropped the kickstand. He turned when he heard Ginny's soft footsteps hurrying down the asphalt driveway.

"Go ahead and get on the bike. Once I disable the security system on the gate and swing it open, we are out of here."

She and climbed on the bike, waiting for his next steps.

He walked over to the alarm box. It was hardwired instead of wireless. Using his pocket knife, pried it open. He stared at the bundle of colored wires. He wasn't an electrical guru like some of the other Guardians. He regretted not listening to Jayden when he was showing him how to disable alarms. Now it was too late. He reached into the wad of wires and ripped them out.

Tiny sparks flew and the light on the box went dark. He grabbed the wrought-iron gate and pulled it open.

Adrenaline filled his veins and he hopped on the Harley and started the engine. Ginny's hands wrapped around his waist and her cheek pressed against his back as she plastered her body against his. He revved the engine and raced through the open gates. He turned onto the street and accelerated.

He glanced down at his watch, mentally ticking off the seconds they had left before Boudier's henchmen would arrive to see what the hell was going on in the house.

The Harley hummed under his fingertips as he raced through the town. He tried to keep off the main streets, but it was going to cost them time. Time they didn't have.

He had no doubt that Boudier would get a full report within minutes about his one and only daughter on the back of a Harley with an Arkansas Guardian.

If they were caught here, there would be no justice for Ginny. There would only be death for the both of them.

He raced through the town. When he reached the inter-state, he didn't dare relax. He checked his rearview mirrors to see if they were being followed. Luckily they were not. Since Boudier had taken over the Louisiana, the state had become enemy territory. An enemy to Arkansas and any other law-abiding state.

What had just happened would send a ripple effect through every aspect of the Were world. Barrett would no doubt be mad as hell. But Jaxon knew the Pack Master to be fair. He would always stand by his Guardians, and right now Jaxon needed him to stand in his corner. If not, then they were all good as dead.

* * *

THEY HAD DRIVEN for a while and Jaxon knew they were getting close to the Arkansas border. A car rumbled up beside him, and he waited for it to pass. When the car didn't make a move to pass, he glanced over.

"Shit." It was Ella. That fucking Witch of Yazoo City. She was driving a tan sedan and grinning like a fucking opossum at him. In the passenger seat was a black cat. The cat howled as she rolled down the window. Its ears were blown back by the wind and didn't look too happy.

Ella met his gaze, smirked, and jerked the wheel to the right.

He hit the brakes to keep her from ramming into them. Ginny screamed and tightened her hold.

"I hate that bitch," Jaxon muttered. He reached inside his holster and pulled out his gun. He flipped the safety and aimed the Sig Sauer at the wheels of the car.

"What are you doing?" Ginny yelled.

"It's either us or her."

"She's an immortal witch, Jaxon. She can't be killed."

"I'm not killing her. I'm keeping her from trying to kill us." He aimed the gun at the tire and pulled the trigger.

The gunshot echoed. The tire blew. Sparks bounced off the asphalt. The car swerved. The cat jumped on Ella's head. Ella screamed. The car went off the road, hit a tree, and came to a stop.

Jaxon slowed the motorcycle and pulled off the road. He glanced over at the car.

"Think she's okay?" Ginny asked.

The driver's door flew open. A very angry red-haired witch with claw marks across her cheek jumped out of the car.

"You motherfucker!" she screamed at him.

"Yep. She's fine." Jaxon pulled back onto the road and sped toward his destination.

* * *

"GET THE HELL OFF ME, you crazy bitch," Ella screamed and shook Nyx from her leg. The cat hissed and released its hold on the flesh of her legs.

"Who are you calling crazy?" Nyx narrowed her yellow eyes.

"You're more offended that I called you crazy than that I called you a bitch?" Ella shook her head and touched her fingers to her burning face.

"It seems we both don't like other people putting labels on us. Besides, you're the psychopathic witch. I'm just the harmless sidekick." Nyx lifted her paw and licked.

"It's borderline personality disorder, not psychopath." Ella glared. "If you're going to diagnose me with a disorder, then make sure it's the right one."

"Whatever." Nyx glanced over her shoulder at the road. "Your werewolf is gone."

"He's not my werewolf." Ella leaned down to the driver's side mirror and winced at the claw marks on her face. "Holy shit, Nyx." She turned back to her cat. "Look what you did to my face."

"Big improvement if you ask me." Nyx smirked.

"What the fuck did I do to get stuck with the likes of you?" Ella asked.

"Well, you were cursed, for starters." Nyx held up a paw.

"Just shut up," Ella spat out. "I don't want to hear it."

"So what's the plan, genius? You were trying to take out that werewolf so he wouldn't capture you and take you back to the cemetery. But all you did was piss him off. For some reason I don't think he's coming back. Now we're the ones in the ditch. For the second time tonight."

Ella squeezed her eyes shut and counted to ten. When she opened them, she glared at Nyx.

"I don't know why you do that counting thing. It doesn't stop you from blowing your top. People like you don't change." Nyx stated.

"People like me?" Ella wished she could conjure up a black pot with boiling grease.

"You know, psychopaths." Nyx shrugged.

"Borderline personality," Ella glanced at her reflection in the mirror again.

"Will you stop looking at it? You'll still get laid even though your face looks like Freddy Krueger kissed you."

"I think I saw a pocket knife in the console of the car we stole. I've got a half a mind to cut your tongue out, cat." Her hands curled into fists.

"See now, that sounds like something a psychopath would do. Murderers are psychopaths. Borderline personalities wouldn't give two flying fucks. They'd just leave," Nyx said smugly.

"Great idea." Ella clenched her teeth and walked out of the ditch. With each step, her heels sank in a little farther into the dirt. "Look at my shoes. I paid a lot of money for these shoes."

"You mean you put a lot of effort into stealing those shoes," Nyx snarked.

"Whatever. They're ruined."

"What are we going to do now?" Nyx walked beside her.

"I'm going to catch a ride with someone who hates cats." She glared at her. "So I'm not sure what *you* are going to do."

"You're just pissed because that werewolf turned you down for that female he had on the back of his bike."

It did sting her ego that Jaxon wasn't into her. But she'd

known the second he had kissed her he was doing it to make that female werewolf jealous. It didn't matter. What mattered was making sure she never ended up back in the cemetery in Yazoo City. She'd spent too many years living in that hellhole. Once she had escaped and made it as far as New Orleans. It hadn't lasted long, and she was soon right back in the cemetery. Then Lucien and his female had come visiting. It was the opportunity she'd needed for her escape. She'd sworn she'd never go back. No matter what.

Which was why she was in Louisiana. If anyone could break the rules and help her, it would be Boudier. She'd heard about his reputation as Pack Master of Louisiana. He broke the rules all the time. Ella had some information that he just might find necessary and intriguing.

She'd planned on showing up at his son-in-law's house and telling John that Jaxon had been with the little wifey. But then he'd ended up murdered before she could talk to him. So she'd followed Jaxon and the murdering wife, hoping to run them off the road and take them captive.

She'd wanted to deliver John's wife to Boudier. All in a pretty package. But Jaxon had ruined it and shot out her tire. Now she was the one who needed saving.

"That's not why I'm pissed. I need that werewolf and his bitch alive. The more leverage I have with Boudier the better position I will be in to bargain for my freedom."

"Why don't you just bat your pretty little lashes and get down on your knees..."

Ella kicked Nyx and sent the cat flying to the side of the road.

"Have I told you today how much I hate you?" Nyx hissed and gathered herself together before joining Ella back on the road.

"Yes. Four times actually." Ella gave her a sweet smile. "But I'm not counting."

"So now what's the plan?" Nyx asked.

"The plan is to get another car and then find that were-wolf. I'm trading the female to Edward Boudier in exchange for my complete freedom. Plus this." She held up the envelope she'd swiped from the bar.

"How do you know he'll grant you amnesty?"

"He'll do it because I'm the one who saw his daughter murder his wife and his son-in-law." She glanced at Nyx. "If I know those fucking werewolves, they will do anything to save the female they love. Jaxon will try to paint a picture that it was self-defense."

"It was. Didn't you see the mom stick that fork in her daughter? Actually, that one was an accident. She fell against her mother and the mom got the short end of the antler, so to speak." Nyx shivered.

"Yes. But I'm going to tell him a different story, a story of murder. Any werewolf who murders their parents, no matter why, is sentenced to die. Not to mention I have the envelope that Ginny left in the bar. I'm sure Boudier will be very happy to get this back. Can you imagine what would happen if it fell into the wrong hands?" Ella pulled the thick envelope out of her bag and waved it in the air.

"So you would lie to the Pack Master to save your own ass."

"It's either her or me, and I'm sure as shit not going to be captured and taken back. I won't be a prisoner anymore. I'd rather face death than that."

CHAPTER 17

"He's bound to know what's happened, Jaxon. I know my father, and he'll have men waiting at the state line." Ginny tightened her arms around Jaxon's lean waist and spoke into his ear.

Jaxon had reassured her that everything would be okay. But her gut told her otherwise. Things would not be okay. She'd set a chain of events into motion that would end them both. If she knew her father, he would kill her in front of the man she loved just to punish her.

He was sadistic like that.

Many nights she woke up, sick to her stomach with the knowledge that her father's blood ran through her veins. She was terrified that she would turn into the same kind of monster that he was.

Every time John would force her to have sex, she was petrified of becoming pregnant. Her body had ceased to be her own. Then the day came when her worst nightmare came true. The day she found out she was pregnant.

She was ruined for Jaxon.

The rush of wind pushed silent tears out of her eyes and

down her face. She was escaping one hell just to face the ultimate hell when Jaxon rejected her.

"Have some faith in me, Ginny," he said over his shoulder.

Faith. That was one thing she'd lost a long time ago. She wasn't sure she could ever find her faith again. Not in him, and certainly not in herself.

"Shit." Jaxon slowed his speed.

She looked over his shoulder. Half a mile up the road, there was a line of vehicles stopped at a police checkpoint. She narrowed her eyes. Fear clawed her stomach.

"I recognize those men, Jaxon. They work for my father."

"Your father has humans on his payroll?"

"My father has everyone on his payroll," she answered.

"Not everyone." He turned the bike around in the highway and headed in the opposite direction. He took the next exit without slowing down. She tightened her hold around his waist.

He didn't go very far on the new road before turning off again. He made several more turns on backroads. She didn't question him, but she hoped his direction was taking them closer and closer to the Arkansas state line.

He slowed his bike and turned onto a dirt road. He kept his speed steady as he drove. He stopped when they reached what looked like a long road heading into a thick patch of woods.

"What is it? Are we out of options?" Fear tickled her gut, and she clung to him. She had a feeling they were going to be found out very soon, and she wanted to memorize the feel of him against her.

"I have a plan." He turned down the rural road.

She squeezed her eyes shut as tree limbs brushed across her face.

"Jaxon, I don't think this leads anywhere. I think it's an old deer trail."

He glanced over his shoulder and grinned. "All trails lead somewhere, sweetheart. You just need to take the right one."

She wasn't so sure about that but decided to keep her mouth shut. She was clearly in a situation where she had no control.

She dug down deep in her gut where she'd buried her hopes and dreams and pulled out the little tiny thread of hope that everything would be okay.

* * *

EDWARD BOUDIER WASN'T a Were to fuck with. He thought everyone knew this.

So when his messenger came and told him that his wife and son-in-law had been murdered and that his only daughter was seen leaving town on the back of a Harley, he'd immediately seen red.

And he then turned and ripped the head off the messenger. All in front of his meeting with his Louisiana Guardians.

"Let me guess who that Were was that was with Ginny." Boudier growled and licked the blood off his hands. He went hard and immediately wanted to fuck. Blood always had that effect on him.

He glanced around the room. All his Guardians avoided making eye contact. Except his Louisiana Assassins.

He narrowed his gaze and cocked his head. "Lorcan."

The Were who was once adamant about keeping his dark hair dyed platinum blonde had since returned to his natural dark color. With his dark hair and blue eyes, Lorcan was startling to look at.

Boudier wasn't gay. He looked at sex as an appetite to be appeased. Like torture and killing. He craved things other Pack Masters would blush at. It wasn't enough to rape a woman. He wanted to hear her scream at the amount of pain he could inflict on her without having her pass out from the pain.

Some thought he was a monster. Others thought a devil.

He knew better.

He was power. Power was all consuming and way better than money, sex or blood.

Power was everything. Being in control made sure things continued to work the way he wanted them to.

"Lorcan, tell me something. Did you ever find out how the Guardian Lucien escaped?"

Lorcan's gaze never wavered from his. His stare was intimidating to most. It would have been intimidating to him if he didn't own the Were, body and soul.

"No."

A smirk played at the corners of Boudier's lips, and he motioned for the Assassin to walk toward him.

"I could have your head on a spike in only a matter of seconds," Boudier said.

"Yes," Lorcan said. "But then you would be down an Assassin and would have to replace me."

He glared. "Everyone is replaceable."

"I'll remember that." Lorcan's words held a deeper meaning, yet his face stayed expressionless.

"Have you seen your brother lately?" He ran his hand down Lorcan's black leather vest. The Were always wore black leather—all the Assassins did, but he was always attracted to Lorcan's look over the other two, Brutus and Killian.

"No," Lorcan answered. "Lucien is dead to me."

"You know, Lorcan, I rather favor you over the other Assassins." Boudier grinned and looked over Lorcan's shoulder to Brutus and Killian.

The other two Assassins stared straight ahead, emotionless.

"I'd rather you didn't," Lorcan said simply.

He cut his eyes at Lorcan. "Yeah? And why is that?"

"Because Brutus is bigger than me and he'll kick my ass when we get out of here for being your favorite."

"Jesus, Lorcan. Show some respect." Brutus cursed under his breath.

"That's why I favor you, Lorcan. That smart-ass mouth you got on you." He stepped closer.

"If you like smart-asses, then Killian is your Were," Lorcan snarked.

"Fuck." Killian breathed out and studied the floor.

The room grew deathly silent.

Boudier fought a grin and then barked out a laugh. "Damn it, boy." He slapped him hard across the shoulder and let out a belly laugh. "You're the only Were I know that can make me laugh on the day I lose my wife and son-in-law."

Lorcan said nothing.

Boudier leaned in closer. "It's not the fact that my wife is dead. I hated that bitch as much as I hated her bitch of a mother. I'm just very disappointed that it wasn't me that got to kill her." He leaned back and addressed the rest of the Guardians and Assassins. "My son-in-law was a bit of an asshole." He shrugged his shoulders. "But he did manage to keep that daughter of mine in line. And he had money. So it was a win-win for me."

"But they both belonged to me." He addressed his Guardians, meeting the steely-eyed gaze of each of them. He needed them to know this was not a joke. He was not fucking around with these assholes.

"And I don't like it when my things are taken from me." He looked at each Guardian, letting his gaze rest on them long enough to let them know he would take them out without hesitation if they even thought about crossing him.

"The penalty for murder is death. There is to be no

Tribunal. This is a clear-cut case of murder. My daughter murdered her own mother. I demand justice. Caroline's blood demands justice."

"What about the Arkansas Guardian she was with?" Brutus spoke up.

He rounded on the Assassin's and met his gaze. "I have plans for that one. I want him brought to me. I will personally peel the flesh from his skin and send it to his Pack Master as a gift."

"You're not ordering a kill on him?" Brutus cocked his head.

"No. I want him alive, and I want you three to bring him back to me in one piece."

He grinned as a gruesome image took root and blossomed in his head. "I want to be the one to rip him apart. One little piece at a time."

CHAPTER 18

*J*axon kept his speed slow through the overgrown path that led farther and farther into the forest. There were a couple of spots where the road was so narrow he was afraid his Harley wasn't going to fit. But luck was on their side, and he managed to get through and keep going.

The trees were thick and mosquitoes were a constant drone near his ear. He was probably going to be eaten up with bites by the time night fell, but he knew he had to keep going. Right now the highway had too many of Boudier's men watching and waiting for them to slip up.

He couldn't slip up. He had to keep Ginny safe. He'd failed her years ago. He wasn't going to fail her now.

He wasn't sure why he'd taken the old road. He'd glanced down at the GPS on his bike. He had seen that there was possibly a way to cross over the Arkansas state line without using the main roads. He also knew that Boudier was thorough and that he would have men watching the smaller roads as well.

He'd taken the dirt road on a hunch.

Growing up in the rural country of Arkansas, he'd loved being out in nature. He knew the country roads like the back of his hand.

Ginny tightened her hold around his waist. She wasn't used to riding a Harley, let alone a riding a Harley in the forest.

He grimaced as branches scraped the sides of his bike. He knew the paint job was going to be ruined by the time they got out of there. It didn't matter. It was a small price to pay to protect her.

The sweet scent of pine and the mustiness of moss filled his nostrils. Leaves swayed as the breeze tickled their delicate green skins, and the rumble of his Harley drowned out any sounds of birds that might be singing in the trees.

The mouth of the road widened, revealing a dilapidated building hidden among the thick grove of trees.

He stopped and killed the engine.

"What are we doing?" Ginny climbed off after him, her eyes wide and uncertain.

"I need to check in with Barrett. Give him an update."

"You mean you want to warn him about me and what I've done." Her tongue flickered out and licked the corners of her mouth. She swallowed and looked like she was ready to bolt.

He placed his hand gently on her slender shoulders. "Ginny. Tell me something."

"What?" She looked up at him with wide eyes.

"Have I ever promised you something that I couldn't deliver?" He wanted her—he needed her—to trust him beyond anything. He knew she was traumatized, but he needed her to have a little faith.

"No. You always did what you said you would do."

"Then hear and trust me when I tell you that I will get you back to Arkansas. Back to where you belong. Trust me."

She blinked and looked at him for a long time. She lowered her head. "It's not you I don't trust, Jaxon. It's me."

He frowned just as his cell phone buzzed. He pulled it out of his jacket. It was Barrett.

He clicked the answer button and held it to his ear.

"Barrett, I was just about to call you. . ."

"Jaxon, listen to me." Barrett tone was clipped, urgent, and unapologetic.

"Okay."

"I need you to get out of Louisiana. I know I told you to get that witch, but the situation has now changed. Get out of Louisiana and make sure you are alone," Barrett demanded.

His blood ran cold. "Is this about Boudier?" How had Barrett found out so fast?

"Yes. And the longer you or any other Arkansas Guardian stays in that state, the higher the risk you are to be found and killed."

"Look, Barrett, the whole thing was an accident. Caroline Boudier wasn't supposed to be killed." He scrubbed his hand across his face. He had to make Barrett understand. He had no other option.

"What did you say? Who was killed?" Barrett's voice went deep. He'd never heard his Pack Master speak like that. Like some bad shit was about to go down.

"Caroline Boudier."

"Boudier's wife was killed today?" Barrett asked.

"Yes, and his son-in-law John." Jaxon frowned.

"Fuucckk." Barrett drew out the curse like a knife slicing into a victim's throat.

"Wait, isn't that why you are telling me to get out of Louisiana?" His stomach knotted.

"No its not. But this just made this whole situation go to DEFCON 1."

Dread filled the pit of his stomach. "Well, I guess what I'm going to tell you next will take it on up to DEFCON 100. I've got someone with me." Jaxon said.

"Please tell me that you have that fucking witch with you, Jaxon. That means I might be able to salvage things with Mississippi."

"No, not her. But she is in Louisiana and did try to run me off the road." He fisted his hands. "Wait. What do you mean, salvage things? I thought we had an agreement with Mississippi that as long as we bring back Ella we would be square with them."

"That was before."

"Before what?"

"Before the Pack Master meeting when Boudier showed up and shit went sideways. Now I'm not so sure we are good with Mississippi. I'm starting to believe that there are a lot of Pack Masters too afraid to stand up to Boudier."

Shit. That wasn't good.

"But what about Alabama? Tennessee? Surely they aren't buying Boudier's bullshit."

"I trust no one," Barrett growled.

Jaxon glanced over his shoulder at Ginny, who was staring up at the abandoned building. He took a few steps away out of her earshot.

"It's Ginny. Ginny McGregor. But you would know her by her maiden name. Boudier." His stomach dropped as he forced the words out of his mouth. This was the worst possible moment to be telling Barrett.

"Drop her off and get the hell out of that state." Barrett ordered.

"I can't. If her father finds her, Boudier would have executed her on the spot."

"Shit, Jaxon." Barrett's growl grew deeper. "Don't tell me that she is the one who killed Caroline and John."

Jaxon took a deep breath and let the next words tumble out of his mouth. "Then I'll tell you I did."

Dead silence sat on the other end of the phone.

Jaxon blinked. "Barrett, are you still there?"

"Jaxon, you need to get the fuck out of Louisiana now. Don't stop. Don't wait. Just get on your Harley and get the fuck out of that state."

"The highway is blocked. The cops have stopped traffic and are checking licenses."

"Then find another road. Any road. Fuck, crawl your way to the state line in a ditch. I don't care how you do it, but get it done."

"I'm on a back road now. Trying to see if there is a way through the woods to cross."

"Good. Do it," Barrett said. "And Jaxon?"

"Yeah?"

"If I were you, I wouldn't be so worried about those cops. I wouldn't even be worried about all those Louisiana Guardians. If I were you, I'd be worried about the Assassins that are going to be hunting down your ass any second."

Barrett ended the call.

Fuck. He'd totally forgotten about the Assassins.

The Assassins were three of the deadliest Weres alive. They were sent out to execute Weres who murdered their parents or spouse. It was decreed in the werewolf law that an Assassin, once sent out on a mission, had to complete the mission before coming home.

Braxton had had the Assassins after him a while back when his father had come up dead. He'd tried to make it to Missouri where werewolves were protected from being extradited. But the Assassins had put a silver bullet in his hide, causing him to lose control of his Harley and fall off the mountain. In the end, evidence showed that a human had killed Braxton's father, and Braxton was cleared of all charges. Barrett had taken exception to the fact that the Assassins had crossed into his state without making him aware of their presence. That's where all the bad blood with Louisiana had begun.

Jaxon studied the ground and then decided to call his best friend. He glanced back at Ginny, who was now leaning against his Harley and waiting patiently.

"Hello?"

"Lucien, I need your help." Jaxon lowered his voice.

"What's wrong, Jaxon? You having trouble with that damn witch? I swear to God, if I get my hands on her, I will strangle her myself," Lucien thundered.

"No, man. It's something else." He cut his eyes at Ginny. She grinned as a brown rabbit hopped in front of her to chew on a bright bunch of green grass. "I need to know if you are still in contact with Lorcan."

There was a short span of silence. "Jaxon, where are you? Tell me you're not in Louisiana."

"I can't do that, bro. You know I'm not a very good liar." He chuckled and then stuck his hand in his pocket.

"Man, you need to get out of there now. Tell me where you are and I'll come get you."

"I can't tell you that. Listen to me. I know that Lorcan helped us get out of Louisiana when Boudier captured you. Do you think he could help me out now?"

"I haven't heard from Lorcan since that night. I've tried calling, but all I get is radio silence. Mom says he hasn't come home either. That's not like him. He might not return my calls, but he always checks in on Mom."

"Well, I have a feeling I'm about to get a visit from him very soon. I need to know where his loyalties lie."

"Jaxon, what the hell did you do?" Concern coated Lucien's tone, making Jaxon's stomach twist.

"Let's just say for semantics there are two dead bodies."

"Well, I know you wouldn't kill your parents because they are in Vermont." Lucien's voice grew deep. "Tell me what's going on. Did you kill someone? And if so, who?"

"Let's say the Assassins are coming for me because of who I have with me. And yes, I killed someone."

"Do I want to know who you have with you?"

"No, but I'll tell you anyway because I'm just that kind of guy." He laughed. "Ginny. I have Ginny."

"Ginny Wilson? Your Ginny?" Incredulity filtered through Lucien's tone.

"Yeah."

"So why do they want her?" Lucien asked slowly.

"Well, they want her because they think she murdered her mother and her husband."

"Husband?"

"They were not mated. It was an arranged marriage,.e, but figuring it'" he assured the Were.

"Did she?"

"No." In his mind, she hadn't murdered them. One was an accident, the other self-defense.

"So then they'll just call a Tribunal. See all the facts before a judgment is found. You know the Were law is very fair."

"That's not all." Jaxon rubbed the back of his neck and studied a clump of dark red weeds near his foot.

"What else, Jaxon? Spill it." Lucien's tone shifted.

"They're after us because of who she is. Of who her father is."

"I thought you said Ginny was an orphan. Raised by her grandmother."

He'd confided in Lucien after a long night of drinking. He'd gotten a good fucking buzz, which almost never happened, and had spilled his heart out to his friend. He'd told Lucien about how Ginny was the love of his life and how she had left him just before they were to be married and mated. He'd said she'd left him a note about how she never wanted to see him again. And that marrying him would be a huge mistake. She said she was going out West to start over on her own. He'd tried to find her grandmother to get some answers, but her house was empty with a *For Sale* sign haphazardly stuck in the yard.

"That's what she thought. Apparently her parents were very much alive. Her grandmother was trying to keep her safe by telling her they were dead. Anyway the father found out Ginny and came and kidnapped her."

"Kidnapped her? What kind of father does that?" Lucien growled.

"The worse kind of male."

"Her father must have some kind of pull to keep her hidden from you all these years."

"Her father is our worst nightmare." Jaxon glanced over his shoulder at Ginny.

"Jaxon, stop with the riddles and just tell me." Lucien sighed.

He took a deep breath and let it out. "Her father is Edward Boudier."

"The Pack Master of Louisiana?" Lucien asked. "Holy fuck."

"Holy fuck is right. And right now I'm trying to get our asses across the state line and back into Arkansas. But Boudier has his men on every main highway and major road doing stop points under the guise of checking driver's licenses."

"Does Barrett know?" Lucien's tone was urgent.

"Yes. He told me to get the fuck out of Louisiana. Which is what I'm trying to do." He shook his head. "Is there any way you can get in contact with Lorcan, maybe feel him out about where his loyalties lie? I mean, shit, man, after he helped get us all out of New Orleans that night, surely he's not still loyal to Boudier."

"I don't know, Jaxon." Lucien's voice was heavy. "I've tried getting in contact with him, but he never calls back."

"You don't think that fucker Boudier did something to him, do you?"

"I don't think he's dead. I mean, we are brothers, and if he had Lorcan killed, I surely would have felt that. Family blood in Weres is strong. Even when we were on bad terms and not talking, I could sense his feelings."

"So can you still sense him? Know how he's feeling?"

"Yeah, but it's really odd."

"What do you mean?" Jaxon asked.

"Lorcan has always been a hothead. That dude has a temper. I could always sense when someone had pissed him off or when someone amused him. But now it's different. It's like he's not letting himself feel one way or another. Like he's indifferent."

"Maybe he's doing that to ensure Boudier thinks he's still loyal. I would have figured Boudier would have had him killed after he helped us escape." Jaxon cringed. "Jesus, Lucien, I'm sorry man, I didn't mean that."

"No worries, man. I know what you meant. To be honest, I thought he would have had him killed too. I was worried for a while, but now I don't know." Lucien's voice dropped. "Listen, I'll try to get in touch with my mom. Maybe she's heard from him. In the meantime, do you have someplace to stay?"

"We're safe. For now." He looked at Ginny and gave her a reassuring smile. "And thanks for all your help, Lucien. I really appreciate it."

"Of course. We might not be blood related, but we are brothers where it counts." Lucien ended the call.

CHAPTER 19

*J*axon stared at the cell phone in his hand. It was a little after noon.

They would have already made it across the state line into Arkansas if the roads hadn't been blocked. But all the detours had cut into their time.

He really couldn't go anywhere until he heard back from Lucien concerning Lorcan.

Lorcan would have the inside scoop, if the Were decided to change his loyalties. Right now he wasn't sure who he could trust.

He shoved the phone back in his pocket and walked back to Ginny, his footsteps muffled by the clumps of dark green grass.

"So what's the plan?" She chewed on the end of her nail and crossed her arms.

"I've got a call in to someone who might help us. Right now we have to stay put. Stay hidden and out of sight."

He looked at the old barn with vines climbing up the windows and weeds crowding the tall double doors. The red tin roof had long faded and rusted, and he was pretty sure he saw some holes, but he couldn't be sure until he got inside.

Thunder rolled overhead. Ginny jumped at the boom.

"Are you kidding me?" She looked heavenward and rolled her eyes.

"Look on the bright side," he said.

"Bright side? What bright side?" She frowned.

"At least we have someplace dry to stay instead of riding in the rain." He grinned.

"You can't be serious about going in there, are you?" She arched her brow. "I don't like hiding out in some snake infested barn."

"Where is your sense of adventure? The Ginny I knew didn't let some little king snake get her rattled." He walked over to his Harley and opened his saddlebags. He dug a round a little and then pulled out a large knife.

"It's not the king snake I'm worried about. I'm worried about the rattlesnake." She pointed at the blade in his hand. "Is that why you have that knife?"

"The knife is to cut down some of the weeds around the door." He smiled and started hacking away at the cluster of weeds blocking the barn doors.

A few field mice scampered out of the bushes and ran off into the safety of the woods. Once the doors were clear of the weeds, he pulled the doors open.

The doors creaked on rusty hinges, and the scent of old hay rolled out. He peered inside the dark building. A couple of old bales of hay were stacked under one of the windows. The dirt floor was strewn with loose straw, and a ladder sat propped leading up to the attic space. He walked the perimeter of the room, kicking the bales of hay and looking in corners for any stray snakes that might be hiding.

"How's it look?" Ginny called out to him.

"It's pretty clean. Hang on and let me look up in the loft."

He braced his foot on the ladder and climbed up to the loft. The floorboards creaked under his footsteps but seemed sturdy enough. The loft was relatively clean except for a couple of old, empty barrels.

He climbed down and walked outside to Ginny.

"I'm going to park the bike inside." He grabbed his Harley by the handlebars and flipped the kickstand. He walked the bike inside, parked it near the window.

"Are you coming in or what?" He turned back to her.

"I don't know, Jaxon. I mean, are you sure it's safe?" Another boom of thunder shook the barn and rattled the windows.

"I'm sure. There's nothing hiding in here to hurt you." He held out his hand and waved her inside.

She hesitated. But when the large, fat drops of rain began to fall, she scurried inside.

He watched as she looked around, assessing their temporary digs.

"It's a long way from what you're used to, I'm sure," he said quietly as he pulled out a blanket from his saddlebag.

She frowned and pointed at the thin blanket. "Do you always carry a blanket in your saddlebag?"

"I do. It's for when I have to work on my bike on the side of the road. Too many times I've had to work on my Harley lying on asphalt. Not the most comfortable thing in the world."

"Oh." She relaxed and smiled.

He caught the look in her eye. He knew what she had been thinking. That he carried it with him to be prepared to sleep with any girl he came across.

"So we wait?" She looked at him and shivered.

"Yeah, for now." He shoved off his jacket and wrapped it around her shoulders. "I'm going to go out to check and make sure no one followed us. Then I'm going to cover up our tracks. I don't want anything leading to us."

He grabbed a rain slicker out of his saddlebag and slipped it over his head. "If you're cold, go stand next to the Harley. The heat from the engine will warm you up."

"Jaxon, be careful."

He smiled and walked back over to her. He placed his hands on either side of her face. His thumbs rubbed the delicate skin on her cheek. Her lips parted, giving him the invitation he sought. He bent his head and gently covered her lips with his own.

He kissed her gently and slowly, holding time in suspension while their bodies became acquainted with each other once again. She moaned under his mouth, sending shivers racing through his body.

God, he'd missed her.

He hadn't realized how much he'd missed her until this very moment. It was like he was slowly dying every day when he was away from her. But now... now, he was beginning to live again, to come back to life.

He wasn't going to let her go. Not in this lifetime or the next.

Her hands slipped around his neck, and she pulled him closer. She opened her mouth under his and he slipped his tongue inside, tasting her sweetness.

His hands went down her back. He cupped her butt and held her against his body.

"Jaxon," she moaned and pressed her mouth to his neck.

Lust pulsed through his body, and his body tightened with lust. He'd never wanted someone as much as he wanted her.

Forcing himself, he pulled away. Disappointment washed over her face and he felt the same way. "Stay here and I'll be right back. I promise."

She nodded and took a step back.

He smiled and headed out the open barn doors. Rain pelted his head and streamed down his face. He broke into a jog down the tiny trail they'd driven up on. He carefully analyzed the road. He spotted their tire tracks. He picked up a fallen branch and ran it across the dirt treads, covering up any sign they'd been here.

Walking back to the barn, he was careful to step in the grass and not the mud. He didn't want to leave any muddy footprints in his path.

Back at the barn, he turned around and swept his gaze across the surroundings.

He didn't smell any danger, nor did he see any. They would be safe here, if just for a while. He doubted that Boudier had the kind of manpower to search every dirt road and every path.

He walked into the barn and shrugged out of the slicker. Ginny stood up from sitting on the Harley and looked at him with expectant eyes.

"It's safe. No tracks at all." He shook out the slicker and folded it up before stowing it back in the saddlebag. He shook his head, sending water droplets flying everywhere.

"Jaxon." Ginny wiped the raindrops from her arms. "I'm going to smell like wet dog now." She smirked.

"Ha ha. Very funny." He chortled.

"How long do you think we'll be here?" She put her hands on her hips and walked around the barn. She kicked a bale of hay and stepped back as if expecting a king cobra to pop out of the old straw.

"Not sure. Lucien is trying to get some intel. It may take a while. We might be spending the night here." He closed and secured the saddlebag and turned back to her.

"Here?" She spread her hands and looked at the dirt floor.

"Well, up there." He pointed above his head to the loft.

"We won't be sleeping on dirt up there, and it's empty and pretty clean."

"Okay." She didn't sound so confident in his decision.

"It's not so bad up there." He turned his attention to the corner of the barn where rain was dripping in from the ceiling. And turned back to her. "Plus, there are no holes in the ceiling in the loft. So it will be dry."

"Give me a minute before you come up." He grabbed the blanket and a smaller bag out of the saddlebag and climbed up the ladder.

CHAPTER 20

Ginny took a deep breath and watched Jaxon disappear up to the loft. This was the last place she'd expected to be today. Their objective, in the middle of nowhere, was to survive, and it if meant spending the night in a dilapidated barn that housed who knew what, then she was up for the challenge.

Something shuffled near the corner. A tiny brown mouse ran over the toe of her boot. She jumped back and screamed.

"What's wrong?" Jaxon's head popped over the edge of the loft and he looked own at her.

"Nothing. Just a stupid mouse." She grimaced and kept her gaze on the floor, watching for any more rodents headed her way.

"He's more scared of you than you are of him," Jaxon said.

"I don't care. Rodents are filthy and carry disease." She scowled and looked around for any movement on the floor.

Jaxon laughed and disappeared back into the loft.

A few seconds later, he called out to her.

"Okay, you can come on up."

She began her climb up the ladder. Though the wood

creaked as she climbed, it felt sturdy enough to hold her weight.

She scrambled over the top of the loft onto the wide plank floor and stood up.

"Wow. This looks cozy." The loft was awash in a soft glow of yellow light from a solar lantern that Jaxon had pulled out of his saddlebag. The blanket was spread out on the floor, and a thermos sat in the middle along with a large bottle of water.

She met his gaze.

He shrugged. "I figured you'd be hungry by now. I have some chili in the thermos and some chocolate chip cookies for dessert."

She arched her brow. "You always make a picnic when you go to work?"

"I didn't make it." He laughed.

Her stomach tightened. Some woman must have cooked for him.

"Granny did. She always cooks for the Guardians, and when she knows we'll be gone on a mission, she makes us take food."

"Oh." She relaxed. "That's really nice." Then she frowned. "Who's Granny?"

"Granny is Jayden's grandmother. She actually used to live in Louisiana with Jayden. But they are in Arkansas now, and she kind of looks after the Guardians as her own grandsons."

She eased onto the blanket and tucked her legs underneath her. A pained smile crossed her lips. "That sounds nice. I'm sure you all appreciate her."

"We do," he said softly. He sat beside her.

"What did you say her grandson's name was?"

"Jayden. Jayden Parker."

"That name sounds familiar. How long have they lived in Arkansas?"

"Not very long. Almost a year."

"Maybe I heard his name from my father talking about all the Arkansas Guardians he was going to take down." She met his gaze. "Jaxon, do you know he has a list? A list of all of Barrett's men. He wants to destroy Barrett and all his Guardians."

Jaxon's gaze hardened. "That fucker can try. But we're not going anywhere."

She swallowed and looked away. "I'm sorry about Heimy and Mitchell."

"You know about that?" Jaxon cocked his head. His muscles tensed in his forearms and strained in his neck.

"John came home one night bragging about what Father had ordered to be done to the Guardian Heimy." She blinked back the tears. "John was the one who carried out the torture of the Guardians. But it was my father who ordered it." She swallowed the lump in her throat. If Jaxon didn't hate her before, surely he would hate her now.

"Your husband did that to Heimy?"

"Yes," she whispered. "He was going to finish Mitchell, but that's when the Arkansas Guardians showed up and found the place." She shook her head. "When he told me about Heimy and Mitchell, he told me if I tried anything, if I tried to get away or tried to kill myself, then you would be the next werewolf they killed." She shook her head.

He reached over and took her hand in his. "What John and your father did had nothing to do with you. It's not your fault. None of that is your fault."

"But this situation that we are in is my fault, Jaxon. I killed my mother and my monster of a husband. The Packs, both Louisiana and Arkansas, aren't just going to let me off with a slap on the wrist. There are consequences." Fear clawed at her stomach, and she wanted to scream.

"Come here." He pulled her into his lap. "Let me tell you something." He brushed her hair away from her eyes and held her gaze. "Everything is going to be okay. I know with everything you've been through and everything you've seen, it's hard to trust someone." He brushed his thumb across her bottom lip. "But I'm asking you to take a deep breath and trust me."

She blinked back the tears burning her eyes. She never cried. She'd taught herself how to push down her emotions until they were under control. Now Jaxon had her wanting to weep like a baby.

She didn't like it. She didn't like not having her emotions under control.

"Say it, Ginny. I need you to say the words."

She took a deep breath and then blew it out. "I trust you, Jaxon."

A smile broke out across his face. "See, that wasn't so hard, was it?"

"Harder than you know." She punched him playfully in the arm.

His eyes narrowed, and the corners of his lips turned up into a smirk. "Oh, yeah?"

He pulled her close and tickled her ribs. She squealed and laughed and tried to get away.

"Jaxon, stop." She laughed and curled up into a ball.

"Not yet." He grinned and caught her arms in one of his hands and pinned them above her head. He tickled her without mercy with his free hand.

"Jaxon!" She squealed.

He finally stopped but continued to hold her arms above her head. He started down at her. His playful expression shifted into another emotion.

Her smile slid off her face as she watched his eyes dilate. She knew what he wanted. But she didn't know if she was ready.

"Jaxon?" She licked her dry lips and stared up at him. Her heart pounded in her chest, and her breathing quickly turned to a pant. She wasn't sure if it was fear or desire filling her chest with butterflies.

It had been so long since she'd been looked at like she was a woman and not something to be possessed.

Something flickered in his eyes and he slowly pulled back and released his hold on her. He got to his feet and went to the ladder.

"Where are you going?" She sat up, her breath but a pant.

"I need to check on something outside. I'll be right back." He climbed down the ladder.

She peered down at him from her position in the loft watching him quickly exit out the large barn doors.

* * *

WHAT THE FUCK was wrong with him?

One minute they were playing around like old times, and the next she was looking at him with fear in her eyes.

Didn't she know he would never hurt her?

He forked his fingers through his hair and walked around the outside of the barn.

He didn't mind the rain soaking his T-shirt and jeans. It least it cooled his body and his libido. He stopped when he got to the back of the barn and looked up at the sky and squeezed his eyes shut.

Thunder rolled and lightning scrawled across the dark sky. The rain was coming down hard and fast now, and he knew there was no way the Louisiana Guardians would be riding in this shit. They would be holed up somewhere, waiting it out. Just like they were.

The Louisiana Assassins... Well, they were a whole other story.

He glanced around the perimeter and didn't notice anything amiss. Taking a deep breath and getting his body under control, he walked back inside the barn.

"Is everything okay?" Ginny called from the loft.

He looked up and met her worried face. He smiled. "Everything is secure." He glanced out the window. "With this downpour, I'm sure the Louisiana Guardians won't be riding."

He reached in his saddlebag, grabbed his phone, and checked to see if he had missed Lucien's call.

His phone showed no calls.

Slipping the phone back into the saddlebag he pulled out the extra set of clothes he always carried with him.

He glanced up and noticed that Ginny wasn't looking down. He pulled his wet shirt over his head and slung it on the seat of his Harley.

He tugged the dry shirt over his head and then unbuttoned his jeans and slid them over his hips. He tugged on the dry jeans and then grabbed his wet clothes. He hung them over the ladder to dry before climbing up.

"You changed clothes." Ginny's eyes ran down the length of him, and he shrugged.

"Yeah. I didn't realize it was raining that hard outside. Good thing I always carry an extra set of clothes."

"I tried the chili. It's really good." She held out the cup from the thermos that she had filled. "I found a fork taped to the side of the thermos. Granny was really smart to do that."

He took the thermos and laughed. "You have no idea. That woman is crazy like a fox."

"Really?" She cocked her head.

"Yeah. She's stubborn and hardheaded, but she loves all the Guardians." He shrugged. "I don't know. She kind of keeps us in line."

"What about Barrett?" Ginny asked.

"She tries to keep Barrett in line, but he doesn't listen."

Her mouth dropped open. "Granny isn't scared of Barrett?"

"Granny isn't scared of anyone." He looked at her, and his smile slipped. He understood what she was getting at.

"Ginny, not all Pack Masters are the same. Not all are like your father," he said softly.

She looked away.

"I don't know who Granny is scared of, but I know who's scared of Granny."

She cut her eyes at him. "Who?"

"Lorcan."

"Lorcan? The Assassin?" Her eyes grew wide. "You must be kidding."

"Believe me, I'm not." He sat down beside her and took a bite of the chili. "The Assassins were sent after Braxton. After they shot him, he managed to hide out at a bed and breakfast in Eureka Springs. Lorcan showed up on the doorstep, and apparently the B&B was hosting some writers and Granny in her B&B. Whatever they said or did to him still has everyone laughing about it."

"They laughed at Lorcan?" She shook her head. "Those writers must have some kind of magic to have that kind of effect on an Assassin."

"You, my love, have apparently never been around writers. They are a different species altogether."

CHAPTER 21

"*I* have a meeting. I'm not sure how long I'll be gone. I need you to cover for me again." Barrett walked over to the secret wall that hid the weapons room and pressed a button. He didn't bother to wait for Damon to agree to fill in for him. He didn't have to. He knew Damon wouldn't refuse.

"What's up? Does this have something to do with the Pack Master meeting the other night?" Damon followed him into the weapon room.

Barrett grabbed a nine-millimeter Sig Sauer and tucked it in the waistband of his jeans. He tugged his leather jacket on and turned to face his Guardian.

"Some things I can't tell you. But there is one thing you need to be aware of." He scrubbed his hand down his face.

"What?" Damon asked

"Jaxon is no longer in Arkansas looking for that witch."

"Where is he?" Damon scowled.

"He's in Louisiana."

"What the fuck is he doing there?" Damon scowled.

"He claims the witch got away from him and he managed

to follow her across the state line. I was hoping he'd apprehend her and get the fuck out of that state before Boudier found out, but there seems to be a problem with that."

"Go on."

"He somehow ended up with Ginny Wilson, his ex-girlfriend... who happens to be Edward Boudier's daughter."

"Fuck. Me." Damon took a deep breath and blew it out.

"Oh, there's more." Barrett narrowed his eyes. "Ginny's mother and her husband are both dead. Ginny did it but he'll sure as shit take the blame." He held up his hand to keep Damon from interrupting. "I'm not so sure Boudier cared that much for his wife, but the fact that his son-in-law was the one financing his trek to power and destruction is not going to sit well with Boudier."

"Shit." Damon shook his head. "How close is Jaxon to crossing into Arkansas?"

"Pretty fucking close. But he can't. Boudier has set up traffic stops on every major highway and road. He's got the police in his pocket and the power to keep looking for them." He pulled his cell phone out of his jacket and hit a few buttons.

"Right now, there is a storm over the area where Jaxon is. He sent a message saying he's somewhere safe."

"Lucien just called and told me that Jaxon reached out to him." Barrett held Damon's gaze. "He is wondering if Lorcan can be of some use in getting our Guardian out of there."

"Jesus. Man, I don't know. I would have thought after he helped us get Lucien out of New Orleans, Lorcan would have stayed in Arkansas and sworn loyalty to you." Damon shook his head. "I don't understand how he can see what Boudier did and still work for him."

"It's fucked up, to say the least." Barrett shook his head.

"You know, your job sucks sometimes, man," Damon growled.

"Yeah. Yeah, it does," he agreed. "Boudier just sent me a text. He wants a meeting."

Damon tensed. "You aren't planning on going by yourself, are you?"

"Yeah."

"No offense, but fuck no. You need to take some backup. That motherfucker could be waiting on you to take you out with a silver bullet in the head." Damon growled, walked over to the wall, and picked up a .45.

"Where do you think you're going with that?" Barrett stepped in front of him and glared.

"With you."

"No. You can't do that. I need you here." Barrett shoved his finger in Damon's chest. "Don't mistake my allowing you to fill in for me as an opportunity to disregard my leadership. You still answer to me."

"And you need to listen to reason," Damon countered.

Barrett glared, and then for the first time in a very long time, he let out a laugh.

"What's so funny? You're not losing it, are you, Barrett?" Damon's brow creased with concern.

"Yeah, Damon. I'm fucking losing it." He sobered and looked at the Guardian. "Who would have thought that you'd be standing here telling me to listen to reason. I remember not so long ago you were about to rip my head off because you thought I was interested in Ava."

Damon scowled. "Yeah well, when people start bandying around words like *mates* and *destiny*, it's hard to see reason."

"I've never let you guys down before. I'm not planning on doing it now."

"Boudier is a sneaky son of a bitch. Don't walk in there thinking he's not going to try something."

"I have no other choice, Damon. My Guardian is in his state. I didn't let him know, and now he'd going to rub that shit in my face. I'm going to try to work out something where I can get Jaxon back without getting anyone hurt. We may have to cut our losses when seeking revenge for Heimy and Mitchell and Lucien."

"Are you fucking serious? You can't just let that shit go," Damon growled.

"Oh, believe me. I'm not letting anything go. I'm just going to let Boudier think I am."

CHAPTER 22

*G*inny stood and left the blanket to walk over to the small window in the loft. They'd been stuck for hours in the dilapidated barn, listening to the rain pelting the tin roof as thunder shook the old windows. The dark storm clouds were giving way to nightfall.

Panic rose in her throat, and she tried not to let Jaxon see her increased breathing. He'd been so focused on waiting to hear back from Barrett for further instructions on when and how they should leave.

Anxiety weighed on her like a heavy stone, and she had forced herself not to fidget in the small space. The more uncomfortable and upset she appeared, the more Jaxon would worry.

She didn't want him to worry about her. They were in enough shit as it was.

Fear clawed at her stomach, and despite his reassuring words that everything would be okay, she couldn't allow herself to believe that.

She was living on borrowed time. Deep down in her gut, she knew that. So was Jaxon. He just didn't know it yet.

Her father wasn't going to let Jaxon live. He would kill Jaxon just to spite her. He'd probably make her watch him die before he killed her too.

Thunder boomed through the sky. She jumped and pressed her hand to her heart and spun around.

"I would have figured you would have gotten used to the sound by now," Jaxon said from his perch on the ladder. He had just come back in from having a look around outside, making sure their little fortress was secure.

"It's hard not to jump when it's so loud," she breathed. "It's been raining for hours. It has to stop sometime."

He stepped onto the loft and pulled his cell phone out of his back jeans pocket.

"According to the weather app, it's going to rain until early in the morning."

"So we have to stay here." Her heart thudded painfully in her chest.

"Until it stops raining or…" His voice trailed off.

She lifted her chin. "Or until we have to make a run for it." Reality settled over her like a sopping wet blanket.

The odds of successfully making a run for it in this weather weren't in their favor. That much she knew.

"Have you heard back from your Pack Master?" She swallowed and looked out the window. She didn't need him to see the fear in her eyes. She'd lived in fear for so fucking long, she should have been immune to it.

That was the thing about faith, hope and second chances. Once she'd gotten the tiniest glimpse of all three, she'd begun to really have hope. She also knew that along with hope came the fear of everything being taken away from her.

This was real life, not a fairy tale.

"No, but I did hear from Damon."

"Who's Damon?"

"He's one of the Guardians. Apparently Barrett has put him in charge while he is taking care of some things."

"What things?" She crossed her arms and gave him a wide-eyed look. "What about taking care of his Guardians? What about trying to find a way to help us?" There was no use trying to keep the fear out of her voice. It had set up residence and didn't plan on leaving anytime soon.

"I'm sure he's doing everything he can. He is in a delicate situation and has to find the most diplomatic way to handle things."

Regret poured through her.

"I'm sorry." She shook her head. "I'm so sorry, Jaxon. We are in this mess because of me. I have no right to say those things to you." She met his eyes. "This is all my fault, not yours. I'm sure your Pack Master is doing what he can to help you."

"And to help you too, Ginny." Jaxon frowned and stepped forward. "And stop saying that. This is not your fault. You have lived in an abusive situation for years. What happened to your mother was an accident, self-defense. You never intended for her to die."

"And my husband? That wasn't an accident," she said softly.

"Yeah, well, that fucker deserved what he got." Jaxon blinked.

Nervous laughter bubbled up inside her chest until it spilled out of her mouth. Once she started laughing, she couldn't seem to stop.

Her laughter was contagious, and soon Jaxon was laughing along with her.

When she finally sobered, she walked over to him and rested her head on his chest.

"Thank you for that. You always did know what to say to

make me feel better," she said softly. She pressed her hand to his chest, feeling his strength radiate into her palm. Just touching him made her feel better, made her feel stronger, like she could take on the world.

His strong arms came around her and he held her tight. He nuzzled his face in her hair as his breathing increased. Her heart pounded faster, and this time it wasn't due to fear or anxiety. This time it was all because of her desire for Jaxon.

She shouldn't even be thinking about such things. They were in a life-or-death situation and needed to be ready at a moment's notice in case they had to leave. But she couldn't explain that to her heart.

"Jaxon." She lifted her face. She slowly trailed her hands up his chest, feeling every ridge of every hard muscle. She felt the pounding of his heart against her palm. She laced her fingers behind his neck and pulled him down for a kiss.

She pressed her lips against his, needing to be near.

He growled and tightened his arms around her, pressing her curves against his muscles.

He fisted his hands in his hair, angling her face so he could kiss her better, deeper.

"More," she whispered and opened her mouth under his. His hot tongue snaked inside, teasing and taunting her with the promise of pleasure and every wicked thing she'd ever dreamed of him doing to her.

He pulled back, his breathing heavy, and gazed at her with dilated eyes.

"I don't want to rush you. I know..." His words tapered off, and she knew where his head was.

"I know what I want, Jaxon. And I want you." He was all she'd ever wanted. He'd been stolen from her on that summer day, along with the promise of their future. He was here, standing in front of her, and she wasn't going to let this opportunity pass her by.

He growled deep and pulled her against him. His mouth slammed down across hers, and butterflies tumbled and swirled in her stomach.

She dug her fingernails into his shoulders, her body alive and pulsing under every brush of his hand.

His hand skirted underneath her shirt, and his fingers glided along her ribcage upward toward her breast. She gasped, and her breathing quickly turned to a pant. The pad of his fingertip caressed her nipple through the lace of her bra, sending pleasure careening through her body.

"Off," he stated and pulled back enough to raise her shirt over her head and toss it on the blanket. His darkened gaze dipped toward her bra, and she could feel herself growing warm all over.

"Your clothes too," she said, her words husky with lust. She grabbed his T-shirt, and he dipped his head, letting her pull the material off and dropping it to the floor. She traced the outline of his hard-muscled chest down to the six-pack above the waistband of his jeans, inhaling his male scent and submerging herself in his heat.

He cupped her face between his hands and forced her to look up at him. They stayed like that, speaking volumes without ever uttering a word and holding onto this moment.

"I never stopped loving you," he said.

She teared up and nodded. "Good."

"That's all you're going to say?" He frowned but didn't stop looking into her eyes.

"No. I've got more to say. A lot more. Right now I need this, Jaxon. I need you." She blinked back the sting of tears and laced her fingers behind his head.

He kissed her and she opened under his mouth, taking the heat to a whole other level.

She sucked his tongue and then kissed him hard and deep, making up for lost time.

She needed to show him how much she loved him, how much she cared. Words were just words, after all. Actions meant everything.

She moved her hand down his shoulders and fumbled with the button on his jeans. She unfastened and unzipped him in a flash, shoving his jeans down past his narrow hips.

She kissed him as she wrapped her hand around his stiff erection. He growled and thrust against her hand. Pleased with his response, she squeezed.

"That's not playing fair. You have me at an advantage." He pulled back and flicked the clasp on her bra, freeing her breasts. "But not for long." He grinned wickedly and then dipped his head. He sucked her hard nipple into his hot mouth.

"Oh, god," she cried out as his tongue swirled around the tight bud. Pleasure built deep in her stomach, and she dug her nails into his shoulder while trying to concentrate enough to squeeze around his shaft.

"I'm nowhere near done." His voice held an edge to it, lustful and hard.

He kept his mouth on her breast as his fingers deftly unzipped her jeans. He shoved them down her legs. His fingers grazed the front of her panties, sending off shocks of pleasure through her body. Her body was on fire, and every stroke and caress added to the intensity of his touch.

He shoved the bra off her shoulders, letting the lace material fall to the floor, and turned his attention to her other breast. He closed his lips around her nipple and sucked.

She clasped his head to her, holding him close and breathing heavy.

"You taste so fucking sweet. Just like I remember." His words came between sucks on her sensitive flesh.

She arched toward him and writhed against his hot mouth.

"Jaxon," she breathed out.

"Keep saying that. Keep saying my name. I want to hear you scream my name when I make you come," he commanded.

She didn't have time to respond before he was kneeling in front of her and pulling her panties off in a heated rush. She steadied herself on his shoulders as he helped her step out of her pants and panties. He shoved the needless articles out of the way and then gazed up at her.

He grabbed her hips and pressed a kiss to her stomach. She rested her hands on his shoulders and balanced herself to keep from falling over.

"You are mine, Ginny." He said the words against the soft flesh of her stomach.

"I always have been yours, Jaxon." She looked down at him. "I love you. That never stopped for me."

His gaze darkened.

He placed his hands on either side of her hips and buried his face between her legs.

She moaned, digging her fingers through his silky blonde hair as his mouth teased the tender flesh. His tongue flicked over her clit, and she nearly came. He sensed her urgency and sucked her clit into his mouth.

"Jaxon," she cried out, pleasure washing over her until she was numb with it.

He pleasured her with his mouth until she rode out her orgasm. Trying to catch her breath, she gazed down at him.

He grinned, his mouth wet with her, and slowly stood.

"Now that the first one is out of the way, the next one will be slower." He grinned and covered her mouth with his.

Ginny looked at him with heavy eyes. Her skin prickled,

and her stomach grew heavy with desire. It was one of the hardest orgasms she'd ever had, and now he was promising her more.

"Just wait a second." She knelt in front of him and smiled from her position.

"Ginny." His voice held a warning.

She was done with warnings. She was going to take what she wanted. Life was too short to hesitate.

"Jaxon." She said his name, then opened her mouth and licked the length of him.

He growled and rested his hand on her head to draw her closer.

After a few more torturous licks, she opened and filled her mouth with him.

She sucked him deep, twirling her tongue along his erection. She didn't use her hands, just her mouth.

"Ahhhhh." He threw back his head, and she could feel him tremble where she rested her fingertips on his hips. His breathing grew rapid.

Pleasure shot through her core and soon she was aching to have him fill her between her legs. She looked up and met his heated gaze.

"It feels too good," was all he managed to say before she felt him lose control. She tightened her hold on his dick and his hips, sucking him as he spilled his release into her greedy mouth.

She finally pulled away and looked up at him. He pulled her up to standing. He cupped her head and covered her mouth with his, kissing and tasting his own scent as he did.

It turned her on even more.

She clung to him as his hand went between her legs, circling her clit.

"We're nowhere near done, baby," he whispered near her

ear before sucking her lobe into his hot mouth. She shivered against him, and she thought she would explode before he made it in inside her.

She felt his dick grow hard once again, straining and lengthening against her stomach. He wanted her as much as she wanted him.

"I need to be inside you, now." He looked into her gaze, awaiting her reply. She knew then, why.

She'd lived under the abuse of a violent husband who took what he wanted with no conscience. Jaxon knew that she needed to be in control of this situation when it came to her body. He was letting her know that this had to be her decision to let him inside, both physically and emotionally.

It shattered the veneer around her heart.

"Yes." She pulled his head down for another kiss, letting him know that she was choosing him and that she would always choose him. She'd never felt as much love as she felt for Jaxon Taylor.

He swept her up in his arms and stood there for a moment just gazing at her with so much love her chest ached.

"It might not be a honeymoon and champagne, but you will always own me, Ginny, my heart and my body." His voice whispered through the old barn.

He was trying to make this as special as their wedding night might have been years ago.

A tear slipped down her cheek, and he bent his head to hers. She buried her face in the crook of his neck and hugged him tight.

He knelt with her in his arms and gently placed her on the small blanket on the old wooden floor. He kissed her as he positioned himself between her legs. His erection, hard and insistent, nudged at her wet entrance, and she widened her legs to accommodate him.

"Now, Jaxon," she whispered against his ear.

He thrust inside her, and she gasped as her body stretched. She was no virgin, but her husband wasn't exactly a large man in that department. Jaxon, on the other hand, had been blessed by the genital gods. Very, very blessed.

He looked down, worry in his eyes.

She pressed the pad of her finger to his lips, silencing any concerns before he voiced them.

"Don't you dare think of stopping. Not now. I've waited all this time for you. I want all of you," she whispered.

He grinned, male pride stretching across his handsome face. He pressed his lips to hers, slowly moving his body against hers and thrusting in and out of her with precision and care.

She moaned as his fingers found her hard nipple, and she clawed at his back when he kissed her neck. He'd always known how to touch her, fondle her, make her sigh. But they'd never actually made love. She'd wanted to save that for their wedding night.

She'd been so wrong to wait. She'd wished a thousand times Jaxon had taken her virginity instead of John.

But now, with his hands on her body and his mouth on hers, all of those thoughts and regrets disappeared like vapor. He was slowly replacing all her regrets with faith and hope in their new future together. A future that in that moment seemed like a strong possibility.

"I'm going to come home to you every night and make love to you like this." He spoke as he thrust, his eyes dark with desire and his voice husky. "You are not getting away from me again. You're mine, and no one is taking you away from me again."

"Yes," she murmured as pleasure stretched across her sensitive flesh. She dug her fingertips into his shoulders and bit down on his neck.

He growled and moved faster, thrusting deep and powerful within her wet heat. Their bodies, slick with sweat, strained and clung to each other. She hungered for him.

Pleasure streaked and built. Promises hung in the dark night, and hope swelled within their tiny barn.

He lifted his head, and in the dim light of the solar lamp, their gazes met. In the small space of time before climax threatened to pull her under and yearning crescendoed, her heart fluttered in her chest.

"Jaxon." This time when she came she whispered his name, promising to be his from that day forward.

* * *

JAXON COULDN'T TAKE his eyes off Ginny as she slept against his chest. They'd made love for the first time in a barn that was about to fall down.

It was perfect.

And it was more than he'd hoped for.

He had found his second chance. With someone he thought had abandoned him.

He wasn't going to let her slip through his fingers a second time. This time, he was going to hold on good and tight.

This time, they were going to make it.

* * *

JAXON SWIPED against the buzz against his head. He hated mosquitoes, and he hated being woken up from sleeping up next to Ginny.

When the buzz didn't go away, he swiped harder. His hand landed on something hard and plastic. He blinked open his drowsy eyes and realized it wasn't a bug but his cell phone ringing.

He quickly disentangled himself from Ginny's arms and legs with regret and answered the phone.

"Hello?"

"Jaxon, what the fuck took so long? You in the middle of something?" Lucien's tone was gruff.

"Please tell me you have good news from Lorcan." He rubbed the sleep out of his eyes and blinked a few times.

"I finally got a message back from him."

"So did you actually talk directly to him?" He didn't have time to play telephone. He needed answers and directions. Lorcan was going to have to be his inside intel to get out of Louisiana in one piece.

"I left a message, explaining things."

"Is that safe? Just leaving a message on his phone? I mean, who knows who else might get it? Or who might be bugging his phone?" He didn't put it past Boudier to keep tight tabs on all his Guardians and his Assassins. Especially since he might suspect that Lorcan had helped them escape. He might be watching him harder than the others.

"I left it in code."

"Code?"

"Yeah. We used to use a code language when we were little. We could have a total conversation in front of our parents. They thought we were talking about girls or football. In reality, we were talking about sneaking out and stealing our neighbor's car for a late-night ride down to New Orleans."

"And here I thought you were straitlaced in a wealthy family." Jaxon snorted. He glanced down as Ginny stirred awake. She blinked and smiled. She sat up when she realized he was on the phone.

"We lived out in the country. We got bored. Sue me." Lucien snarked.

"Since your family is filthy-ass rich, I'll be sure to do that. But right now I need a way out of Louisiana and back into Arkansas."

"He says that your best bet is to leave now. While it's raining. He says there is minimal security on the smaller roads. Boudier has rerouted the majority of his men to the interstates and the highways. He suspects you'll have to cross into Arkansas by the interstate because of the heavy rains."

Jaxon glanced out the window and scowled. The thunder and lightning had eased up, but it was still raining. He was not looking forward to riding with Ginny in this mess.

"Okay. There's a road a few miles from here where I can possibly cross. I've studied the map, and that's the closest thing to us besides the interstate."

"Do that, then." Lucien's tone dropped. "Jaxon, you are running this by Barrett, right? I mean, he did tell you to have me get you hooked up with Lorcan?"

Jaxon's gut twisted. He hated lying, but he had to get Ginny back to Arkansas safe and sound.

"Barrett told me to do whatever it took to get back to Arkansas. That includes talking to Lorcan." Jaxon scrubbed his hand down his face. "Look man, when I get back home, I'm going to owe you big time for this."

"Nah. Besides, you were there in New Orleans helping me get out. We're Guardians. It's what we do." Lucien ended the call before Jaxon could respond.

"Is everything okay?" Ginny pulled her knees up to her chin and looked at him with wide eyes.

His head nearly exploded with the love he felt for the woman in front of him. He'd never loved anyone as much he loved her.

"I've got good news and bad news." He cocked his head.

"What's the good news?" She arched her perfect eyebrow and studied him.

"We have a way out of Louisiana and back into Arkansas."

"And the bad news?" She bit her lip.

"We have to leave now." He glanced over his shoulder and out the window at the rain pelting the glass. "And we have to ride in this."

CHAPTER 23

$\mathcal{E}$dward Boudier sat behind his elaborate gold desk and listened to the current updates from his Guardians as to the whereabouts of his worthless daughter and that fucking Arkansas werewolf she was with. His Guardians had never been inside his office before. He could smell their fear filling the room.

None of them knew about the call he'd gotten only a few minutes ago from a particular witch from Yazoo City who was proving to be quite an asset. He usually didn't fuck with witches, but this one was going to prove very useful indeed.

He picked up the crystal glass of sherry and swirled the garnet liquid, watching it change colors in the light.

"What do you mean, you lost sight of them?" He continued to gaze into his glass. This was no ordinary glass. It had come all the way from France in the 1900s when his ancestors had settled in New Orleans.

"Sir, we've continued to monitor the roads and inter-states. We've had no sign of Jaxon trying to cross into Arkansas. It's probably the rain that's keeping him off the

186

roads somewhere until this weather clears up." Manny's voice droned like the buzzing of cicadas.

"Tell me, Manny." He lifted his gaze and looked around his office, which was filled with priceless paintings, ancient artifacts, and swords from countries all around the world. "If you were on the run, would what would you do?"

Boudier let the silence fill the room. He knew his other Guardians were waiting for Manny's response. He knew they were waiting to see what he was going to do to Manny if he gave the wrong response. He also knew that though they were loyal, they were also scared of him. And that was how he kept control of his state and control of his wolves. Keeping them scared to keep them loyal.

"If I were on the run, I would..."

He stood from his desk and held up his hands, silencing Manny. Tension thickened in the room like a good New Orleans roux.

"Tell me, Manny. If you were on the run from me. What would you do?"

Manny blinked and then spoke. "I would continue trying to find a way to pass into Arkansas."

Boudier smiled. "Would the rain stop you? Would you take the time to stop and find some romantic spot to hide away with my daughter while you fucked her into oblivion?"

"No, sir."

He narrowed his eyes on Manny, anger sparking like a match in his gut. "Are you saying my daughter is not fuckable?"

"No sir, I didn't imply..." Manny's eyes grew wide and he cleared his throat.

"Are you saying that you want to fuck my daughter?" Boudier growled. Sometimes these Guardians were fucking animals. Unable to control their urges and lusts.

"No, sir." Manny shook his head furiously and held his

hands up and bowed his head. "I would never disrespect you or your daughter like that."

He cut his eyes from Manny to study the audience in the room. He knew they were waiting to see his response.

"What about you, Brutus?" He cocked his head at his lead Assassin. Brutus looked like he belonged in the military with his buzz cut, black fatigues, and no-bullshit attitude.

"I am trained to track down and execute. That is my job, and it's my only job." Brutus met his gaze with steely-eyed determination.

"I see. So you don't have time to fuck." He nodded approvingly. "I like that. I like that a whole lot."

He turned his attention to Killian, his other Assassin. "Killian, what about you? I'm awaiting your answer with bated breath."

"I am an Assassin. I've taken vows to uphold any order that you give. Like my brother Brutus, execution is my job."

Boudier cut his eyes over at Lorcan. He walked the room until he stopped right in front of his third Assassin. He smirked and pointed his finger in Lorcan's direction. "Lorcan. Same question."

"Sir, I, like my fellow Assassins, am trained to kill. I don't have time to fuck anyone," Lorcan deadpanned.

Boudier broke out into a smile. "As usual, I'm not disappointed by your smart-ass mouth, Lorcan." He slapped the Assassin on his back and leaned in. He measured his next words carefully before he spoke. "Let's not forget that those who betray me face the cruelest punishment imaginable. Worse than death."

Lorcan didn't blink, nor did he flinch. That meant the Assassin was on the up and up and hadn't been behind Lucien's escape. Or maybe Lorcan was a really, really, really good liar.

Whichever it was, Boudier was going to find out.

He stepped back and walked back over to his desk. He picked up his glass of sherry and took a sip. He stepped back in front of Manny and held out the glass to the Were. "Drink?"

"No, sir." Manny's eyes grew wide. "I'm on duty and not worthy of such expensive liquor."

"Go on. Take it. I insist." He shoved it in Manny's chest, forcing the Guardian to take it.

Manny held it out and blinked.

"Try it." He ordered.

Manny lifted the glass to his lips and took a sip. The Were winced slightly but covered it up and fixed a neutral expression on his face.

"A lot of people don't like sherry. It's more of an after-dinner drink. Or served in the afternoon with cookies." He smiled. "I know in Charleston they serve it like that. With cookies. It's a genteel sort of thing that I like to keep alive. I am very fond of traditions. It's what separates us from the animals, so to speak." He smiled and looked to his audience of Guardians.

"Look around my room, gentlemen. Everything in my office has value." He pointed to the painting to his left. "That painting right there is from a famous artist in France. I paid over twenty thousand dollars for that piece." He turned and nodded at the tablets that looks as if they were made out of cement. "And that. That right there was discovered in a pyramid in Egypt. In the pharaoh's tomb."

He walked over to the wall where his most prized swords hung. "And here. Right on my wall near my desk. Swords from every country." He ran his finger along the tip of a Samurai sword. Blood welled and dripped from his finger onto the floor.

"It's sharper than any sword you will ever find. Enough pressure, and it will take my finger clean off my hand." He cocked his head and popped his finger in his mouth, sucking the coppery blood from the tip.

"Why do you think I keep these things?" He waited for a response, but no one said a word.

"Give up? I'll tell you." He waved his hand around the room at all the items he'd just discussed.

"You see, everything in here has value, whether it's a painting, an artifact, or a sword. It holds value." His gaze landed on Lorcan. "Even my Assassins hold value because they carry out a special function. They're probably my favorite objects in the room."

He had to hand it to Lorcan. The Were didn't flinch or break eye contact.

He took the sword and walked over to Manny and touched the metal to the middle of the Guardian's chest. Not hard enough to break the skin—just enough pressure to let him know he was there.

"Tell me, when should I expect Jaxon captured and my daughter returned to me?" He cocked his head.

Manny swallowed.

"Before dawn, sir." A bead of sweat rolled down his temple and bled into his T-shirt.

"Well then, I suppose you all should get going. He's not going to get caught with all you assholes standing around here holding your dicks." He snatched the glass out of Manny's hand and tossed it against the fireplace. The crystal broke into a thousand shards. It was going to be a bitch to get out of the carpet.

Everyone in the room turned and hurried to the door.

"Except you, Manny," he said slowly. "You stay."

Manny turned his wide eyes on him and looked around the room for some allies. What Manny didn't know was that in the Louisiana Pack, there were no allies. Boudier had made sure of that.

The best way to control his werewolves was to have their undivided loyalty to him and not to each other. Barrett Middleton was a weak and foolish leader to encourage his Guardians to rely on each other. All it did was make the Pack weak. A weak Pack wouldn't bother to protect their Pack Master.

That's why he demanded complete loyalty to him. It ensured his survival. And the survival of his Pack.

"Sir, I..." Manny swallowed and blinked so fast that he thought the Were was going to burst out in tears in front of him. Manny was a pussy. And he didn't tolerate pussies.

"Come now, Manny. You didn't seriously think I was going to let you walk out of this room, did you?" He grinned and then turned to see his Assassins still standing in the room.

"Lorcan, what should be done with Manny?" He gave the Were a pointed look.

"If he is found lacking, then you should get rid of him," Lorcan said without emotion.

Boudier narrowed his eyes. "Good answer."

"But if you execute a Were without enough evidence, then it may raise questions among the other Guardians," Lorcan continued without putting inflection in his voice. He sounded like he was reading a how-to book on fixing a sink.

"Is that so?" He slowly walked toward Lorcan. Brutus took a deep breath and Killian frowned. He knew what the other Assassins were thinking. Or he used to. It seemed like it was getting harder and harder to read these fuckers. On the outside, they all looked ready to ride and die for him, for his causes. But who the hell knew. Lately, with all this trouble with Arkansas, he'd heard of some murmurs of unease within his own ranks.

Now with his wife and son-in-law murdered, he knew there would be some within his Pack who thought he was going to be a weak leader. They'd think about leaving the Pack.

He wasn't weak. He'd never been weak. Even as a child. If the human population knew some of the shit he used to do as a child, they would declare him a psychopathic serial killer and have him locked up. But humans were stupid and easy to manipulate with money and the promise of power. Civilian Weres, even more so.

"Tell me, Brutus. What is your opinion on Manny?" He turned his cold gaze on the leader of the Assassins. "Should I execute him? Or let him off with a warning?"

"You've never let anyone off with a warning, Pack Master." Brutus returned his cold stare.

Boudier felt a large grin cover his face. "You know what, Brutus. I'm thinking about letting you be my favorite Assassin instead of Lorcan." He glared at Lorcan. "You know, I liked you better when your hair was blonde. The way you have it makes you eerily similar to that bastard brother of yours." He knew he should have ordered his son-in-law to kill Lucien when he had the fucker in his hands. But no, John couldn't just kill the Were and be done with it. He needed time to play with his prey.

He gripped the sword and ran it through Manny's stomach. Manny gasped in shock and looked down at his gut. Blood poured out, soaking his shirt and dripping onto the floor.

"Sorry, Manny. You've outlived your usefulness. As I said, I don't keep anything around that isn't of any value to me." He smiled broadly and pulled the sword out. Grabbing the handle with both hands, he swung the large sword and decapitated the Guardian in one swift move.

Manny's head landed on the floor with a thunk. His body crumpled to the floor.

"Well, that was anticlimactic." He propped one hand on

his hip, leaned against his sword, and shook his head. "I wish there had been more time to make Manny understand the seriousness of the situation. But I've got shit to do." He looked up at the Assassins.

"Which one of you wants to volunteer to clean this shit up? It's going to be a bitch to get out of my antique rug." He should have made sure Manny was standing far enough away from his rug before he started swinging.

"I'll do it." Lorcan went for the door.

"Hold up, Lorcan." He studied the werewolf, looking for any signs of deceit. He found none. But that didn't mean shit.

"I've got a better use of your time than wasting it cleaning this up." He still needed his Assassins. "Make one of the other Guardians do it. I want all of you on the road. Find Jaxon and bring him to me."

"What about Ginny?" Brutus asked.

"What about her?" Boudier shrugged.

"If we find them together, shouldn't we bring them both in?" Killian frowned.

Boudier thought for a minute and then looked at his Assassins.

"You're right. Bring Ginny to me unharmed. And make sure Jaxon is with her. I want to make sure she gets to see her lover as I peel the flesh from his body. Females don't seem to find males attractive without their skin." He grinned as his stomach fluttered with excitement. "And after I kill Jaxon, then give Ginny to my Guardians to do with as they please." He nodded slowly as the excitement built. "I do mean that in the most carnal sense."

"I'm sure she won't last a full day once they get ahold of her. She risked everything for love. Now I want her life in exchange."

CHAPTER 24

*L*orcan kept his gaze straight ahead as he walked out of the Boudiers' house and into the dark starless night.

"Lorcan, what the fuck is going on with you?" Brutus called out from behind.

He didn't bother slowing his stride until he stopped at his Harley Davidson Breakout. He turned and met the angry looks that both Brutus and Killian were shooting him.

"I'm doing what I'm told. Following orders." He kept his expression neutral despite the rage boiling deep in his gut. He hated Boudier. He hated being in Louisiana under Boudier's thumb. But he had no choice. Although the Pack Master didn't really have any evidence that Lorcan had helped Lucien escape, Boudier was paranoid enough to suspect him.

Lorcan had family in Louisiana, and he couldn't just up and leave them vulnerable to whatever Boudier would do to get his revenge.

"Stop it, man." Killian shoved him enough to get his attention.

"Stop what, Killian?" He held the Were's gaze.

"Dude, it's us. Just us standing out here with no one else around." Killian glanced over his shoulder toward the house. "Look, tell us what happened with Lucien."

Lorcan held his hand up to stop whatever the fuck Killian was about to say. "I don't know what you are implying, but you need to shut your fucking mouth right now. Lucien is no longer my brother. He left his family for Arkansas. He betrayed us. If you think I'm waxing sentimental over missing my brother you are wrong."

Killian sighed, letting Lorcan know he wasn't buying what he was selling.

"You have to know your place, Lorcan. We are Assassins. Ours is a coveted position that only the elite can fulfill." Brutus elbowed Killian out of the way and got in Lorcan's face.

"I'm sure that look on Manny's face when he had Boudier's sword cutting his guts meant he sure wished he were one of us. One of the elite." He didn't bother keeping the sarcasm out of his tone. Let them think what they would. He knew he couldn't trust any of them. Not even Brutus and Killian.

"There are whispers"—Brutus lowered his voice—"that you helped Lucien escape from New Orleans."

Killian cocked his head and met Lorcan's gaze. Lorcan looked from one Assassin to the other and shrugged his shoulders. "There are always whispers, Brutus. You should hear what they say about you when you're not around."

"I don't give two fucks what they say about me. I know who I am, and I know my place."

Lorcan curled his fingers into fists at his sides and leaned toward the massive Assassin that he'd come to think of as a brother. "And maybe I now know my place, Brutus. You seem to think that all this shit that's been going on is based on justice and order. But you know damn well it's not. Intimidation, torture, and murder is no way to rule a Pack."

"Lorcan," Killian hissed and looked around to see if anyone was watching them.

Lorcan only smiled. "Don't worry. I'll do my duty and my job. It's what I have sworn my allegiance to." He straddled his Harley and started the motorcycle. "It's strange."

"What's that?" Brutus narrowed his eyes.

"We are sworn to execute justice, to defend our Pack. But really we murder the innocent and defend Satan himself." He looked back at the house and shook his head.

"We better be getting on the road. The ride to hell is going to be a long one." He sped out of the driveway and onto the road, leaving his words hanging in the air.

* * *

"WHAT DID YOUR BROTHER SAY?" Barrett leveled his glare at Lucien. He'd ridden toward the Louisiana and Arkansas border with Lucien at his side. Getting Jaxon back into Arkansas was his first priority.

They pulled of the road and into a small gas station. They needed to gas up their bikes before getting back on the road.

"Lorcan said that it would be best if Jaxon tried to cross the border now. From the GPS on Jaxon's bike, it looks like Jaxon's not far from where he needs to cross into Arkansas." Lucien frowned and glanced away.

"What is it, Lucien?" Barrett didn't need Lucien holding back any kind of information. Not now. It could mean disaster for everyone.

"Barrett, you need to understand that I'm getting all this from Lorcan. And I'm not exactly sure where his head is at. I've not seen him since…"

"New Orleans. I know." Barrett propped his hands on his

hips and stared into the darkness. They'd pulled to the side of the road so he could talk with Lucien. He glanced over his shoulder. The rest of his Guardians were still sitting on their Harleys, waiting for orders.

"I hate to say this, but how do we know…" Lucien gave him a pained look.

"If we can trust him," Barrett finished for him. "I'm thinking the exact same thing." He ran his hand through his hair, knocking the drops of rain from his head.

"Here's the thing, Lucien. We need to get Jaxon back. I'm not losing any more Guardians or having any more Guardians tortured. After Jaxon is back, then I'm going after Boudier myself."

"You won't exactly be by yourself. All your Guardians want a piece of that fucker too," Lucien growled.

A ghost of a smiled brushed Barrett's lips. He nodded at Lucien. "How are you doing?"

"All healed up. You could never tell that Boudier's men tried to filet me like a fucking trout."

"He will get what's coming to him. Trust in that, Lucien," Barrett said and looked away.

"This whole thing is going to be one massive shit storm. Blowback on everyone." Barrett crossed his arms. "I'm fucked if I go after Boudier, and I'm fucked if I don't."

"I don't get why the other Pack Masters aren't upset about this." Lucien shook his head.

"Because they don't want to be in Boudier's crosshairs." He shrugged. "I know all of them, and they are not bad men. They are afraid if they go after Edward Boudier then he will come for them and their Guardians. No one likes to lose men."

"Except Boudier. That fucker could care less if his Guardians live or die." Lucien snarled.

"And from the sound of it, he doesn't intend on keeping

them around for much longer." Barrett met Lucien's gaze. "My advice to you is to warn Lorcan to get out before this shit goes sideways. Tell him I always remember debts. And I haven't forgotten what he did to help us in New Orleans."

He clamped a hand on Lucien's shoulder. "Now let's go get Jaxon out of there and back to safety."

* * *

GINNY STRADDLED the Harley and wrapped her arms around Jaxon's waist. She wasn't sure she was going to be able to hold on in this weather, but she prayed she would be able to.

Unease snaked up her spine and seeped into her flesh. She tightened her grip on Jaxon as he started up the motorcycle. She squeezed her eyes tight, trying to ward off the sense that something was wrong. She didn't want to stay here, but she didn't want to leave either. She knew her father, and she knew he wasn't the kind of man to give up something he considered to be his.

After her father had found her and murdered her grand-mother, Ginny had fallen into a severe depression. She'd mourned her grandmother, the woman who'd raised her, yet she was glad to discover that her mother was alive. But after a while, Caroline had begun to resent the fact that Ginny talked of her grandmother so much.

Her mother began to change in other ways. She'd grown colder, more distant. Ginny had always thought that it was because her father controlled every aspect of her mother's life, from what she ate to where she went to how she dressed. But now she realized it was something else too. Her mother had let whatever good she'd had left rot and mold and blow away until the only thing that was left was the need to survive at any costs. Even the safety of her daughter.

Ginny opened her eyes and squinted as Jaxon made his way down the tiny trail back to the road they'd turned off of.

The occasional crack of thunder and spray of lightning across the sky didn't make her jump this time. She was getting used to it, but she still didn't like the idea of riding in the rain and the slick road conditions.

"Hang on." Jaxon spoke to her across his shoulders.

She nodded and interlaced her fingers, locking them in place. She laid her head against Jaxon's back and held on tight as he turned onto the road. He increased his speed and hit just about every freaking pothole in the dirt road.

She let out a deep breath and tried to focus on the positive.

At least they were moving.

At least they were together.

And for right now, at least they were alive.

* * *

"ARE you sure you don't want me to come?" Damon scowled as he got a quick update from Barrett.

"Yes. Stay at the Compound until I get back. Understood?" Barrett barked out.

"Got it, boss." Damon frowned and ended the call. He felt Ava's arms wrap around his waist as she scooted up behind him in bed. Barrett's call in the middle of the night had awakened him from a deep sleep of uneasy dreams. Dreams he couldn't shake.

"Everything okay?" Ava murmured near his ear.

"I think so." Even if it wasn't, he sure as fuck wasn't telling Ava that. Ava was headstrong to the point of being a danger to herself. If she even sensed something was going on with the Arkansas Guardians, she'd load up Granny and the other females and charge straight into danger.

"That was just Barrett checking in." He turned his head, buried his face in the crook of her neck, and inhaled deep. His body immediately reacted to her sweet scent and his dick hardened.

"You don't have to leave, do you?" She glanced at the clock on the nightstand.

He grabbed her and pulled her around until she was sitting in his lap. She laced her fingers around his neck and grinned at him.

God, he loved her. The way she looked at him with love never got old to him. She never ceased to amaze him.

"It's already three in the morning. I should go ahead and get up." He cupped her face.

"Does Barrett get up at three to go to work?" She arched her eyebrow.

"I'm beginning to think the bastard never sleeps." He rubbed his thumb across her full bottom lip.

She sucked the pad of his finger into her mouth, eliciting a groan from him.

"Ava," he warned.

"Just give me fifteen minutes. Thirty, at the most." She smirked and pulled the lacy camisole over her head. He'd gotten to bed after midnight, and she'd been fast asleep. He hadn't wanted to disturb her. He'd been content to stand over the bed and stare down into her beautiful face.

"You make it hard to say no, Ava." He ran his hand down her neck to her chest. His finger tweaked her nipple until she was panting with desire.

"I just make you hard," she whispered, slipping her hand behind the sheet that hid his erection. Her cool fingers found him, tightened around his shaft, and squeezed.

He growled, knowing they'd have sex at least two more times tonight before he left.

He dipped his head and sucked her nipple into his mouth. She moaned as he flicked his tongue across the hot, taut bud.

She held his head to her breast as he sucked, teasing and tasting her like he'd not had her in a while. His desire for her knew no bounds. She was something he couldn't get out of his system, something he constantly craved.

He couldn't imagine a life without her.

He stood with her in his arms. The sheet slipped to the floor, revealing their nakedness.

He turned back to the bed, and she wrapped her legs around his waist, rubbing her wet core against his length.

He laid her gently on the bed and thrust inside her body.

He groaned as her muscles tightened around his dick and squeezed.

She dug her fingernails into his back and bit his ear. "More," she demanded.

He wanted to go slow, to savor her, but when she felt this good, it was a struggle to even think clearly.

He pistoned his hips, driving himself deeper and faster inside her hot body.

A thin sheen of sweat covered their bodied from the sexual friction, and he gripped her hips tight. He pulled back just enough to see her face. He needed to see her face.

Her lips parted and her eyes dilated. He knew what was next. Her body tensed around him, squeezing him with such delicious pleasure that it was almost impossible to hold back his own orgasm.

"Damon." She breathed out his name as she climaxed, her body tensing around him and then going limp.

He growled and buried his face in the crook of her neck, spilling his seed deep inside her willing body.

Exhausted, he collapsed on top of her. She wrapped her arms around him and stroked his back with the tips of her fingernails, lulling him into a state of calm and peace.

"Stay," she whispered near his ear.

He leaned on his elbows and looked down into her green eyes. "Duty calls."

"Fine, but one more time." She arched her brow, and he was already getting hard inside her. "And this time I'm on top."

CHAPTER 25

*B*arrett stopped his Harley and killed his engine near where Jaxon would be crossing into Arkansas. He stepped off his bike and shook his head, sending water droplets flying in the darkness. Lucien followed suit.

Barrett squinted into the darkness down the long silent stretch of highway.

There were no lights, no sounds of vehicles moving along the empty road. The rain had stopped but not before drenching him to the bone. Some werewolves hated riding their Harleys in the rain, hated the unpredictability of the weather. But not him.

No, riding his Harley in the rain was like stripping him bare of all the sins and secrets that he'd buried a long time ago and kept hidden for no one to find. Rain was cleaning, healing, and revealing.

Where he'd grown up, the rain always held a hint of ocean as it fell to the earth.

He reached inside his jacket pocket and pulled out his phone. Thankfully, his phone was protected in a waterproof case and safe from the elements. He glanced down at the phone and noted the time.

"Almost three o'clock," he murmured. "Where are you, Jaxon?"

From behind him, the distant hum of an engine had him turning. Three sets of headlights bobbed toward him, growing bigger as the motorcycles came into view.

He gritted his teeth when Jayden, Braxton, and Zane pulled up and stopped.

All three killed their engines and slid off their bikes.

"What the fuck are you doing here?" Barrett growled. "I don't remember inviting you assholes to come along."

"Yeah, well, we're like genital warts." Jayden beamed. "Shows up when least expected. And completely unwanted."

"Speak for yourself, asshat." Lucien shot back.

"It looks to me I have three fucking Guardians that can't seem to take orders. Maybe you all would like to find another home? Like Antarctica." Barrett glared at all of his Guardians.

"Nah, it's too fucking cold in Antarctica." Jayden shook his head and stuck his hands in his jeans pocket. "Besides, I can't leave Granny."

Zane looked like he was fighting a laugh, and Lucien had enough sense to avert his gaze.

"Let's just say we're here as a preventative measure." Braxton said.

"Like penicillin?" Jayden pulled out a sucker and stuck it in his mouth.

"Yeah, for your genital warts." Zane snorted.

"I think you've got your STDs mixed up. I think you need penicillin for syphilis." Braxton grinned.

"Well, you would know." Jayden pointed his sucker at the Were.

"Don't let the blue hair fool you. I'm very selective about who I sleep with. Braxton crossed his arms.

"WHEN DID YOU GET HERE, BRAXTON?" Barrett turned his glare on the Guardian from Eureka Springs.

"Late tonight." Braxton frowned and scrubbed his hand across his blue tipped hair. "Or is that early this morning? Hell, I don't know. All I know is these guys said there might be some problem with Louisiana Pack Master, so I figured I'd tag along. I know what an asshole he can be."

Zane turned and frowned. "Braxton, why do the civilians of Louisiana put up with Boudier's shit? Word on the street is he's looking to eliminate his Guardians completely."

"Beats me." Braxton shrugged and studied the ground. "I remember my old man used to brag on Edward Boudier all the fucking time. I guess he used to beat his old lady too. Maybe that's why he looked up to him. Birds of a feather and all that shit." Braxton's eyes hardened, and Barrett knew the Were was thinking about his mother, who'd turned her back on Braxton. Even after he'd been acquitted of murdering his father, Braxton's mom refused to talk to him. Braxton said he didn't mind, that he counted himself lucky to have Kate, but Barrett knew that it bothered him.

Barrett couldn't understand a mother turning her back on her own child.

Didn't make any fucking sense. Maybe the whole bunch of Louisiana werewolves had been poisoned into thinking it was okay. Maybe they were all brainwashed.

Barrett turned and gave his focused attention to Lucien. "Are you sure this is where Lorcan told Jaxon to cross?"

"Yes."

Barrett punched the app on his phone and a green-and-white screen popped up. A tiny red dot was slowly approaching. A million thoughts ran through his head. He knew Edward Boudier wouldn't give up his chance to get one of Barrett's Guardians this easily.

That was the feeling he couldn't shake.

"Be ready." Barrett squinted toward a bobbing headlight headed straight toward them from a distance away. The faint hum of a Harley's motor drifted out into the night and rested on Barrett's ears.

"That's him. I'd know his Harley anywhere." Lucien let out a breath and nodded. "That's a good sign right?"

"Sure it is." Jayden's tone was tense, but he shot everyone a reassuring smile.

"Is he expecting us to be here waiting for him?" Braxton looked back at him.

"I've not talked to him since I gave him the coordinates that Lorcan gave me." Lucien looked at Barrett, his face twisted with worry and concern.

He was worried, and for damn good reason.

Barrett knew Lucien didn't trust his brother any more than Barrett did.

"Look alive, Guardians." Barrett stepped forward and brushed the heel of his hand against the butt of the Sig Sauer holstered to his chest. He didn't put it past Boudier to use humans instead of his Guardians as a shield. He'd made it clear that he hated humans more than his own kind. But he also knew that Boudier wouldn't hesitate to kill all of them if it kept his ass safe.

The guy was a psychopathic pussy.

The roar of the engine drew closer, and the headlight grew wider. Barrett continued to scan the area for any movement. He inhaled deep, trying to get a better read on his environment, but he still didn't smell any danger.

Yet the hair on the back of his neck continued to stand on end.

He didn't like this.

"Who's that with him?" Jayden cocked his head as the motorcycle continued on its path to them. "Looks like some chick."

"That's not just any chick." Barrett narrowed his eyes. "That's Ginny."

"Who the fuck is Ginny?" Jayden glared.

"It's Edward Boudier's daughter," Barrett said.

All the Guardians turned and faced Barrett. Their eyes widened, and he could tell from their scent they were on alert after what he'd just told them.

"You're fucking with us." Zane's tone was harsh.

"I wish I were." Barrett said.

"Wait, *Ginny*." Jayden frowned and looked back at the approaching motorcycle. "The Ginny that was supposed to mate with Jaxon years ago?"

"Apparently her father didn't know she existed. Her mother had tried to hide her at the grandmother's house in Arkansas. But he found her." Barrett stated.

"Shit. So Boudier shows up and..." Jayden frowned.

"He killed the grandmother." Barrett narrowed his eyes. "He took Ginny back with him. Force her to write a note to Jaxon saying she didn't want to marry him anymore and was leaving for California."

"So why the fuck didn't she leave her father?" Jayden asked.

"Because once you are involved in abuse like that, it eats away at your soul. I'm sure she stayed in Louisiana because Boudier said he would kill Jaxon. It was his leverage. Abusers are like that." Braxton crossed his arms and looked back at Barrett. "So for Ginny to agree to leave with Jaxon, that right there tells me some major shit went down."

Barrett nodded.

"So are you going to tell us?" Zane asked.

"It's on a need-to-know basis. Right now, you don't need to know," Barrett growled. "All I need to know is that no matter what happens, you stand with the Pack." He rested his gaze on each and every one of them, forcing them to meet and hold his gaze.

"You know we will, Barrett." Zane cocked his head. "But it would be great to get a heads-up on what the fuck's going down."

"You'll find out soon enough." He wasn't about to tell them about the murders. Nor that Ginny had committed them. He sure as shit wasn't going to tell Lucien that if protocol prevailed, then the Assassins, including his brother Lorcan, would be showing up in their state seeking justice. No matter how fucked-up it was. No. They were just going to have to wait and let this whole thing play out.

He tensed as the Harley barreled toward them. He dialed Jaxon's number and watched the Were's response. In the dark, he saw Jaxon's cell phone light up and Jaxon read the text that the Arkansas Pack was up ahead.

Like he expected, Jaxon didn't stop but continued on his course.

A set of headlights appeared behind Jaxon and quickly accelerated.

"Fuck," Barrett murmured. This was not good.

"Zane and Jayden, see if you can get a lock on that vehicle with your gun." Barrett reached in his holster and pulled out his gun. Zane and Jayden stepped off the road and grabbed their rifles off their Harleys. They each took a knee and aimed, looking through the scopes.

"It looks like a Hummer. Military style," Zane answered, keeping his sights on the truck. "Want me to take out the tires?"

Barrett flexed his fingers around his gun. "Wait." He knew that the Hummer was too close to Jaxon. If the Hummer ran off the road, there was no guarantee that it wouldn't take Jaxon with it.

"Barrett?" Jayden kept his gun aimed at the target.

"They're too close to Jaxon," Barrett growled. "Can you see who's driving that truck?" He glanced over at Zane and waited for an answer.

"I can't tell, it's too dark. But one of the passengers has a cell phone up, and it looks like it's Boudier." Zane kept his gun aimed and looked over at Barrett with a question in his eyes.

Barrett knew that look. He knew what Zane was asking without actually saying the words. Saying it out loud was dangerous and criminal, and yet the wheels in Barrett's head began turning swiftly.

He only had to give Zane a look, a quick nod of his head that would be indiscernible by the other Guardians. Zane had been with him from the beginning. He was a strong Guardian and a damn good soldier. And he would do whatever Barrett commanded.

If he gave the go-ahead, Zane would take out Boudier with one shot. It would start a war that would consume not only their Pack but every Pack in the South.

He wasn't willing to risk that.

He held Zane's gaze and shook his head. Zane hesitated and then looked back through his scope.

Barrett held his breath as the Harley got closer. Jaxon was almost home. Almost home.

"Hang on, what's that? Behind the truck?" Jayden asked.

"What?" Barrett demanded. Three motorcycles appeared from behind the truck. They passed the truck while the truck fell back, letting the Harleys get closer to Jaxon.

Barrett growled and looked over at Lucien. "Tell me that's not the Assassins?" He already knew the answer. Deep in his gut he knew.

"That can't be." Lucien shook his head. "He wouldn't do that." He looked at Barrett with wide eyes and blinked.

Nausea rolled over Barrett's stomach.

Time slowed and lengthened.

If he ordered his Guardians to shoot the truck or the Assassins, then Boudier's men would turn their weapons on Jaxon. He had no doubt that the fucker already had a gun aimed at Jaxon. If he made his men hold their position and wait then it might be too late. Boudier might be waiting for Jaxon to cross before shooting him in front of Barrett, which would be the ultimate *fuck you*.

"Keep your guns trained on them, Jayden and Zane. No matter what happens, you don't fucking cross the state line." He holstered his gun and straddled his Harley.

"But..." Zane frowned and started to stand.

"Fucking do what I say, Zane," Barrett growled. He turned his attention to Lucien. "You stay here. If Boudier sees you, it's going to remind him of what went down in New Orleans. Plus, I don't want you anywhere near Lorcan. Got it?"

"Got it." Lucien nodded and continued to hold his gun up at the approaching caravan.

"Braxton. You come with me," Barrett ordered.

Braxton straddled his Harley and started then engine. The bike roared to life.

Barrett eased onto the road with Braxton at his side. He slowed as Jaxon approached.

Barrett stopped in the middle of the road and got off his bike. Braxton followed. They waited as Jaxon approached.

"Be steady, Braxton." Barrett stepped in front of his bike as Jaxon slowed and then stopped in front of him.

"Jesus, Barrett, what are you doing? We need to get out of here." Jaxon hissed.

"Stay where you are, Jaxon." Barrett glanced at Ginny on

the back of the bike and then turned his attention back to the three motorcycles and the truck stopping in front of them.

"Barrett…" Jaxon tried to talk, but Barrett held out his hand to silence his Guardian.

"Trust me." He narrowed his gaze on the three Assassins. All three had killed the engines on their bikes and were stepping off.

The one named Brutus led the trio, with Killian and Lorcan flanking him. They stopped a few feet from Barrett.

"Barrett." Brutus acknowledged him with a growl and then turned his glare on Braxton.

"Hello, boys. You guys miss me?" Braxton smirked and gave a little finger wave.

"You need to have better aim, Killian," Brutus told the Assassin who'd tried to kill Braxton and missed.

Killian narrowed his eyes at Braxton.

"Where are your other Guardians, Barrett?" Lorcan asked, his expression neutral.

"Oh, they're here. And I'm pretty fucking sure that Lucien has a gun pointed right at your head," Barrett stated.

The other two Assassins looked at Lorcan and then back at Barrett.

"I'm not too worried," Lorcan said.

"Yeah. Why is that?" Braxton crossed his arms over his chest and glared.

"Lucien always sucked at shooting." Lorcan shrugged.

"Maybe he did when he was in Louisiana. But I assure you all my Guardians know to kill on sight when needed."

Barrett didn't miss the longing in Killian's eyes as he looked on the Harley that was once his. After Braxton had been found innocent of all charges of murder, Barrett had forced the Assassin to give his bike to Braxton as a recompense. Plus, he did it to piss Boudier off, since he would be footing the bill for a new Harley for his Assassin.

The Hummer stopped behind the Assassins' bikes.

Every muscle in Barrett's body tensed as Boudier stepped out of the passenger side of the truck.

He wasn't sure what the fucker had planned, and he knew enough to keep his gaze locked on him.

CHAPTER 26

"*B*arrett," Edward Boudier snarked, "looks like you've got a problem."

"Actually, it looks like we both have a situation." Barrett propped his hands on his hips and held Boudier's stare.

"Hmmm. I don't think so. You see, your Guardian right there"—he pointed to Jaxon—"has my daughter on the back of that bike. And I'm going to need you to hand them both over to me."

"That's not going to happen." Barrett kept his gaze on Boudier.

"Ginny, as Pack Master of Arkansas, I need to ask you a question. And I want you to answer honestly," Barrett said.

"Okay." Her voice was shaky as she answered.

"Ginny, have you been in any way, shape, or form abused or assaulted within the state of Louisiana?"

"Ginny, you better think before you speak, girl," Boudier growled.

Ginny looked at her father and then back at Barrett. The color seemed to drain from her face. He knew she was terrified of her father.

"Ginny. I asked a question." Barrett held her gaze and waited.

"Yes, sir. I have." A single tear slid down her face, and she tightened her hold around Jaxon's waist. Jaxon narrowed his eyes at Boudier. The Were looked like he wanted to kill Boudier.

"Ginny. When you were abused or assaulted, was it by or at the hands of your husband?" Barrett looked back at Boudier and then looked at Ginny. "Or any other family member?"

Ginny took a deep breath and held Barrett's gaze. "Yes, sir. Both my husband and my father physically abused me."

"You fucking bitch." Boudier snarled and took a step forward. Lorcan stepped in front of him and held up his hand.

"Under the circumstances, do you think it's wise to take action, sir?" Lorcan cocked his head.

"Lorcan, you are treading on very thin ice. Do not forget who owns your ass," Boudier growled.

"I meant no disrespect." Lorcan dropped his hand and stepped to the side.

Barrett studied Boudier's group of Assassins. He couldn't get a read on Lorcan, despite the fact that the Were had helped them out in New Orleans. He still belonged to Louisiana, which meant Barrett still didn't trust him.

Brutus stood silently still. For a brief second, a look of discomfort had crossed over his face at Ginny's accusation that not only had her husband hit her but her father—his fearless Pack Master—had done the same.

Killian was easier to read than the others. His eyes widened and he looked at Boudier. That Assassin was clearly shocked that Ginny had been abused.

Either Edward Boudier had kept a tight lid on how his

daughter had been treated or maybe he had trained his Guardians to accept how he ran his household.

"As Pack Master of the state of Arkansas, I am hereby taking this female into my protective custody until a Tribunal is called to assess the accusations made against the state of Louisiana." Barrett leveled his gaze on Boudier.

"Wait a fucking minute. You are not taking my daughter anywhere. And you sure as shit won't be taking Jaxon after what he did." Boudier raised his voice.

"And what exactly did Jaxon do?" Barrett could feel the blood rushing into every cell of his body. The urge to shift into wolf was almost too much to contain. He clenched his muscles, ready for whatever Boudier was going to throw his way. He didn't put it past the fucker to shift and then order all his men to open fire on his Guardians.

"Jaxon murdered my wife and my son-in-law." Boudier's satisfied smirk grew wide, and he looked to Jaxon to deny it.

Barrett gritted his teeth. He waited for Jaxon to deny it but he knew damn well Jaxon would go to his death and not deny it in order to save Ginny.

He looked at Jaxon. Jaxon lifted his head and said not a word.

Barrett cut his eyes at Ginny.

Her eyes grew wide, and she started to open her mouth. She met Barrett's gaze and he gave her a look. She got the gist of not saying anything to contradict what her father had said. She buried her face in Jaxon's back and tightened her arms around him.

"Isn't that right, Jaxon?" Boudier asked.

"Jaxon, don't answer that question," Barrett commanded.

"I demand a Tribunal to assess and judge the charges set against Jaxon. Until then, I will take them into my custody." Barrett stated.

"I demand justice now," Boudier shouted, his voice

echoing into the night. He took a step toward Barrett. "Assassins, I want Jaxon shot right now. Make sure you fucking do the job right this time."

Brutus stepped forward and drew his gun.

Barrett stepped in front of Jaxon and Ginny. Lucien followed and stood beside Barrett, his gun aimed right back at the Assassin.

"I can give him an order to shoot you both and then kill Jaxon. Step out of the way, Barrett," Boudier ordered.

"You give that order. My men are watching us right now, and I'm pretty fucking sure they have you in their crosshairs. Shoot at me and they will take you out first." Barrett fisted his hands at his side.

Boudier growled and glanced back up the road, trying to make out whether Barrett was bluffing or not.

"Let them go." Lorcan stepped up, put his arm on Brutus's, and lowered the gun.

"What? Are you disobeying me?" Boudier screamed.

Lorcan turned and looked at the Pack Master. "No. I'm merely suggesting that now is not the time to get your revenge." He looked back at Barrett. "Let Barrett have his Tribunal. The truth will come out. And when it does there will be a demand for blood. Such an atrocious act will always pay in blood. No one can outrun justice. Isn't that right, Barrett?"

Barrett wanted to plow his fist right into Lorcan's face. And then rip his heart out and eat it.

"And what better way to get your revenge and justice than in front of all the Pack Masters?" Lorcan added.

"What do you mean?" Boudier cocked his head.

"Let Barrett call a Tribunal. But invite all the Pack Masters: Mississippi, Tennessee, Alabama, even Kentucky. Let them see for themselves that justice still reigns and that no one is above the law. I daresay that once Jaxon is tried and found guilty, Barrett would face no better humiliation and torture than watching his own Guardian die in front of everyone." Lorcan shrugged. "And we can make it as quick or slow as you like."

Boudier studied Lorcan as quiet fell across the group of werewolves.

A slow smile broke out across Boudier's face, and then he slapped Lorcan across the back and laughed.

"Have I told you lately that you're my favorite Assassin?"

"Not lately," Lorcan deadpanned.

Boudier turned his gaze back on Barrett. "I'm going to do something I rarely do. And that's take advice from one of my men. Lorcan had a good point. I think I'd rather destroy you while the world watches. I mean, it's really no fun if I kill Jaxon right now without an audience." Boudier shrugged. "Besides, I have my evidence. And all you have is a couple of liars." His gaze slid to his daughter. "Ginny, don't forget that when this is all over, you'll be coming home with me. Where you belong."

Ginny cringed and buried her face against Jaxon. She trembled as she wept silent tears.

Barrett turned his glare back on the Pack Master. "Hear me now, Boudier. You won't get your hands on that girl. Not ever again." He cut his eyes at the Assassins. "And you assholes are no better for following a sadistic leader who couldn't give three fucks whether you live or die. We are all collateral damage as far as he is concerned."

"We follow a code. A code of responsibility and honor," Brutus growled.

"Yeah. I'm not so sure your Pack Master is all about honor. At least, according to what I've seen," Braxton shot back, all the while keeping his gun aimed at the Pack Master's head.

"Enough," Barrett growled. "The Tribunal will take place

at Petit Jean at midnight." He knew he needed enough time to secure the place and make sure no one else would be there.

"Fine. Gives me plenty of time to gather my evidence and witnesses to prove my case." Boudier smirked.

"Witnesses? Don't you mean liars?" Braxton said.

"I love it when my enemies doubt my sincerity. It makes the victory that much sweeter." He clapped his hands together and smiled. He turned and walked back to the truck. Once he slammed the door, the driver backed up and headed back down the road the way they'd come.

"You do realize that your brother is up there with a gun, don't you?" Barrett looked at Lorcan.

"You forget. I no longer have a brother. I have my Assassins." Lorcan walked back to his Harley and straddled it. He started up the engine and waited until Killian and Brutus did the same.

All three Assassins turned their bikes around and followed after the truck.

Braxton put his gun away.

"Barrett..." Jaxon started to speak, but Barrett knew time was of the essence.

"Jaxon, I need Braxton to take Ginny up to where the other Guardians are. I need to talk to you alone."

"No. I can't leave her." Jaxon shook his head and rested his hand on her thigh.

"It's okay, Jaxon." Ginny raised her head. "You two need time to talk."

"Are you sure?" Jaxon frowned.

"I'm sure." She gave him a smile and got off the back of the Harley.

"Hi, Ginny. I'm Braxton." Braxton walked up, held out his hand, and smiled.

Ginny looked at his blue hair and tattooed arms and then his hand. She took his hand and shook it. "Nice to meet you."

"Let's get you back to the rest of the Guardians." Braxton straddled his Harley and waited for her to climb on before starting the engine.

She stared at him for a second. "You're the one my father sent the Assassins after."

He gave a grim smile and nodded. "Yes, that would be me."

"And Barrett helped you," she said softly.

Braxton looked up at Barrett and then back at her. "Yes. He did. I think he can help you too, if you let him."

She nodded and climbed on behind him.

Barrett's stomach knotted. He wasn't sure how the hell he was going to help Ginny in these circumstances. But he knew his Guardians were counting on him to fix the situation.

He watched as they rode back up the hill where the other Guardians were waiting.

Jaxon got off his bike.

"Is she going to be okay?" Barrett asked.

"With everything she's gone through, I hope so." Jaxon's voice was heavy.

"Are you going to be okay?" Barrett looked at his Guardian.

"I guess that remains to be seen with tomorrow's Tribunal."

Barrett turned and gave Jaxon his full attention. "I need you to tell me everything. The whole truth, and don't leave anything out."

Jaxon cringed and looked away.

"I know you think you're helping her by taking the blame." Barrett glared.

Jaxon's head jerked up.

Barrett shook his head and gave Jaxon a hard stare. "Listen to me. I need to know everything. And I mean every

JODI VAUGHN

fucking thing. Boudier is going to come out full force with whatever evidence he claims to have. I can't be blindsided by anything. Do you understand?"

"I understand." Jaxon lowered his head and studied the ground.

"So spill it."

"I took Ginny home after the witch stole her car. She wouldn't let me drive her directly to her house. She said she didn't want her husband to know she'd been out with me. So while I was gassing up my Harley, she took off on foot. I followed her, careful to keep my distance. I just wanted to make sure she got home okay." He scrubbed his fingers through his hair.

"And then what?"

"I saw her go into the house. They have a large gate around their property but I managed to drive in before it closed. I know I should have left, but I couldn't. Not after I saw her bruises. Anyway, I searched the property to see if I could see anything before I headed inside the house. Once inside, I found Ginny. That's when I knew for certain that her husband had been beating her. She was scared to leave him all these years because her father told her if she did, he would kill me."

Jaxon shook his head. "Jesus, Barrett. She stayed all those years suffering at the hands of her husband to keep me safe. I told her to come with me that she didn't have to live like that anymore. I finally convinced her. I'm not going to let her down by letting her take the blame."

"So how did the mother happen into all this?" Barrett frowned.

"She wanted to tell her mother that she was leaving and convince her to come to Arkansas as well. I slipped out of the house before she saw me so they could talk. They argued, and Caroline stabbed Ginny in the back with a silver fork."

"Shit." Anger flared in Barrett's gut. "Her own mother?"

"Yeah. Caroline said she wasn't going anywhere. I heard Ginny scream and was on my way into the house. By the time I got inside, Caroline was dead, impaled on some silver antlers that John kept on the wall. Ginny and her mother were fighting and Ginny stumbled into her mother. Her mother impaled herself right through the head. It wasn't Ginny's fault. It was clearly an accident."

"Good." Barrett nodded. Maybe there was a way out of this for his Guardians. "So how did John end up dead?"

"We were fighting and he bit me. He had silver fitted over his teeth so he could bite his enemy and infect him with silver."

"Who the fuck does that?" Barrett knew Boudier was crazy, but what John had done was insane.

"He was about to kill me when Ginny grabbed the other silver antler sconce and hit him with it. It went through his head."

Fuck.

"So she killed her husband."

"Yes, but it was self-defense. You can explain to a Tribunal that this was an act of self- defense and an accident." Jaxon pleaded.

"So Boudier is saying that you killed them because inflicting punishment on you is the same as inflicting punishment on me." Barrett rested his hands on his hips and took a deep breath.

"I'll take the blame. I'm willing to do that. But Barrett, you got to promise me that he won't ever get his hands on Ginny again. Not ever," Jaxon stated.

Barrett jerked his head. "Do you realize what you are saying? Boudier is going to demand his payment in blood. Blood. Your blood."

"I know." Jaxon nodded. Sadness crossed his eyes and

filled his voice. "But I can't live knowing that Ginny is back in Louisiana, suffering at the hands of her father. I won't live that life again. I'd rather be dead."

"You're a fucking fool, Jaxon," Barrett growled.

"I'm not a fool for standing for something I believe in. I believe in Ginny. I believe that we could have a life together. And even if that fucker kills me tomorrow, then I'll be willing sacrifice myself for her." Jaxon lifted his chin. "If dying for someone you love is foolish, then I'd gladly do be foolish."

Barrett felt his eyes widen. He was never falling in love, and he sure as shit wasn't ever getting mated.

Jaxon snorted.

"What's so fucking funny?" Barrett thundered.

"I was just thinking that when you get mated, the world is going to stop turning." Jaxon grinned.

"That shit's not happening. I got enough pussy-whipped werewolves to deal with as it is. I sure as hell need to be clear-headed to keep you assholes in line." He glared.

"Whatever," Jaxon murmured under his breath.

"So do you know what kind of evidence that asshole could have to prove that you were the one who killed them?"

"I don't know. I mean, the only thing I could think of was maybe he had cameras in the house? But even if they do have video, it's going to show Ginny is the one who killed them. So it doesn't make sense for him to bring a video." Jaxon leaned his head back and looked at the blackened sky.

"We need to get back to the Compound. Everyone needs to rest and get ready for tomorrow night." Barrett straddled his bike.

"Barrett, promise me that you won't let Boudier take Ginny." Jaxon put his hand on Barrett's shoulder.

Barrett tensed.

"I know I'm asking you to sacrifice one of your Guardians

in order to save your enemy's daughter." Jaxon lifted his chin. "But if you can't promise me that Ginny won't be safe, then I'll go ahead and cross back over into Louisiana right now. I'll walk right up to Boudier's door and lay down on his altar. No Tribunal, no hearing, nothing."

Barrett shook Jaxon's hand off him. Fury and regret tore through his chest.

His own Guardian was willing to face the gates of hell to save the woman he loved.

It didn't seem fair, and it sure didn't seem right. But Barrett respected Jaxon's choice.

"I swear after tomorrow night, Ginny won't ever have to fear her father again." Barrett started the Harley and took off down the road.

CHAPTER 27

That night the Guardians drove back to the Compound in Little Rock.

Jaxon didn't say anything to Ginny. He'd said just one thing to her as she'd climbed on his bike. He'd told her everything would be okay.

It was the first time he'd ever lied to her.

She'd protected him for years. He was prepared to do whatever it took to protect her.

He wasn't ever going to let her put her life at risk for him again.

She slid her hand up to his chest, her palm resting over his heart. He smiled. It was something she'd always done when they were young. She said it was her way of connecting with him. Like she was seeing into his soul.

She leaned forward and pressed a gentle kiss to his neck. It sent shivers down his back in all the right places. He wished they were already in Little Rock.

He glanced at the time on the dash of his Harley. In another hour they'd be home. They'd probably be there before dawn.

He planned to take his time making love to her.

After tonight, he knew without a doubt that tomorrow wasn't guaranteed…

* * *

LUCIEN ROLLED his tense shoulders and reached for the door to his old room in the Compound. After he'd mated with Catty, he'd gotten a house off base. But tonight he knew his fellow Guardians needed him here in case something happened.

He was exhausted and couldn't wait to crawl into bed. He opened the door and stopped. Catty stood when she saw him.

"Hey, what are you doing here?" A warm feeling swept through his chest at the sight of her. "You should be at home in bed."

"I figured you would spend the night here since you got in so late. So I decided to wait up for you." Catty cocked her head and walked toward him. "I've never been inside the Guardian Compound. It's different than I thought."

He grinned and pulled her into his arms. "What were you expecting?"

"Dirty, grimy, scary." She laughed and pulled back to look around. "But this room looks better than my apartment in New Orleans. Silk sheets, minibar, 70-inch TV with curved screen."

"We also have an outdoor and an indoor pool." He grinned and kissed her.

She moaned against his lips and slid her hands down the front of his chest.

He pulled back and rested his forehead against hers.

"Lucien, what's wrong?" Her voice, soft and gentle, tugged at the recesses of his heart.

"Just work."

"No." She pulled back to look him in the eyes. "No, I feel like this is different. I spoke to Ava earlier, and she's on edge too. This thing with Boudier is dangerous. I feel like we are getting ready to go to war."

"I don't want you to worry, Catty. Barrett knows what he is doing." Lucien hoped to god that Barrett could pull off a miracle.

"I talked to Haley. She heard from Jayden that Jaxon didn't come back alone. He came back with Boudier's daughter." Her eyes widened ever so slightly. "You know, when I lived in New Orleans, people knew he had a daughter but no one ever really saw her. And you certainly didn't discuss her."

"No doubt. He married her off to gain his wealth. Apparently he also promised the son-in-law that he would be next in line for Pack Master."

"He's full of shit." Catty snorted. "Boudier would never give up his position. Never."

"I don't doubt that." Lucien took a deep breath. "There's a Tribunal at midnight tonight."

"Ava told me."

"I wonder why you bother asking me anything at all since you have your own intel going on." He laughed.

"I'm sure we don't know everything." She gave him a look. "What's the Tribunal for?"

"Catty, I…"

"Relax. Damon already told Ava about the Tribunal for Jaxon. He's accused of killing Boudier's wife and son-in-law." She blinked as her eyes began to water. "What about Boudier's daughter? How did she cross over without Boudier going ape shit?"

"Barrett declared his protection for her since she admitted her husband and her father physically abused her."

"That motherfucker," Catty spat out.

He grinned at her fierceness. "I couldn't agree with you more."

"I've never been at a Tribunal before. Can I go to this one?"

"No." He narrowed his gaze. "It can get ugly, and I don't want you to see that."

"Lucien, I'm not a child." She shrugged. "Besides, I've seen worse."

"I don't care. Catty, you're not going."

She let out a long-suffering sigh and gave him a look that implied she was far from pleased.

"Fine." She crossed her arms and sat on the bed. "I guess you want me to leave too."

"No. Stay." He felt the same tenseness in the air as she did. Something bad was coming, and it was headed straight for Arkansas.

"You're not going to get in trouble for having me here, are you?"

"Nah. I saw some of the other females sneak into the Compound." He snorted.

"Ugh, they totally stole my idea." She crossed her arms and scowled.

"It's almost dawn. We need to try to get some sleep before noon. I'm sure Barrett will call a meeting with the Guardians to make a game plan." He pulled his shirt over his head and tossed it on the floor.

Her pupils dilated, and he pulled her into his arms.

Lucien kissed her hard. When he pulled back, he looked into her eyes. "But right now, it's just you and me. And I don't want to waste another second without you in my arms."

* * *

SKYLAR CRACKED OPEN an eye when she heard the unmistakable sound of footsteps. She jerked out of the bed and turned on the light that sat on the nightstand. She grabbed the hammer she'd left lying on the small table.

"Skylar, it's me," Zane's familiar voice called out from the doorway.

"You scared the crap out of me, Zane." She pressed her hand to her heart. She placed her hammer back on the night-stand. "What are you doing here?"

"I was trying to find you. You weren't at home, so I figured that the only other place you'd be is here." He grinned and stepped into the room.

A small smile broke out across his face, and her heart sped up a little at the sight of him. It always did.

She'd worked for months on SKYLAR'S HOME. It was a home for runaway girls who'd slipped through the cracks and had nowhere else to go. Skylar had been one of those girls after suffering years of abuse at the hands of her father. Now her mission was to protect other girls.

"What's up? I thought you were going to be gone all night." She frowned. Something was up. She could sense it.

"It's almost dawn," he said softly. He walked to her and gathered her up in his arms. "We need to get back in bed."

"Zane, what's wrong?" Skylar touched her fingertips to his whiskered cheek. She knew him inside and out. "Are you okay?"

"I am."

"Are the others okay?" She swallowed. "Did Jaxon come back? I thought Barrett was going to make sure Jaxon got back across the Arkansas border."

"Jesus. Where are you getting your information?" Zane gave her a wide-eyed look.

She shrugged.

"Well, since Damon's been in charge, I'm going to assume that Ava is the one who told."

"And Granny." She didn't want Ava to take the blame alone. "I think Granny has some kind of hacking ability when it comes to computers. Ever since that online dating episode, she's been glued to that computer like crazy."

"Ugh. Don't remind me." He rubbed his hand across his forehead.

"You didn't answer me. Is Jaxon back?" Her heart thudded in her chest. Jaxon was like a brother to Skylar, and he was a good friend to Zane. She didn't want anything to happen to the Were.

"He's back, and he's got Ginny with him."

"Who is that?"

"Apparently it's Jaxon's former love and Edward Boudier's daughter."

"What?" A shiver ran up her spine.

"There's a Tribunal at midnight. I need to be ready for it."

"A Tribunal?" Her heart sunk to her toes. "For what?"

"I'm shocked Catty hasn't filled you in." He smirked.

"My cell phone has been off." She snatched up her cell phone and turned it on. "There are three missed calls from Ava and two from Catty."

"Do I need to call her?" she asked.

"No. She's probably asleep with Damon."

Skylar grinned. "Asleep? Or in the same bed?"

"You're right. They're doing what I want to be doing with you." He cupped her cheek.

"Zane, what's wrong?" She gripped his wrist. "Tell me about the Tribunal."

His face fell and he looked away. Zane was always so in control of his emotions—he didn't let anything bother him. But tonight something was off.

"Boudier is accusing Jaxon of killing his wife and his son-in-law. They are calling a Tribunal to present evidence." Zane swallowed.

"So what's Barrett's plan? What's he going to do?"

"Skylar, I don't know." He raked his hands through his hair.

"Zane, do you trust Barrett?" Skylar cocked her head.

"Of course I do, it's just this is bigger than just presenting cases and arguing. Blood will have to be spilt." He rubbed his hand down his face. "There is no getting out of this."

"When I was kidnapped and held in that building, I thought that was going to be the end of my life. I figured that was how my luck was supposed to go, since I had just found you and discovered what love really is." She swallowed back the emotion that filled her throat.

"I had given up hope. And then you showed up with Barrett and all the Guardians. I couldn't believe it. It was like something out of a story. I didn't know who they were, but they were willing to face danger for me.

"What I'm trying to say is there is always hope. This Pack is built on it. Just because you can't see what's coming up ahead doesn't mean there isn't light."

He smiled and pulled her into his arms. His mouth slammed down across hers. His hand slid up her T-shirt as he found her breasts.

He broke the kiss and looked down at her with such love in his eyes.

"I'm the luckiest male alive to have you."

She grinned. "I know. Now let's go to bed."

* * *

BRAXTON HEADED to the empty room at the Compound. It was one he occasionally used when he was in town. He stopped short when he saw a beautiful blonde leaning against the door with a bag in her hands.

"Kate." He felt a smile spread across his face, and he didn't bother stopping it.

"Hey, yourself." She smiled and pushed off the door. She wrapped her arms around his neck and pulled him down into a kiss.

He held her close, loving the feel of her small body against his.

"What are you doing here?"

"I got a call from Ava. She said something was up and that you would appreciate me coming down for a few nights." She smiled. "Besides, I missed you."

"You just saw me this morning before I left Eureka Springs."

"I know, but I always miss you when you are away on a mission."

"I'm glad you're here." He wrapped his arms around her and held her tight. She always had a way of making him feel better with just her presence.

"Me too." She pulled back and opened the door to his room. They stepped inside.

The room was awash in a soft yellow glow from the sconces that hung on either side of the bed. The oversized couch in front of the large TV was warm and inviting.

She sat the bag on the coffee table and pulled out a bag of cookies.

"I thought you might be hungry, so I brought some things from home." She smiled.

He grabbed one and took a bite. He moaned as the sweet confection melted on his tongue.

"I haven't had anything since this morning," he admitted. He'd been too worried about the shit that was going to go down between Arkansas and Louisiana to eat.

"Ava told me about Jaxon and the Tribunal." She cocked her head, trying to read his expression. It was a habit she had with him. "She also told me about Ginny."

"Yeah?" He didn't know what else to say.

"Did you talk to Ginny?" Kate's soft voice soothed his soul.

"A little." He shook his head and frowned. "She apologized to me for her father sending the Assassins to kill me."

"She knows what kind of animal her father is, then." Kate nodded slowly.

"Did Ava tell you that Boudier physically abused Ginny? And so did her husband."

"Yes. And I'm glad her husband is dead. Surely the Tribunal will see the evidence and not convict Jaxon." Kate said.

"It doesn't work like that, sweetheart." He took her hand, brought it to his mouth, and placed a kiss there.

"Braxton, don't lose hope. We seem to find ourselves in shitty situations that we don't think will ever work out. Like when I thought the B&B was going to be foreclosed on. And just when I couldn't see a way out, you showed up."

"That reminds me. Who is watching the Bella Luna while you're here?" He frowned. He knew she didn't like leaving someone else in charge of the B&B. She'd fought too hard to hold onto it, and she was pretty much a stickler for details when it came to running her business.

"Remember those authors?" She bit her lip, trying to suppress a smile.

"The crazy ones?" He arched his brow. A bunch of authors and Granny had descended on the Bella Luna in search of a writing retreat. He'd expected the older ladies to be quiet and reserved, but once they got all liquored up, they were like a Viagra tornado. They'd even managed to scare Lorcan away when he'd come looking for Braxton.

"They're really nice, Braxton. Besides, I told them I wouldn't charge them if they just watched the place while I was gone. They were glad to do it." She shrugged.

"I'm glad you're here." He needed to be with her tonight. "Barrett wants to meet with us around noon."

"So we need to make the most of what time we have." Her pupils dilated as she ran her hand down his chest to his groin.

His body tightened to the point of pain. He wanted to take her slow and deep tonight.

"Now take off your clothes while I open the wine."

* * *

JAYDEN STOOD outside the Compound looking up into the night sky. He was physically tired, but his mind was racing with every possible outcome of the Tribunal. He knew he needed to go inside and get some sleep, but he wasn't sure he'd be able to. Since Haley had come into his life, he didn't like sleeping in a bed without her.

"Jayden, are you going to stand outside all night, or are you coming inside?" Haley's voice had him turning around.

"Babe, what are you doing here?" She was standing at the entrance to the Compound.

"Waiting on you." She walked toward him. Her tight jeans and white T-shirt made her look like a fucking angel. His angel.

"I thought I'd spend the night here with you since you couldn't come home." She bit her lip and looked at him under her lashes.

He grinned and pulled her against him. "You know, I've never had a woman in my room at the Compound. Barrett never allowed it."

"I knew I liked Barrett." She smirked.

"I'm glad you're here." He brushed her blonde hair out of her eyes. His heart still melted a little every time he looked at her.

"Ava told me what happened with Jaxon. She said they are calling a Tribunal."

"Ugh. Damon tells Ava way too much." He groaned.

"Damon didn't tell her. Granny did." Haley brightened.

He rubbed his hands across his eyes. "My grandmother is going to get my ass kicked out of the Guardians."

"Your grandmother is the glue of the Guardians. She's the only one tough enough to keep you all in line." Haley arched her brow.

"You may be right." He admitted. "The crazy glue."

"Jayden, are you okay?" She frowned. "I've never seen you like this."

"Like what?" He tried to give her a reassuring smile.

She studied his face. "You are worried about Jaxon and the Tribunal."

"Maybe." He lied. His gut was burning with the unknown outcome. He knew damn well that the likelihood of Jaxon getting off without punishment was unimaginably small.

"Surely they won't find him guilty," Haley said.

"The penalty for murder is death, Haley." He said the words he'd been thinking about on the ride home.

"Tell me this, Jayden. The Tribunal is always fair, right?"

"Yes."

"So how could a Tribunal find someone guilty of murder when it was self-defense? If Jaxon killed those people, then it was self-defense. Plus, he was trying to get Ginny out of that abusive situation and safely into Arkansas."

"Yes, but Haley, the people killed are her mother, who is the wife of the Pack Master, and the Pack Master's son-in-law."

"Who were both horrible, sadistic werewolves, I understand." Haley crossed her arms over her chest. "When I lived in Louisiana and still had the good graces of my parents, I met her mother."

"You did?"

"Yes, at some kind of charity event they used to make me go to." She shook her head. "Boudier held it every year, claiming the purpose was to raise money for the Pack. But in reality, all that money went into his pockets."

"What kind of person was she?"

"Caroline Boudier was self-absorbed and selfish. I remember seeing Ginny at one event. Her husband refused to let her leave his side the entire night. She wasn't allowed to talk to anyone without her husband present. Seemed like an asshole to me."

"No doubt."

"I trust our Pack Laws, and I trust the judgment of the Tribunal." Haley wrapped her arms around his neck. "I also know that you've got to be up in a few hours, so we need to get inside and you need to get some rest before tonight."

He grinned and swung her up in his arms. "Oh, there will be no sleeping. Not with you in my bed."

* * *

AVA RAN to Damon as he entered the room in the Guardians' Compound. Since Damon had been filling in for Barrett, Damon had moved her into the Compound to his old room.

She'd been unable to sleep since Damon had gotten the update from Barrett. She'd stayed awake in the room while Damon stayed in Barrett's office waiting for everyone to get back to the Compound.

"Hey." Damon's rough voice seemed to vibrate through her body, making her feel safe.

"Hey, yourself." She looked up at him. "Did you talk to Barrett? What did he say?"

"Ava, you know as much as I do. Tribunal is at midnight. Jaxon will stand trial. And no one is saying it, but I'm guessing that he's taking the fall for Ginny." Damon took a deep breath.

"Oh, god." Her heart pounded in her chest. "Barrett can fix this, right? I mean, he's the Pack Master and the Tribunal is on Arkansas soil, so we have the upper hand. Plus, there's the fact that he was defending himself protecting Ginny."

"Yeah. If I was on the Council I would not demand Jaxon's life."

"Jaxon's life?" Her eyes grew wide. "Surely that won't happen."

He hugged her tight. "Why aren't you asleep?" Damon frowned.

"Because I wanted to wait up for you. I wanted to see you." She bit her lip.

"Well, I'm here now, so let's go to bed."

"Wait." She pressed her hand to his chest. "Damon, there's something want to talk to you about." Her stomach tingled.

"What is it?" He cocked his head and stared at her.

"Sit down."

"Shit, Ava, tell me." He grabbed her by the arms. "Did Jaxon skip out? Did Barrett call?"

"No. Nothing like that." She pointed toward the bed.

He eased onto the bed and she sat beside him. She swallowed back her nerves and took a deep breath.

"I'm pregnant."

CHAPTER 28

"A baby?" Damon's heart did something funny in his chest. His breathing increased.

"I know, we haven't talked about starting a family, and it's kind of a bad time with everything going on in the Pack." She chewed her lip and glanced at the ground.

"A baby?" He tested the words on his tongue. They settled into his chest, warming him from the inside out.

"Yes, a baby." She took a deep breath and met his gaze. "Please say something. Other than the word 'baby.' You look like you might be sick." She frowned and took his face between her hands.

A slow grin grew on his face, and he pulled her into his arms. "You're having my baby."

"Yes. I am." She cupped his face between her gentle hands. "I'm not that far along. I just found out today when I took a pregnancy test." She swallowed and looked into his eyes. "Are you mad?"

"Mad? How the hell could I be mad? You're having my baby." He buried his face into the side of her neck and inhaled. It hit him. The scent of her pregnancy.

Ava was pregnant. He should have recognized the signs. Her increased appetite and sex drive. She'd even lost interest in wine.

His body hardened fast and he all he wanted was to pull her jeans down and bury himself in her body.

She moaned and rubbed against him.

"Damon." She breathed out his name and tugged his T-shirt out of his jeans. She ran her fingernails up his bare stomach to his chest, scraping against his flesh and making his blood pulse.

He rid himself of his shirt and tossed it on the floor. He growled as he tore at her shirt, rending it in two.

She looked at him and grinned. "That's more like it." She quickly tugged her jeans off while he did the same.

She jumped and wrapped her legs around his waist. He grabbed her tight butt and positioned her over his erection. She dug her heels into him and impaled herself on his cock.

She moaned and he pressed her back against the wall, thrusting himself into her willing body. She dug her nails into his back, clawing and scratching with lustful desperation. He growled, thrusting faster as a thin sheen of sweat covered both their bodies.

Fingertips traced over muscled and smooth flesh as they discovered each other again, tasting and savoring their love. The connection they'd always had seemed to grow a thousand times tighter now that they were going to be a family. A family never to be broken.

It almost brought tears to his eyes.

"You're mine. Now and forever." He growled and then covered her mouth with his.

He felt her quiver as her climax washed over her fast and hard. She laid her head against the wall, shivering as pleasure swamped her body.

He quickened his pace, thrusting deep inside her body. Lust licked the pit of his stomach and he growled as he came.

"That's a pretty good warm-up." Ava lifted her head and stared into his eyes. Her pupils were dilated. He knew that look. She wasn't done with him yet.

"I heard that females who are with child are unusually…"

"Horny?" She finished the sentence for him and smiled.

"Yeah." He grinned as he trailed his finger down between her breasts and circled a pretty pink nipple.

Her eyes drifted shut and she moaned.

"We should definitely get all the sex in that we can now. Who knows how much sex I'm going to get once the baby arrives." The thought had his chest expanding with pride.

"Oh, that's not going to change. You have to promise me sex at least twice a day." She looked at him and sucked his finger into her mouth.

His cock stirred. He wanted her again.

"Twice a day? That's all?" He arched his brow.

"I don't want to tire you out with your job as Guardian and being a new father and all." She pressed her lips to his neck and sucked.

His body tightened and he was ready to have her all over again.

"Baby, I have enough stamina for all that and you." He kissed her hard, and when he pulled back to look at her, his heart nearly exploded with all the love inside his chest.

"I love you, Damon," she whispered.

"I love you too." He carried her to the bed and laid her down. "Now let me show you how much."

* * *

BARRETT WATCHED his Guardians filing one by one into the Compound. He had seen the females sneak inside. He'd had a hard rule about no females in the Compound where the Guardians slept, but that was before so many of them had mated up.

He had to remind himself to act pissed tomorrow at his Guardians for allowing the females in. In reality he didn't mind. He knew his men needed whatever encouragement they could get tonight, and if the females could deliver, then then so be it.

He frowned and wondered what it would be like to be mated. He'd never given it a thought for himself. He didn't need the distraction, nor did he want the inconvenience. He had a job to do, and having a female around twenty-four-seven would just get in the way of his purpose. And his purpose was to bring order and peace to Arkansas.

He would need to brief Damon on what was to be expected at the Tribunal, but he knew that the Were was with Ava.

He would talk to him later. He headed toward the woods located behind the Compound. He needed to be somewhere solitary and think. He couldn't do that locked up in his office or some other room.

He kept walking away from the security lights toward the dark. He blinked, letting his eyes adjust to the darkness. His footsteps soon left the concrete for the grass, and he was walking farther into the thick woods.

Mosquitoes buzzed near his ear, and an owl hooted from her perch on a nearby branch. He lifted his face as a breeze of summer air whirled across him. He stopped when he came to a large oak tree near a small pond.

The pond was overgrown with weeds and shrubs. He doubted there were any fish in the water, but he was pretty sure there was more than one water moccasin gliding across the surface.

He pulled his phone out of his jeans pocket and dialed in a number.

"Hello?"

"Ryker. It's me." He looked up at the sky and was struck by how completely void of stars it was. Not even the moon was out.

"Barrett. What's up?" Ryker asked.

Barrett's gut twisted, and he fought back the sense of dread that he'd been feeling all day long. Even before the showdown with Boudier, Barrett had been getting a very bad feeling that something big was to go down between the Packs. Something he didn't think he could control.

"How's the situation with the Fae in Vermont?" He blew out a breath and waited for the report.

"If you would have told me a week ago I'd be in New England fighting alongside an army of fairies against an army of demons and a sadistic Fairy Queen, I would have told you to fuck off," Ryker said.

Barrett snorted. "And now?"

"While I don't like to get involved with other species' problems, I have to say it was a hell of a fight. Those fucking fairies are pretty damn strong," Ryker admitted. "And that Celeste, well, she not only can fight, but she can heal people. Never seen anything like it. Not to mention she's hot as fuck. But married. Definitely married."

"I wouldn't be messing around with Celeste Nordstrom, Ryker. Her husband, Eric is not known to share anything, and I'm sure when it comes to his wife, he'd kill a fucker," Barrett stated.

"You know Eric Nordstrom?" Ryker asked.

"He's a past acquaintance." Barrett didn't tell Ryker that he'd once done business with Eric. They were both from wealthy families, and their pasts were very similar.

Ryker didn't need to know that. None of his Guardians did.

"Where are you?" Barrett asked.

"I'm crossing the Mississippi River Bridge back into Arkansas. I should be at the Compound in a few hours," Ryker said.

"Well, don't stop at the Compound in Little Rock. I need you to head on to Petit Jean State Park."

"What the fuck are we doing there? Cooking hotdogs?" Ryker groused.

"There is to be a Tribunal. And that's where it is to be held."

"Fuck. A Tribunal? For what? Jaxon crossing across the state line?"

"Let me catch you up." Barrett quickly filled Ryker in on all the details of what had happened.

"Are you fucking kidding? Man, Boudier isn't going to let Jaxon walk away from punishment. That asshole is going to demand blood," Ryker said.

"I know."

"Do you have a plan? Please tell me you have a plan."

"Glad you asked. Because I'm going to need to you to be ready for anything when the time comes." Barrett studied the ground.

"Anything, man. Whatever you need. I'm there."

"Good." Barrett wasted no time and ended the call.

Now he had to get ready. To hope for the best and prepare for the worst.

CHAPTER 29

"*Y*ou should get some sleep." Jaxon looked at Ginny and nodded toward his bed. He'd been the last of the Guardians to head into the Compound. He had hung around outside after they'd arrived as all the other Guardians had introduced themselves to Ginny. He was glad that they all seemed to welcome her into their Pack and didn't judge her for who her father was.

"The Arkansas Guardians are different from the Louisiana Guardians." She eased onto the bed and looked at him under her lashes.

"How's that?" He sat in the chair by the TV and pulled off his boots.

"They spoke to me."

He stopped what he was doing and looked at her. "The Louisiana Guardians don't speak to you?"

"No, they're not allowed." She shrugged. "Apparently, my father and husband didn't want them associating with me." She looked at the ground. "But I wonder if it's because they hate me simply because of who my father is."

"But the Louisiana Guardians are loyal to him."

"They are loyal out of fear. Not out of undying love or commitment." She licked her lips. "I didn't realize that a Pack could be welcoming." She rested her hand on her stomach.

"How are you feeling?" He walked over to her and sat next to her on the bed. His gaze drifted to her stomach.

"My stomach feels a little crampy, but I'm fine."

"Crampy?" He frowned. "We have a doctor here at the Compound. I can send for him so he can check you out and make sure you're okay."

"No, I'm fine. I've had these cramps before." She shook her head. "It usually happens after John gets angry and..." Her voice trailed off.

"He hit you knowing you're pregnant." He tried to keep the anger out of his voice, but the bitterness was still there.

"I never told him I was pregnant. He made it clear early on that he didn't want children. He saw a baby as a threat to his opportunity to be next in line for Pack Master." She looked at him. "I didn't even tell my father I was pregnant."

"Boudier doesn't know about the baby?"

"No." She stood and walked over to the window.

"Can I ask you something?" He stood and waited until she turned around and faced him. "How do you feel about the baby?"

She folded her arms across her chest and took a deep breath. "At first I was horrified, knowing that I was carrying part of John inside me. I worried the baby would turn out like him. I didn't want him at first." She glanced down at the floor. "But as the weeks went by and the baby survived despite the beatings, I began to see her—or him— as a survivor. Like me." She looked up at him.

He nodded. He could understand that.

"Do you hate me because I'm carrying another male's child?" She asked, the tone of her soft voice uncertain.

"What?" His chest clenched at her question. "I could never hate you. I love you."

Silent tears slid down her cheek. She didn't bother wiping them away but let them find their course to her clasped hands in her lap.

"After everything that I've done to you, leaving you without telling you why, marrying another male, and now carrying his baby, I don't understand how you could still love me." She shook her head and looked at the floor. "I'm not the perfect girl you fell in love with. I'm ruined."

"Listen to me." He tilted her chin up with his fingertip, forcing her to look into his eyes. "I want you to hear what I'm going to say because I'm only going to say this once."

She blinked, her attention on him.

"You're not ruined. You are perfect. And you are perfect for me. I will love that baby inside of you because it's part of you. I could never hate you or the child you are carrying. That child is going to need a father and, Ginny, I want to be that for her or him. I want a life with you and that child and the many other children who will fill our home. That's what I want. But I need to know if you want the same things." His swallowed back the emotion in his throat. He spoke the words without hesitation, and he meant them with all his heart.

"Jaxon, I love you." She wrapped her arms around his neck, burying her face into his chest.

He held her tight, her body snug against his own. He could feel her heart beating against his like they were one. His chest swelled with emotion, and a sense of complete joy washed over him.

The struggle they were going to face over the next twenty-four hours would determine their fate forever. But in this moment, he pushed those thoughts away, determined to stay in this moment with her.

He bent his head, pressing her lips to hers. She relaxed in his arms, melding her curves to his edges. She sighed and opened under his lips. He dipped his tongue into the sweetness of her mouth, teasing her tongue with his and eliciting a moan.

Her hands slid down his chest. Her fingers found the bottom of his T-shirt and she tugged it up. He broke the kiss long enough to pull his shirt over his head and toss it on the floor.

Her fingers were everywhere, touching and caressing and teasing.

His stomach burned with desire to have her underneath him and to make her his in every possible way.

He lifted her shirt over her head and then stood, pulling her up with him. She reached up on tiptoes and pressed her mouth to his in a heated kiss.

Her fingertips fumbled with the zipper of his jeans before she managed to shove them down his hips. Her cool hand wrapped around the length of his hard cock and squeezed.

"Easy," he groaned and thrust into her palm. He wanted this to last, to make love to her until daylight. He wanted this seared into his memory forever.

She moved her hand and shimmied out of the rest of her clothes leaving them in a pile on the floor. She stood there before him, naked, with only her blonde hair flowing across her shoulders.

She looked like an angel. His angel.

He couldn't wait any longer. He took her in his arms and kissed her. He picked her up and carried her to the bed. Laying her in the middle, he hovered over her. She caressed his face and pulled him down for a slow, sensual kiss.

He sheathed himself in her body, melding them together as one. He moved slowly against her as they made love in the shadows of the darkened room. Time seemed to be suspended, and reality only consisted of them in their own little world.

His fingertips memorized the soft curve of her hip and the shape of her soft breasts. He dipped his head and captured her nipple in his mouth. She moaned as he sucked the hard bud, teasing her with his tongue.

How had he lived all these years without her? How had he existed?

She moved under him, arching her body and straining toward him. She hooked her ankles around his thighs, forcing him to drive himself hard and deep inside her willing body.

Urgency boiled in his blood as pleasure soaked through every cell of his body. He forced his body into submission, to hold off his own pleasure until she found hers.

She arched and dug her nails into his back as she climaxed. He thrust faster, matching her pleasure with his own and spilling his seed into her body.

He continued to move until they'd ridden out their orgasms together. Exhausted, he pulled her trembling body against his and cradled her in his arms.

He held her close and forced his racing mind to shut down. He needed to find his own rest. Even if it was for a few hours. He needed his strength, and he needed to be prepared for whatever Boudier was about to throw their way.

CHAPTER 30

*B*arrett had arrived at Petit Jean State Park hours before his Guardians. He'd left Damon at the Compound to update the Weres about the Tribunal set for midnight. The Guardians were set to arrive that afternoon to start securing the area high on the mountain where the meeting would take place.

He squinted up at the sun beating down on his back like a relentless bitch. He stared down from his perch on the mountain to the waterfall below. It had to be at least a hundred, a hundred and twenty feet down from where he stood.

He had notified the Southern Pack Masters of the time and place of the Tribunal. Besides Arkansas and Louisiana, the other states that would be present would be Mississippi, Alabama, and Tennessee. Even Milfred Jones, the Pack Master of Kentucky, had agreed to come to the Tribunal, although it had taken some convincing. Milfred hated taking sides and getting involved. He wanted to stay out of everyone else's business and wanted to be shown the same courtesy.

Barrett couldn't blame him. But things were different

now, and all the Pack Masters knew that whatever went down tonight at the Tribunal would somehow affect them all.

"I wouldn't get too close to that edge, man. The fall won't kill you, but it will hurt like a motherfucker," Ryker said.

Barrett turned and faced Ryker. "Have you been updated by Damon?"

"No. I drove straight here because you told me to. Besides, you're my Pack Master, not Damon." Ryker crossed his arms, and Barrett could tell the Were was studying him behind his sunglasses.

"Tribunal starts at midnight. The Pack Masters will arrive around eleven."

"What about the Council?" Ryker asked.

"They will be here and will rule with the final decision." Barrett turned his gaze back out across the state park.

The gray mountains dotted with green trees jutted out of the ground and rose to the sky. The rhythmic splash of the waterfall below and the scent of dirt and leaves and nature surrounded him. Usually, just being in nature calmed him, allowed him to be more in tune with what he needed to do in certain situations. But not today. Today he was as conflicted over how he was going to get Jaxon free of the charges brought by Boudier.

Barrett knew that Jaxon hadn't killed Caroline or John. And he also knew that the Were wouldn't let Ginny take the blame either. He knew Jaxon well enough to know that he would go to his death declaring Ginny's innocence.

The only way he was going to get out of having Jaxon killed was to try to talk to Boudier and broker a peace. If he gave Ginny back to her father it might appease him enough that he'd let Jaxon go. He hated doing that. It went against everything he believed in. But he couldn't let another Guardian die.

Ryker's cell phone buzzed.

"Fuck." Ryker scowled.

Barrett turned and his heart rate increased. "What is it?"

"Things just got complicated." Ryker lifted his gaze from the phone.

"Things were already complicated," Barrett growled.

"Well, things just got fucking complicated." Ryker shook his head. "Just got a text from Damon. Did you know that Ginny is pregnant?"

Barrett's stomach dropped.

"Why the fuck didn't Jaxon tell me?" Barrett growled.

"Jaxon just told Damon." Ryker shook his head. "Said he didn't want Ginny to be at the Tribunal tonight because of her condition. Boudier doesn't know she's pregnant."

"She has to be there. She has to confront Boudier about the allegations she made against him. If she doesn't go, then Boudier will ask the Council to have her returned to him." His gut twisted. This was worse than he suspected.

"The Council will order you to return Ginny if she doesn't show and present her case. Boudier will kill her once he gets his hands on her," Ryker stated.

"No. He'll torture her for betraying him. He'll make sure she stays alive so he can make her pay for the rest of her life." Finality settled over Barrett like a death shroud.

Boudier would be outraged once he found out about Ginny's pregnancy.

"So what do we do?" Ryker asked.

He had no choice. Barrett walked down the trail back to where he'd parked his Harley. "Make sure my Guardians are all accounted for when they start arriving. Boudier wants blood. So we give him blood."

* * *

Damon rode toward Petit Jean State Park. Barrett had ordered him to stay behind and watch over the state while the Tribunal was held. But his conscience wouldn't let him. Besides, he figured since he was filling in for Barrett that technically made him temporary Pack Master. And being Pack Master meant he didn't answer to anyone.

He'd called Ava and told her where he was going. She'd been shopping with Haley for her wedding. He was glad she was distracted from the crap that was going on. He told her to buy a new outfit while she was out.

He saw the signs for the state park, slowed his speed, and turned.

After tonight, he was afraid they would be going to war with Louisiana.

After tonight, none of them would be safe.

* * *

"Hey, Jack." Barrett stood near at the top of the mountain where the Tribunal was to be held. In another hour, fates would be sealed and debts would be paid.

"Barrett, I got your message," Jack Welbourn said. The Pack Master of Mississippi's tone was flat. He sounded unlike the genteel alpha that Barrett had come to know. "You have to give me more information about Boudier."

"No. The time for talking has passed." Barrett glanced down at his cell phone and noted the time in the dark. He looked up across the sky. "It's actually really beautiful out here."

"Yeah, well, that's what they say about a hurricane. That right in the center of it all, it's calm." Jack forked his fingers through his hair. "Tonight is nothing but a shit hurricane."

"I think if you're patient enough you still might catch your witch." Barrett looked up at the starlit sky. Out here in the middle of nowhere, the sky was putting on one hell of a display. It was the perfect night for a Tribunal.

"Ella?" Jack jerked his head in Barrett's direction. "She's here?"

"I got some intel that she's coming." Barrett shook his head. "That witch of yours is the one who holds the key to all this. She is Boudier's witness. She is going to say that she saw Jaxon kill both Caroline Boudier and John. She's going to stand up in the Tribunal and lie."

"Jesus Christ." Jack's eyes widened. "But why would she do that? Why would she help Boudier? She hates our kind."

Barrett narrowed his eyes at the older Pack Master. "Can I trust you, Jack?"

Hurt flashed through Jack's eyes. It was the reaction that Barrett needed.

"Of course. I know things went to shit at my house, but I have always had your back, Barrett. I've always sided with you. To say that I'm not trustworthy is very offensive to me. You know you can trust me."

"I know. I needed to ask it. I needed to see your reaction." Barrett gave him a little smile.

"How did I do, smart-ass?" Jack cocked his head.

"You passed… for now." Barrett narrowed his gaze a little.

"After all these years, I should have known that in your most critical hour as Pack Master you would still be busting my balls." Jack chortled.

"Yeah, well, I have to have something to entertain me." Barrett shrugged.

Jack chuckled, and the tension between them was gone.

They stood there for a few minutes saying nothing, just taking in the night air and staring back at the beautiful sky.

"I'm going to ask you to do something. Something you might find difficult." Barrett turned to look at Jack.

"You know I'll do what I can to help. Anything. Just tell me." Jack's face creased with concern.

"Before I ask you, I need a blood oath, Jack." Barrett pulled out a knife from the back of jeans. He wasn't allowed to carry a gun to the Tribunal, but a knife was acceptable.

"Are you shitting me?" Jack arched his brow. "Just when I thought we were having a moment, you ask me something like that."

"You'll understand later. Quit bitching and cut your fucking hand. Let's get this shit over with. Then you can bro out as much as you want." Barrett sighed.

"Ugh, with this new vernacular. I'm not sure what *bro out* means, but if it involves getting a drink, I'm in." Jack held out his hand and then hesitated. He narrowed his eyes on Barrett. "And I don't want some girlie drink like wine either. I'm a scotch and bourbon man. Always have been, always will be."

"Jesus, will you just give me your hand?" Barrett lifted his eyes to the sky.

"Fine. But don't cut too deep. I'm on a blood thinner and I'll fucking bleed like a stuck pig." Jack scowled at him.

"Pussy," Barrett murmured as he took the knife and brought the blade across Jack's palm. Blood came to the surface and dripped out of the cut.

He turned the knife on himself and made a cut in his own palm, slashing a large cut across the flesh. His hand stung and he squeezed his hand, making the blood come faster. He held out his hand to Jack.

Jack sighed but stuck out his hand, and they shook. Barrett held on and looked Jack in the eyes. "This blood bond is unbreakable. For the next twenty-four hours, you will be unable to break our deal or reveal what was said between us. Agreed?"

"Agreed." Jack nodded.

Barrett released his hold and glanced down at his hand.

"So tell me." Jack took a silk handkerchief out of his jacket pocket and pressed it against his palm.

"You won't interfere in the judgment of the Tribunal."

"I swear it," Jack said. "I'm not sure why you need a blood vow for that. No Pack Master has ever interfered with a Tribunal ruling."

"And I expect you to stand with the ruling this time as well. Just so we're clear." Barrett held Jack's gaze.

"Barrett, do you mind telling me what the fuck is going on?"

"The fact is, Boudier will demand retribution for the killing of his wife and son-in-law. There is nothing for the Council to say but to uphold that."

"So you're going to let them have Jaxon even though we both know the daughter probably did it." Jack glared. "Hell, why don't you just give him the girl. That's what he wants anyway."

"No. That's not what he really wants. What Boudier really wants is to watch me suffer." Barrett glanced up at the sky. A shooting star whizzed across the twinkling canvas, and he wished that there was something else that could be done. "There's more. Ginny is pregnant."

"Holy fuck." Jack scrubbed his hand across his face.

"You tell me, Jack. If you were in my position, would you give Ginny over to Boudier? Knowing what kind of life she would suffer at his hands?"

Jack scowled and then studied the ground.

"No, you wouldn't." Barrett chuckled. "We are more alike than you think. You would do anything to protect your Pack."

"I would. But I don't know if I could hand over one of my men. Even if it would save the rest of them."

"The life of one versus the life of the many." Barrett closed his eyes and inhaled deep.

"I won't interfere with the ruling of the Tribunal. Is there anything else you need me to do?" Jack propped his hands on his hips.

"I have a briefcase over there by that rock. You need to grab it and take it to the Tribunal. Don't let anyone else touch it. When the time is right, I want you to open it and hand over the contents to the Council."

"How will I know when the time is right? You're being awfully vague here, Barrett." Jack scowled.

"Trust me, Jack. You'll know." He clasped his hand on Jack's shoulder and nodded. "And one more thing. When the shit goes down tonight, I'm going to need help holding back my Guardians. I would greatly appreciate it if you could position your Mississippi Guardians beside mine. They're not going to be happy with the outcome. They will fight to save their own. They might even come after me." He gave him a wry smile. "So I need you to hold them back. Use whatever force. Just don't let them interfere. Okay?"

"You have my word." Jack nodded. "You will have a hard time ruling over Arkansas when your Guardians see that you handed Jaxon over to Boudier. They will feel betrayed." Jack shook his head and clasped Barrett's hand in his. "I don't envy you the choice you have to make tonight, Barrett. But I'm here to stand beside you."

"I appreciate it, Jack." He gazed up at the sky again. "I'm sure my Guardians will get over feeling betrayed soon enough. We all eventually do."

CHAPTER 31

"I'm not so sure we should be here, Granny." Ava shoved her hands in her jeans pockets and continued to walk up the steep trail up to where the Tribunal would be held. "I don't see any other females." She cut her eyes at the Guardians from the other states jogging up the hill in a uniform line.

"Pish posh. I've never been to a Tribunal, and I promised Ginny I would look after Jaxon." Granny turned her sad eyes on Ava.

"Stop doing that," Haley said.

"Stop doing what?" Granny frowned.

"Stop giving everyone that look. You know, that look that says everything is not going to be okay." Haley wrapped her arms around her chest and continued walking with them.

"Everyone needs to calm down," Catty said from behind. "Barrett is in charge, and he always finds a way out. I mean, we're the good guys, right?"

Ava glanced over her shoulder at her friend. "Catty's right. I'm just worried what Damon is going to say when he finds out I came."

"How's he going to find out?" Granny frowned. "He's back at the Compound. Looking after things. Besides, we'll just watch things from behind those trees. The Arkansas Guardians are already around the Tribunal circle. There's no way they can see us, so there's no way that Damon will find out."

Ava tried to relax. Granny was right. Besides, she was more worried about Ginny than what Damon would say about her coming tonight.

Before she left, she'd gone to visit Ginny with Granny. Ginny had stayed behind in the Compound in Jaxon's room. Jaxon had posted a guard at her room to make sure she didn't try to leave.

As soon as Ava had entered the room, she'd recognized Ginny's scent. The female was pregnant.

Ginny had been wary of them at first, but after a while she'd warmed up to Granny and then Ava. While Granny had gone to the kitchen to fix them some tea, Ava took the opportunity to confide in Ginny that she too was pregnant.

Ginny was distraught over Jaxon's situation. She'd told them that Jaxon was innocent. Ava really didn't need her to say anything. She already knew in her heart that Jaxon was taking the blame for the woman he loved.

Ginny had tried to convince them to sneak her out of the Compound so she could see Jaxon, but they refused. Instead, Granny offered to go herself and stand by Jaxon's side.

"I don't understand why Ginny isn't here. I mean, isn't she supposed to speak against Boudier?" Catty asked.

"Jaxon made Barrett promise not to let her come tonight. So she's at the Compound with a guard at her door," Ava said and looked around the small trail.

"What the fuck are you all doing here?" Barrett stepped out from the tree line and blocked their path.

"Barrett, you scared me half to death." Granny clutched

her chest and pursed her lips together. "I think I just aged another twenty years."

"All of you are going to turn around and leave now." Barrett didn't smile, and his voice held an edge that Ava had never heard before.

"But I promised Ginny that I would come and stand with Jaxon," Granny insisted.

"No. Leave now. All of you," Barrett commanded. He looked over his shoulder and waved. From out of the thick forest, a couple of large Weres stepped out.

"Who are you?" Granny lifted her chin and assessed the Weres in front of her.

"This is James and Michael. They are Mississippi Guardians. They will escort you back to your vehicle." Barrett turned to leave, but Ava placed her hand on his arm.

He jerked away at the contact and took a step back.

Something was wrong. Ava knew it.

"Do what he says, Granny," Ava said.

"But I promised…" Granny raised her voice.

"Please, Granny. Do what Barrett asked. I'll be along in a minute." She looked at the older woman.

"Fine." Granny relented. "Come on ladies, let's go." She turned and headed down the mountain trail with Haley and Catty. The Guardians followed behind.

She waited until they were out of earshot.

"Barrett, what's going on?" Ava asked.

"Leave, Ava. Go home to Damon." He closed his eyes and lifted his face to the night sky. The moon was bright, and she could see the stress etched into his expression despite the darkness.

She'd never seen Barrett so on edge.

"Don't bullshit me, Barrett. It's just me and you." She leaned in closer and lowered her voice. "Can you get Jaxon out of this?"

Barrett met her gaze. "Boudier has a witness who will say she saw Jaxon commit those murders."

"Boudier is a lying sack of shit. He probably bribed someone to lie." She crossed her arms over her chest.

"It doesn't matter. He has a witness," he glared. "Don't you understand? Blood must be paid for those two murders. It is the Pack Law."

A shiver of dread ran through her, and she took a step back. She'd never seen Barrett this angry.

"I need to be alone, Ava. Before this starts." He looked at her. "Go back with Granny and the girls."

Dread settled in her stomach like an anchor. Barrett couldn't save Jaxon. Jaxon was going to die.

"Okay. I'll go back." She nodded and started down the path. She glanced over her shoulder as he disappeared back into the woods.

She turned around and followed him.

She couldn't let him face this alone.

She had to do something.

CHAPTER 32

"Should we wait on Ava?" Catty asked Granny and then froze.

Coming up in front of them were the Louisiana Assassins and a very familiar female.

A female that Catty hated with a vengeance.

Ella. The Witch of Yazoo City.

"Keep moving, female" the Guardian named James growled, but Catty wasn't having it.

Ella spotted her and her eyes widened. She quickly recovered, fixed a smirk on her face, and stopped.

"Well, you're looking well, Kitten." Ella tossed her red hair over her shoulder and smirked.

"The name's Catty, you psychotic bitch." Catty lunged, but one of the Assassins stepped in front of the witch, blocking Catty. The Mississippi Guardian James, held Catty back.

"Back off, female." The large Assassin, she believed Brutus was his name, glared at her.

"You gonna make me, asshole?" Catty shook off James's hold. Her hands curled into fists. "I have a score to settle with that bitch. She put a sword through my chest, and I intend to pay her back."

"Not tonight you won't," Brutus said. He looked from her to the other women. "She's under the protection of Edward Boudier. She is a witness for him in the Tribunal."

Granny shoved her way past both the Mississippi Guardians and stepped up to Brutus. She shoved her bony finger in his chest and growled. "If she's on his side, then she must be a liar. I know Jaxon and he would never murder anyone... without a damn good cause." She lifted her chin to make her point.

"Lady, I don't know who you are, but you better get that finger out of my chest," Brutus growled.

Catty stepped up beside Granny. "If you so much as lay one finger on her, I'll rip your fucking head off."

"Language, Catty," Granny chided. "Besides, if anyone is going to rip heads, it will be me."

"You won't touch these females, Brutus. Barrett has ordered us to make sure they get back to their car unharmed." Michael, the Mississippi Guardian, stepped up beside them. He narrowed his gaze on Brutus. "You three males could use some manners when it comes to talking to a lady."

Brutus growled.

Catty looked past him to the one who looked familiar. Very familiar.

Her chest tightened when he met her gaze.

"You should know your brother is finally healed from what Boudier did to him. I can't imagine staying loyal to a Pack Master who tried to have your brother skinned alive. But then again, you are nothing like Lucien. You won't ever be half the male he is." Catty turned and headed down the trail. If she'd stayed any longer, she would have shifted into wolf and torn Ella's throat out.

Then she would have gone after Lorcan.

* * *

ELLA WATCHED as the group of females headed down the trail.

"Sounds like you make friends super easy," Lorcan said.

"Sounds like you need to shut the fuck up." Ella gritted her teeth and wrapped her leather jacket tighter around her. "Boudier said he was going to meet with me before the Tribunal, so I suggest you three pretty boys get to moving. I'm sure he doesn't like to be kept waiting."

Brutus ignored her and kept walking. Brutus never said anything other than a grunt or two. Killian didn't make eye contact. He'd probably heard about her powers of glamor and didn't want to get caught under her control. She didn't tell him that he didn't need to worry. She could only glamour humans.

She squeezed her eyes shut and sucked in a deep breath. She could feel her power fading, and she knew she was going to have to spill some blood soon to keep from being sucked back into the cemetery where she was cursed to spend all eternity.

She cut her eyes at Lorcan. While all the Assassins were eye candy, Loran was pretty hot. Even she had to admit that. Plus, he had a smart-ass mouth. She appreciated a man who could verbally spar with her.

They continued up the trail and then turned off into the woods. They walked a further until they came to a break in the trees. She saw a small, rusted trailer sitting under a tree. It was large enough to carry a motorcycle, and judging from the dust and weeds growing up around it, it had long been abandoned.

They stopped in front of it. Edward Boudier stepped out from behind a tree.

"Well, well, well. The Witch of Yazoo City." Boudier smiled and clasped his hands together. "We meet at last."

"I have a name. It's Ella. And if you expect me to testify for you, then you're going to have to provide a blood donor." Her vision began to blur and she squeezed her eyes shut and tried to stay conscious. "I don't have much longer before I'm sucked back to the cemetery. Once I'm there, you don't have a witness. There will be no getting me out of there again. Jack Welbourn will make sure to have someone guard me to make sure I don't get out again. He seems to think I'm on a killing spree."

"Ah yes. That." Boudier's creepy grin grew wider. "It seems I'm the reason he thinks that."

Her eyes popped open. "What? Why would he think that? I didn't drain them, nor did I kill them. They were very much alive when I left them."

"Because, my dear, I've been following you. Every time you took blood from a victim, I ordered my Guardians to kill them." Boudier sighed and looked around.

"Why would you do that?" Her mouth dropped open, and she took a step back.

"Because it was the only way I could ensure that all the other Pack Masters knew you were dangerous. I know you've wanted your freedom for a long time, and I wanted to make sure the other Pack Masters would never broker a deal with you."

"You killed people so people would blame me for it." She felt like she'd stepped into a trap.

"Yes. You see, I have this reputation for willing to work with, how do you say it? The unsavory. And once I made you into a psycho killing witch, I knew it was only a matter of time before you would come to me wanting my help. And see, it worked. The cameras at John's house put you outside the house at the scene of the crime. You are going to be my star witness to the crimes against Jaxon Taylor."

"I'm not psychotic. I'm borderline personality, you dumb shit," she spat out.

His grin faded. "Be careful, Witch. I don't allow anyone to talk to me like that. You want your freedom and you need a blood donor. I can offer you both in exchange for your testimony and something else of mine that I know you have."

Her eyes widened ever so slightly, and then she fixed an innocent look on her face. "I don't know what you are talking about."

"Yes, you do. The packet that Ginny dropped off at the bar. The packet you stole." He glared.

She shut her eyes. She'd been holding onto it to use as her leverage against Boudier. Now the tables were turned.

He laughed. "You don't have much longer. I can see how weak you've become. Agree to my terms of being my witness and saying that you saw Jaxon murder those two people, and I will give you the blood you need and the freedom you seek."

She swallowed. "How will you give me my freedom? I saw a bunch of fucking Arkansas and Mississippi Guardians on our way up here. I'm practically surrounded by them."

"Under the Pack Law, a witness in a Tribunal will not be harmed and is under the protection of the Pack Master involved. Once you give your statement, I will give you immunity from all past crimes." He grinned and nodded to the Assassins. "Ask them if you don't believe me."

She looked at Lorcan. He simply nodded.

"Fine. I'll testify. But I need blood." She clenched her hands together and took a deep breath. "The envelope you want is hidden underneath the seat of the car I arrived in."

"Perfect. I'll send a Guardian to retrieve it. Now to uphold my end of the bargain." He waved his hand in the direction of the trailer. "Your salvation, my dear, is inside that trailer."

Boudier snapped his fingers, and half a dozen Louisiana Guardians stepped out from the shadows.

A Guardian stepped forward and tugged the door open. She squinted, but it was too dark to see inside. She took a step forward.

"Now," Boudier said behind her.

She was shoved inside. She fell inside the cramped trailer. A large figure fell on top of her, and the door slammed shut. She was trapped in darkness.

"Get the fuck off me." She wheezed, shoving at the massive body of muscle on top of her.

He grunted and rolled off.

"A Guardian. What the fuck? So your own Pack Master offers me your blood." She felt around in the dark. "How do you feel about that?"

"Not too fucking thrilled," Lorcan replied, his tone even.

"Lorcan?" Her knees buckled and she slumped to the floor.

"Yeah. Do you need a knife or something?" Lorcan asked.

She was so stunned she couldn't speak for a few seconds.

"A knife?"

"For the blood. The blood you need to keep you here." He spoke slowly, like he was explaining something to a child.

"A knife would be good," she said carefully. "Did you volunteer for this?" She couldn't imagine the Assassin volunteering to give his blood.

"No. Take this." He grabbed her hand and pressed the blade into her palm.

She took the knife and felt her way around his body. The dude was built like a freaking wall of muscle. She grinned and dipped her hand past the waistband on his pants.

He grabbed her hand. "Easy. I don't want anything down there cut."

"Wasn't going to cut there. Just checking out the situation." She smirked.

"Well, don't."

"Fine." She sighed. "Where can I cut you?"

"You're asking?" His tone was one of disbelief.

"Yeah, well, I've never actually had anyone volunteer." That wasn't totally true, but he didn't need to know.

"Do my neck. Then it will be easier to cut my throat after you're done."

"I'm not cutting your throat. Jesus." She was fading fast. She sliced the blade against the side of his neck. Immediately the coppery scent of blood filled the tiny trailer. She leaned in and pressed her cheek to his bleeding neck.

He stiffened. "I thought you didn't drink blood."

"I don't, you idiot. I do, however, need to feel it on my body." She laid her forehead on his shoulder. He could almost hear his pulse beating in his chest. "Relax. I know you're a werewolf. You'll heal quick enough."

"Not this time," he said solemnly.

"What do you mean?" She frowned but didn't lift her head.

"After you are done with me, Boudier's Guardians will come in and put a silver bullet in my head. To finish me off."

Her eyes popped open, and her power was back. She lifted her head. With his blood, she could even see him in the dark. "Why would they do that? Guardians don't kill their own kind. Not within their state."

"In Louisiana they do. When given an order by Boudier the Guardians they will do what they're told." He winced and pressed his hand to his still-bleeding neck.

"Why would Boudier order that?" Her stomach twisted. She knew she was making a deal with the devil, but she would do anything to keep from going back to that cemetery.

"Because he knows I helped my brother escape. He

suspects I helped the Arkansas Guardians get out of Louisiana." He shrugged. "He may even suspect that I helped get Jaxon across the border before we caught up to them."

"Did you?" She froze.

"I'm not telling you." He glanced at the closed door that would lead to her freedom. "You need to go. Boudier is waiting for you. If he suspects we talked, then he won't hesitate to end you."

"Well, I'm a little hard to kill." She bit her lip.

"No doubt." A small grin crept across his lips.

"I'm not safe with him, am I?" She waited for his answer.

He stared at her hard and then slowly shook his head. "No one is."

She heard movement outside and some yelling.

"When they open that door, run. Don't look back," he said.

"Why are you doing this? Why are you helping me?" She didn't trust anyone. Least of all a shifter.

"It's my way of trying to make up for my past," he said.

She leaned down, pressed her lips to his, and kissed him long and hard. He didn't fight her or shove her away. She pulled out an envelope out of her jacket and tucked it inside his leather jacket. When she pulled back, she winked. "Thanks for the blood, sugar."

"Well I really didn't have a choice." Lorcan said.

"This is yours." She handed him the knife back. "Take care of yourself, Lorcan."

The trailer door creaked open, and she bolted out into the darkness.

CHAPTER 33

"The Council has heard the testimony from the witness for Edward Boudier. The Witch of Yazoo was shown at the scene of the crime. She gave testimony that she saw Jaxon Taylor break into the house and murder Caroline Boudier and John McGregor. We would now like to hear from Barrett Middleton's witnesses regarding the charge against Guardian Jaxon Taylor." One of the ten Council members spoke, his voice echoing in the cave.

Barrett alone stood in front of the Council while Jaxon stood off in the shadows with his hands chained behind his back. The meeting was closed to the other Guardians. Only the Pack Masters were allowed entrance. Once the verdict was announced, they would move near the top of the peak where the Guardians were gathered in a circle to see the outcome.

"I'm afraid I have no witness." His stomach clenched.

The council members looked at one another and frowned.

"But how will you counter the accusations made against Guardian Jaxon Taylor?" one of the Council said.

"I am here as a character witness."

Boudier snorted. "Are you serious?"

Barrett ignored Boudier and addressed the Council directly. "May I continue?"

"Go on."

"Jaxon has never harmed an innocent civilian since I've known him. He's one of my finest Guardians and has done his job without reproach. The death of Caroline Boudier was an accident. I believe the crime scene results will show that she fell and impaled herself."

"That's not what my witness saw," Boudier yelled out.

"Let Middleton speak," one of the Council members admonished. He waved his hand for Barrett to continue.

"Your witness is a liar. I suspect you brokered a deal with her so she wouldn't have to go back to the cemetery." Barrett glared at Boudier.

"As far as John McGregor goes, John attacked Jaxon first, and he bit him with his silver teeth."

"Silver teeth?" One of the Council members cringed and looked at Boudier.

"My son-in-law was a bit... quirky." Boudier shrugged.

"The death of John was self-defense. It was either kill or be killed," Barrett stated. "I would have done the same if I were in his position."

The room grew quiet.

"If you please, I have a witness who is here of her own volition, despite the fact that Arkansas and Mississippi have planned to do her harm." Boudier waved at Ella.

Ella cringed and took a step back as if she realized she had picked the wrong fucking horse in this race. But it was too late now.

"Barrett has no witnesses, and Jaxon himself has admitted to killing two Weres—one who was my wife." Boudier fisted his hands at his side. "I demand justice. I demand blood for what was taken from me."

Barrett tensed, waiting for the Council to speak. He cut his eyes over at Jaxon. He was still standing there with his head held high, like he was determined to die for his female.

The Council members turned their backs to him and whispered and murmured among themselves.

Every second that ticked by made his chest hurt even more.

The Council finally turned around and faced them. Barrett tried to get a read on them, but it was impossible. They were as somber as priests.

"A verdict has been reached in this Tribunal. Once it is stated, it cannot be taken back or changed. It's final."

Silence.

"We have found that Edward Boudier had demanded justice for his wife and son-in-law. And it is by law that we demand a blood debt be paid by an Arkansas Guardian. A life for a life."

"Yes!" Edward Boudier let out a triumphant shout, and it echoed in the cave they were standing in.

Nausea swamped over Barrett hard and fast, and he forced himself to stand there.

"Barrett, you've been a great leader of Arkansas and we commend you on that. But Jaxon's life has to be sacrificed for the crime he has committed."

"What you are saying is that you need an Arkansas Guardian to die for Boudier? Despite the fact that Boudier is a danger to his own kind?" Barrett said.

"The Council's verdict is final," one of the Councilmen said with conviction.

"Don't look so sad, Barrett. You've got lots of other Guardians. You won't miss one." Boudier smirked.

"You are not allowed to speak, Boudier," one of the Council chided. "You've had your say. Now we must see the punishment through."

Barrett looked at Jaxon, who didn't make eye contact. Jaxon stared straight ahead. A single bead of sweat rolled down his temple and onto his shirt.

Barrett walked over to where Jaxon stood, and suddenly two the Louisiana Assassins appeared out of the shadows to escort Jaxon out.

Barrett glared at Brutus and Killian. "I will walk out with Jaxon."

They stepped out of the cave and onto the top of the mountain, where Guardians from Tennessee, Mississippi, Alabama, Kentucky, Louisiana, and Arkansas waited. The Council walked out first, followed by Boudier. Barrett waited a second and fell into step with Jaxon at his side.

"I'm sorry, Barrett. I've let you down." Jaxon murmured. "But I couldn't let her die. She's pregnant."

"I know." Barrett cleared his throat as they stepped out into the clearing at the top of the mountain.

The Council members lined up to address the werewolves. Silence fell over the crowd.

"The verdict is guilty. Arkansas must pay Louisiana a death in exchange for the two lives Boudier lost."

Rumblings and murmurs rose up among the Guardians. Only the Louisiana Guardians were silent.

Barrett searched the crowd until he found Jack Wellbourn. The Mississippi Pack Master stared back at him with the briefcase clutched in his hands. He let his gaze drift over to his Guardians. As promised, Jack had positioned his Mississippi Guardians in between each Arkansas Guardian.

He stepped forward to address the crowd, but a female screamed. He looked toward the woods.

"Wait! Wait!" Ava came barreling out of the woods and dodged Brutus, who tried to prevent her from running up to Barrett.

"Ava. I told you to go..." Barrett glared down at her. And then froze as her scent hit him. Ava was pregnant. How had he not recognized this before?

He must have been too caught up in trying to figure out a way to get Jaxon out of this mess.

"You can't kill Jaxon. It's not right." She looked up at him with tears in her eyes.

He looked upward into the sky. "Ah, you women. You never trust me."

"You found a way out of this?"

He lifted his head to the crowd and froze when he spotted Damon edging closer to the middle. Damon frowned when he saw Ava.

Barrett hadn't known Damon would show. But it was then he knew it was fate. It was then he knew what he had to do.

Barrett leaned down and looked her in the eye. "Promise me when this is over that you will take care of Damon. He's a good male. Don't let him feel guilty for any of this."

"Feel guilty? I don't understand." His eyes widened. "What are you talking about, Barrett?"

"I'm sorry for what I'm about to do. I hope you can forgive me one day, Ava." He grabbed Jaxon and shoved him toward the line of Mississippi Guardians, who caught him before he hit the ground. Jack's eyes widened, yet he didn't move.

Barrett grabbed the silver knife out of the waistband of his jeans and seized Ava. He clamped a hand down on her mouth and held the knife to her throat. His gut twisted and turned as she tried to break free.

He had to do this to save Jaxon.

He had to do this to save his Pack.

He had to die to save the future of Arkansas.

"What the fuck are you doing, Barrett?" Damon broke through the line of Kentucky Guardians. "Get your fucking hands off her."

"You do know, Damon, that Ava was always supposed to be mine, right?" Barrett called out over the roar of the crowd.

Everyone went silent.

"Get your fucking hands off her now, Barrett." Damon growled.

Barrett didn't move. He knew the only thing Damon would kill him over was Ava. Damon and Ava and their little one on the way would protect the state of Arkansas. They would be the future of the Pack.

Once this was over, they would find the paperwork that legally gave Damon control as Pack Master in case of the Barrett's death. They would also find enough evidence on Boudier to send him to his death as well.

But first someone had to die.

In order to save Jaxon, he had to die.

In order to protect his Guardians, Barrett was willing to do it.

Barrett leaned down to Ava's neck. To everyone else, it looked like he was kissing her.

"I'm sorry. This is the only way I can save Jaxon. It calls for a death. They will get a death. Not his. But mine." He pressed the blade to her neck, enough to draw a drop of blood.

"Forgive me, Ava. Take care of Damon," he whispered.

A demonic growl erupted. Damon lunged and shifted into wolf in midair.

Barrett timed it just right, and right before Damon landed, Barrett shoved Ava out of the way and turned the blade of the knife to his chest. The weight of Damon shoved the silver blade into his chest, ripping apart the chambers of his heart as it sliced through the muscle. Something flickered in Damon's eyes, and he backed away from Barrett. Barrett's heart slowed, and he could feel the blood pouring out of his chest. Unimaginable pain sliced through his chest as the silver began to poison him. He fell to his knees. He only had seconds before he would be dead.

Barrett looked at the crowd. Jack looked horrified at what had happened. He looked over to where his Guardians stood. Mississippi Guardians were holding back Braxton and Jayden, who were trying to get to him. Zane had shifted and was growling and biting the five Guardians holding him back. Lucien had started a fight, and it took three Mississippi Guardians to hold him down. Jaxon, still in chains and restrained by the Assassins, sank to his knees, yelling and screaming at the top of his lungs. Ava started toward him, and Damon in wolf form was pacing back and forth, unsure of what had just happened.

Barrett got to his feet. He was acutely aware of the silver poisoning what was left of his heart. He struggled to breathe and coughed up blood. It wasn't finished. Not yet. He looked at the horrified expression of the Council and walked backwards to the edge of the mountain. He didn't want his Guardians to watch him take his final breath.

"You hereby have your blood debt. Paid. In. Full." The heel of his boot found the edge of the mountain. He held his arms out to his side. He looked up at the sky one last time before he felt the last beat of his heart.

He fell back into nothing.

He didn't hear the screams of Ava or the wails of Jaxon. He didn't hear the curses of his Guardians trying to break away from the Mississippi Guardians restraining them. He didn't hear the yells of Boudier saying it wasn't Barrett who was supposed to die. It wasn't even the sounds of the crowd demanding the council do something. Anything.

The last thing he heard as he looked up at the starlight sky was the howl of the wolf who had killed him.

CHAPTER 34

Silence swept across the crowd of Guardians and Pack Masters from all the Southern states as Barrett fell off the mountain.

"What does this mean? I don't understand, what does this mean?" one of the Mississippi Guardians yelled out, breaking the silence.

"It means that Barrett died for me," Jaxon said from his position on his knees.

"Has that ever happened? Has a Pack Master ever sacrificed himself for one of his Guardians?" a Kentucky Guardian asked.

"I don't give a shit about that." Boudier spoke up. "I still demand the life of Jaxon Taylor."

"Not so fast, Boudier. You can't demand Jaxon's life. Barrett just paid the debt. It's paid in full." Jack Welbourn held the briefcase in his arms. He still couldn't believe what he had just seen. Couldn't get over the fact that Barrett had sacrificed himself.

All eyes went to the Council. One of them cleared his throat.

"Jack is right. If someone sacrifices himself for a death debt, then it is considered paid in full."

"Fuck!" Boudier screamed and fisted his hands like a toddler.

Everyone looked at him.

"But the law also states that if a Pack Master vacates a position, then a current Pack Master may claim it as his own. I claim the state of Arkansas as my own." Boudier glared at the other Pack Masters, daring them to challenge him.

Anger burned in Jack's gut.

"I'm afraid that's not going to be legal. Not in this case." Jack rested the briefcase on a rock and opened it. He hadn't told Barrett that once he'd given him the suitcase, he'd sneaked a peek inside. He already knew what legal documents he would find. The blood vow he'd made to Barrett wouldn't let him reveal this information until now.

"You see, I have the legal paperwork of Barrett Middleton putting Damon Trahan as next in line as Pack Master should anything happen to him." Jack waved the document in the air and then handed it to the Council.

"But Damon killed him," Boudier said.

"As I recall, you killed the Pack Master of Louisiana to gain the power." Jack narrowed his gaze on Boudier. "It's how a lot of these assholes get into power."

Murmurs swept the crowd.

"Brutus and Killian, kill Jaxon. I demand it." Boudier screamed until he was red in the face.

"Yeah, see, that's a no-go on that." Killian stepped in front of Jaxon, blocking Boudier's view. "When you tried to kill Lorcan, that's where I drew the line in the sand."

"You worthless piece of shit." Boudier spat out. "Brutus, kill Jaxon, now!"

"Fuck off." Brutus stood beside Killian and rested his

hand on the silver knife he carried in a holster next to his gun.

"You killed one of your Assassins?" Jack looked over at Lucien. He knew Lorcan and Lucien were brothers. Lucien's face was dark with rage and retribution.

"Tried. He tried to kill me." Lorcan stepped out from the shadows. "You all should also know that the Witch of Yazoo City never killed any of her victims. She bled them enough to keep her power but left them alive. Boudier had someone following her and ordered anyone she took blood from killed. He wanted everyone to think she was a killer."

"But she testified for him," Jack said.

"She admitted to me that she lied. She lied in order to secure her freedom. Boudier promised her freedom from the cemetery if she lied for him."

Murmurs rose up around the crowd, and Boudier began to shift his weight from foot to foot. It was the first time the Pack Master looked uncomfortable.

"Release Jaxon," Lorcan ordered. Killian nodded and quickly unlocked the chains.

"You are under no power to order…" Boudier stated.

"You forget. As Assassins, we are judge and jury. We might be deadly killers, but we are well versed in the Pack Law. I dare anyone here, including the Council, to come up against us."

Everyone looked at the Council.

"Lorcan is right. Jaxon is free to go," one of the members said.

"I also have something else that might be of some value." Lorcan smirked and pulled an envelope out of the back of his leather jacket. "Before Ella, er… the Witch of Yazoo City left, she gave me something. Something of Boudier's." He waved it in the air and walked over to Jack.

"You need to read that," Lorcan said.

"What is it?" Jack asked as he turned the envelope over in his hands.

"It's a hit list from Boudier. You see, he has a hit list of all the Guardians and Pack Masters he wants taken out." Lorcan looked at the Arkansas Guardians.

Boudier's eyes grew wide and he took a step back.

"And your name is on there too, Jack. In fact a lot of the Pack Masters' names are on there. Seems like Edward Boudier was wanting to take out a lot of werewolves to increase his territory."

Jack gritted his teeth. "Take him into custody." His Mississippi Guardians stepped forward and grabbed Boudier.

"Take your fucking hands off me. Now!" Boudier screeched.

"I would love to declare a Tribunal on account of everything presented today." Jack looked at the Council.

"Granted," the council said unanimously.

CHAPTER 35

"Fuck. I shouldn't have worn heels for this." Ella stumbled on the rocks and finally gave up, bent down, and tugged off her heels. She stood and glared at the figure lying on the ground.

"You better be worth my Louboutin's." She eased her way over to the lifeless figure and bent down beside him. Because she'd had Lorcan's blood, she could see pretty well in the dark. It wouldn't last, but she didn't need it to.

She bent over the large Were and grabbed the knife sticking out of his chest. She tugged.

It didn't budge.

She stood over him, straddling him, and gripped it with both hands and pulled. It finally slid out of his chest.

She cringed as she looked at the bloody knife. She wasn't sure what to do with it, so she stuck it in the back of her skinny jeans. She leaned down and brushed the hair out of his face.

The majority of his blood was on chest. When he'd fallen off the mountain, he'd crushed the back of his skull in, but his face was still pretty. She liked a good-looking face. He certainly had one.

She ran her hand down his chest to his wound. It wasn't healing, and she wondered if it was too late. Maybe he'd gotten too much of the silver inside him. Maybe he really was dead.

She stood and looked down the rest of his body. Her gaze landed on his crotch. Even dead, he was still sporting a bulge in his pants.

She bit her lip and looked around to make sure they were alone. She bent down and put her hand on the front of his jeans.

"Very nice, Middleton. Even in death, you're hung like a horse." Maybe she could make a mold from it.

She stood and grinned.

"Let's go, big guy." She grabbed him by the legs and tugged his body toward a nearby cave.

"Took you long enough." Ryker groused from inside the cave.

"Well, if you had gotten off your ass and helped me drag him, I would have been here a lot sooner." Ella glared at the werewolf.

"Besides, I don't even know if I can bring him back. Blood magic is a tricky thing. He might not come back the same." She dropped his legs and propped her hands on her hips.

She looked at Ryker. "So you knew Barrett was going to sacrifice himself? And you let him? That's pretty fucking... sick. Even if I do say so myself."

"I suspected. I wasn't sure." Ryker knelt beside Barrett's body.

"Do you feel any life in him at all?" He looked up at her.

Her heart tugged. "I'm not sure. The silver has saturated his heart, and his skull is crushed. I don't think there's a spell for that. I'm sorry." She was.

"That's why I brought in a backup. You can come out now, Celeste," Ryker said.

A stunning blonde stepped out from the depths of the cave wearing a beautiful red dress and high heels. Ella immediately hated the woman.

"Nice shoes." She studied the blonde's heels.

The blonde hurried over to Barrett's body and knelt. She looked up at Ryker.

"I'll do what I can. But I can't promise anything," Celeste said.

"I've seen what you can do. I'll take anything you've got," Ryker said and then looked up at Ella.

"You two have not been introduced. Ella this is Celeste Nordstrom. Celeste, this is Ella, the Witch of Yazoo City." Ryker grinned.

Ella arched her brow. "Are you a witch too?"

Celeste narrowed her gaze. "No. I'm a fairy."

"Are you shitting me? I thought fairies only existed in story books." Ella snorted.

"Watch it, witch." Ryker snarled. "Show some respect. She's not that kind of fairy."

"What kind are you then?" Ella crossed her arms and glared.

"If you're not careful," Celeste took a step toward her, "I can be the dangerous kind."

CHAPTER 36

*F*our weeks later...

"How's Damon doing?" Granny gave Ava a hug before stepping inside the Compound in Little Rock.

"Not good. He hasn't shifted back. It took all of our Guardians and a few of the Mississippi Guardians to restrain him and get him in the back of the eighteen wheeler." Ava sighed and led the way down the hallway. "We had to put him in the holding cell."

"Why?"

"Because it was the only thing strong enough to hold him. He tore a huge hole in the side of the trailer before they could get home." Ava stopped and looked at her. "They had to use a tranquilizer dart to get him the rest of the way home.

"He won't say it, but he blames himself for Barrett's death." A tear slid down Ava's face. "I don't know how to help him. He won't listen to me."

"Oh honey." Granny pulled Ava into a tight hug. She felt Ava shudder with silent cries as she held her. After a long minute, Ava pulled back and wiped her eyes.

"First of all, this is not your fault or Damon's." Granny pursed her lips. "Barrett made a choice. He sacrificed himself for Jaxon." Her chest ached with such grief she thought it would burst right open. Now was not the time for mourning or for tears. Now was the time for strength and courage.

"Where are all the Guardians?" She lifted her chin.

"They're here, in their rooms. No one has left the building since we got Damon home."

Granny nodded. "I talked to Jack Wellbourn and he has his Mississippi Guardians stationed in Arkansas to help out until Damon can settle into his position."

"Jack's been very kind." Ava nodded.

"I want you to gather our Guardians. Tell them Damon is going to meet them in the gym." Granny lifted her chin and hooked her purse on the crook of her arm.

"Damon doesn't want to see anyone, Granny. I've tried." Ava shook her head.

"He will. You run on now, tell them to meet in an hour." She drew back her shoulders. "But first, take me to Damon. I want to talk to him."

* * *

DAMON TREMBLED as he paced back and forth in front of the bars of the holding cell. The tranquilizer they'd shot him had worn off and adrenaline now filled his veins. His wolf eyes darted around the darkened room.

Ava had come to see him and tried to talk to him. Her grief and sorrow had filled the room like funeral flowers. It had been too much for him. He refused to shift back into human form, preferring to stay as a wolf.

Every time he shut his eyes, he kept seeing Barrett falling off the edge of the mountain with that hideous knife stuck in his chest.

Ava had told him afterwards what Barrett had said. He'd asked for Ava's forgiveness and he'd told her to take care of Damon.

Every time he thought about it he wanted to scream.

Barrett had paid Jaxon's debt with his own life. And put Damon in charge as Pack Master.

How could he live with Barrett's death on his hands?

The creak of the metal door filled the empty space. He jerked his head toward the door and snarled.

"Look here, mister." Granny stepped into the room wearing a bright yellow muumuu and carrying that white plastic purse on her arm. "Don't you dare growl at me." She stepped closer and narrowed her eyes at him.

He sighed and sat back on his haunches.

Granny stepped up to the bars and stuck the key in the lock.

His eyes widened as she swung open the door and stepped inside with him. She shut the door behind her.

"I'm here to talk." She pointed her bony finger in his face and glared. "And you are going to sit there and listen."

He let out a low growl at his displeasure. She pressed her lips into a thin line.

"Damon, that's enough."

He looked away. He wasn't in the mood for a lecture. He just wanted to be left alone.

"Barrett knew what he was doing when he sacrificed himself for Jaxon. He was one of the best Pack Masters I had ever known." Granny lifted her chin. "Damon, you need to know something. You didn't kill Barrett. He planned to die."

Damon jerked his head towards the old woman. Of course he killed Barrett. He was the one who landed on him and shoved the knife into heart.

"Barrett had papers drawn up months ago in case anything happened to him. He knew months ago that he wanted you to be the next Pack Master. He saw your potential. Most of all he saw your courage and strength." She cocked her head.

He studied the ground.

"As Pack Master it is time for you to rule. Your Guardians need a leader. And you need your Guardians."

But how could they want him as their leader?

"I want you to look inside yourself and see if Barrett was right about you. See if you have the courage to step into that role." She nodded. "I see the greatness inside you. Even if you don't."

She reached out and ruffled the fur on the top of his head and smiled.

"You've got a lot of people counting on you, Damon. Ava and your child and your Guardians. They are waiting in the gym for you." She walked to the iron bars and opened the door.

She stepped outside and left the door open. "You know in your heart this is the right thing to do."

He listened to her footsteps as she walked away, leaving him alone.

* * *

DAMON AVOIDED LOOKING in the mirror in the hallway as he made his way towards the gym. His stomach clenched. He wasn't sure what he was walking into and he didn't know yet what he was going to say.

"Damon," Ava's soft voice had him stopping in his tracks.

He turned and faced her.

She was pale and there were dark circles under her beautiful eyes. He frowned.

"Are you okay?" He asked.

"Yes." She nodded. "Damon, I . . ."

"Stop." He held up his hand. "I don't want you to apologize for being at the Tribunal. The outcome wouldn't have been any different. Barrett still would have died for Jaxon."

She looked at the ground and nodded.

She looked so tiny and frail. He couldn't take another second of the awkwardness between them.

He closed the distance and took her into his arms. She clung to him and buried her face into his chest.

"I was so scared, Damon. Scared that I wasn't going to get you back." She sobbed.

"What did I tell you? You're never getting rid of me." He said softly.

She looked up and let out a chuckle. "Good."

He bent his head and covered her warm lips with his. She held on tight as he kissed her slow and deep. When he pulled back he stared down into her eyes.

"I need to ask you something. Something serious."

"Okay. What is it?"

"How do you feel about me being Pack Master? I know you didn't like it much when I was just filling in. Now it would be permanent. So I need to know how you feel about it. Because if you're not all in, then I won't accept it."

"Are you serious? Has anyone ever turned down the position?" Her eyes widened.

"No, not that I know of." He shrugged.

Ava let out a slow breath and looked into his eyes.

"I'll stand by whatever decision you make." She cupped his cheek. "I think you would make a great Pack Master. I think this state needs you now more than ever. I think the Guardians need you. I think you were always meant for this, Damon."

Her words humbled him. He swallowed back the emotion

welling up in his throat. Now was not the time to be crying like a pussy.

Now was the time for strength.

"I love you." He said.

"I love you, too." She smiled.

CHAPTER 37

*D*amon walked into the gym with Ava at his side. The Guardians who had been talking amongst themselves turned when he entered. The room went silent.

He walked to the front of the room and faced the Guardians.

"I have something I need to say." Damon addressed the room.

"When I was first admitted to the Arkansas Guardians, I was a little shocked. After being kicked out of the Louisiana Guardians I didn't think another state would take me. But Arkansas did. Barrett did." His throat ached. He swallowed and continued.

"I was shocked when I found out Barrett left me as Pack Master. Even though I filled in for him only a few times, we never talked about who would be next in line. I never asked. I guess I just thought he would live forever." A ghost of a smile crossed his lips.

"To be honest if I could relieve that night, I would change the outcome. And Barrett would be standing here giving everyone hell."

A soft laugh erupted through the gym.

"I can't change the outcome. But I can honor Barrett's wishes in accepting the position as Pack Master." He looked around the room.

"But before that decision is final I want to know how you all feel about that."

"That's not how it's done, Damon. You don't need anyone's approval." Zane said.

"I know. But I would like to know I have it all the same." He lifted his chin. He knew in his heart that even if just one Guardian voted against him, he would step down.

"Does anyone have anything to say?" He scanned the room waiting for someone to denounce him as Pack Master.

"I have something to say." Jaxon stepped forward.

Jaxon hadn't shaved and he looked like he hadn't slept in a week. Jaxon looked like Damon felt.

"I feel like I need to turn in my resignation. What Barrett did was for me. I don't deserve to hold the title Guardian anymore." Jaxon raked his fingers through his hair.

"So you're going to quit. Just like that." Damon curled his hands into fists. "Let me tell you something Jaxon. If you quit now, then Boudier wins. If you leave your brothers then everything Barrett did was for nothing."

Jaxon's head jerked up. "How can I live with what I've done?"

"What you've done is protected Ginny from an abusive father and husband. What you've done is taking her back when she's pregnant with another male's child. What you've done is show a willingness to die to save a female that you love. That's not weakness. That's unimaginable strength." He narrowed his eyes. "And if you so much as think your ass is leaving the Guardians, I will beat you into submission. You got that?"

Braxton and Jayden snorted.

"I would listen to him, Jaxon. You don't want to spar with Damon." Lucien acknowledged.

"You are part of the Arkansas Guardians, Jaxon. We are a family. We stick together." Damon stated.

Emotion flashed through Jaxon's eyes and Damon knew he was touched by the outpouring of support.

Jaxon nodded. "Well then. I'll stay on one condition." He stared at Damon. "I'll stay as long as you are my Pack Master."

This time it was Damon who was having a hard time controlling his emotions.

He put his hands on his hips and looked at the ceiling in an attempt to gather his emotions.

When he looked back at all the Guardians, they'd stepped closer.

"I guess what we are saying is that we would all be honored to have you as our Pack Master." Zane said. "Barrett knew what he was doing by choosing you."

"Yes, please say you'll do it." Jayden scowled. "I'm tired of all these Mississippi Guardians in our state. It's too crowded."

Everyone laughed and the tension in the room drifted away like smoke.

Damon nodded. "As Pack Master of Arkansas I will do my best to protect our state and our Weres. I'm honored to have you all as my Guardians."

A cheer went up around the room and each Guardian took turns to knell before Damon. Zane had retrieved the insignia ring from Barrett's office and placed it on Damon's hand.

"As your first official act as Pack master I have a request." Jaxon asked.

"What is it, Jaxon?" Damon frowned.

"I want you to mate me to Ginny. Today." Jaxon stated.

JODI VAUGHN

A smile crept across his face and he nodded. "I would be honored. But first catch me up on what's going on in Louisiana."

Lucien stepped forward. "They are holding Boudier for attempted murder against all the Pack Masters and Guardians. I've heard from Lorcan and he said they had to move him to Texas because of all the death threats against him."

"Should have just put him in a room with all his Louisiana Guardians. I'm sure after this they would be more than willing to kill him and save us the time."

"No doubt." Lucien snorted. "I'm sure when the Tribunal is held it will be one hell of a show."

"So who's in charge of Louisiana? Now that Boudier has been relieved of his duties." Damon asked.

"The Southern Pack Masters will be taking turns over seeing the state. Right now Jack Wellbourn is in charge and then after a month you'll oversee it." Zane offered.

"What about the Assassins? Are they staying in Louisana?"

"For now. I talked to Lorcan and he said the reason he'd stayed with Boudier for so long was he tried to get my parents out of the state before he left. He knew that Boudier would kill our parents."

"So he wasn't being disloyal to Barrett." Damon nodded.

"No, he was trying to protect my mom. Now that Boudier is gone, he'll stay until he figures out his next move." Lucien shrugged.

"Good." Damon nodded. "I need people I can trust. Like Lorcan. I need to talk to him and see if he has any idea where that Mississippi witch ran off to."

"Damon, there's something else." Zane lowered his voice. "Ryker is missing. We think he's trying to cope with everything that's happened. Want me to go look for him?"

"No. Give him space. He'll come back when he's ready."

"Jack Wellbourn wants to meet with you at your earliest convenience. Just to go over some things." Braxton said.

"I'll call him tomorrow." He smiled a little. "But first I need to get Jaxon and Ginny mated.

* * *

JAXON TIGHTENED his hold on Ginny as he stepped into his room at the Compound. The ceremony had been quick. Just as he liked it. He couldn't wait another second to start his life with Ginny.

This time he wasn't going to waste a second.

"I wish we had a place of our own. It feels weird carrying you across the threshold at the Guardian Compound." He looked down at her.

"I don't care where we spend our honeymoon. As long as we're together." Ginny pressed her lips to his. "Besides, I'm not sure we can afford to get anything right away. I never had any money of my own. Maybe we can find a deserted barn to live in." She giggled.

He walked over and set her gently on the bed.

"Actually I was going to talk to you about that." He walked over to the kitchen counter and picked up the envelope as he fought a smile.

He knelt beside the bed so he could be eye level with her.

"What's that?" She eyed the envelope suspiciously.

He grinned. "Actually you do have money. A lot of it."

"What are you talking about? I never had money. My father gave me a meager allowance and when I married John he controlled the money."

His smile grew. "And when John was killed all of his wealth went straight to you."

"What?" She opened the envelope and stared at the words

written by every member of the Council declaring her as beneficiary of John's money.

"It has to be at least.."

"Eight million dollars. Not including property." Jaxon said. "And that doesn't include your father's estate. Once he is found guilty, you will also inherit that. You are a very wealthy woman."

"Oh my God." Her mouth fell open.

"It's yours to do with it as you wish." Jaxon cocked his head. "Although as a Guardian I do make pretty good money so it's not like we're broke."

"Really?"

"Yeah really good money. But I don't like to brag." Jaxon grinned.

"I never imagined that this would happen." She looked at him with tears in her eyes.

"What? That you would be filthy rich."

"No. I don't' care about that. I already know what I want to do with John's money." She lifted her chin. "I want to donate it to SKYLAR'S HOME. I want to make a difference in someone else's life. I want to give the help that I couldn't get."

The love he felt for her expanded a thousand times until he thought his chest would explode.

"Ginny Taylor. You are the most perfect female I'd ever met. I don't deserve you. But I'm going to make it my mission to show you how much I love you every single day.

"You better, Jaxon. Because this time I'm never letting go."

The End

HER WEREWOLF ALPHA CHAPTER 1

*P*ain ricocheted through his body like lightening. But it was his chest that hurt like a mother fucker. He tried to pry open his eyes but it was impossible. He felt like he'd been stuck, suspended between consciousness and reality.

He tried to remember what had happened. But his mind was one black screen. He swallowed and winced at the pain in his throat.

It felt like someone had shoved shards of glass down his throat.

He tried to lift his arm but his body wouldn't obey.

"You really shouldn't be moving around like that." A distinctive female voice whispered near his ear.

"Oh and it's no use trying to talk. Because you can't. Not yet."

What the fuck? What did she sound so familiar? And why couldn't he remember how he'd gotten in this situation.

"Looks like it's going to be just me and you for a little while, wolf." She said softly.

Her hand went between his legs and she palmed his dick.

"I have to say I've had my eye on your for a while. While you are recovering and in my care, we'll get to know each other better." She leaned down and licked his ear.

"Get away from him, Witch."

Ryker. Thank God.

"I was just making him comfortable." She groused.

"With your hand on his dick? I don't think so." Ryker growled.

"Well until we can leave, we are just going to have to learn to get along." Ella said. "And if you play your cards right, maybe me and you can learn to play well together."

"No fucking way. I don't roll with psychopathic witches." Ryker snorted. "And if I see you groping Barrett again I'll cut your fucking hand off."

"I'm a borderline personality!" Ella shrieked. "Not a psychopath."

"Well whatever you are, you need to get that fucking cat under control. It clawed my leather jacket to shreds." Ryker yelled.

"She's just bored." Ella said. "Besides I don't control Nyx."

The drone of arguing voices had him drifting off to a dreamless sleep.

ABOUT THE AUTHOR

Jodi is an USA TODAY bestselling author and a National Readers Choice Award finalist for best paranormal. She is the author of the Werewolf Guardian Romance series and writes paranormal romance as well as contemporary romance.

Born and raised in Mississippi, her deep Southern roots and love of the paranormal led her to write Southern Paranormal novels. When she is not conversing with characters in her head, she can be found at her home in Northeast Arkansas with her handsome husband, brilliant son, a temperamental swan, and yellow lab that is fond of retrieving turtles when duck season is over.

Find her on Facebook, Jodi Vaughn, author.
Follow her on Twitter and Periscope @JodiVaughn1
Sign up for her newsletter and check out her website
http://jodivaughn.com/
Find her on Instagram at VaughnJodi

ALSO BY JODI VAUGHN

Werewolf Guardian Romance Series
Her Werewolf Bodyguard (book 1)
Her Werewolf Protector (book 2)
Her Werewolf Defender (book 3)
Her Werewolf Champion (book 4)
Her Werewolf Hero (book 5)
Her Werewolf Mate (book 6)

The Vampire Housewife Series
Lipstick and Lies and Deadly Goodbyes (book 1)
Merlot and Divorce and Deadly Remorse (book 2)
Bullets and Booze and Dead Suede Shoes (book 3)
Aces and Eights and Dead Werewolf Dates (book 4)

Veiled Series
Veiled Secrets
Veiled Enchantment

Somewhere Texas
Saddle Up
Trouble in Texas
Bad Medicine

Somewhere in Paradise

www.ingramcontent.com/pod-product-compliance
Lightning Source LLC
Chambersburg PA
CBHW032153190626
46814CB00005BA/1976